Praise for Lawrence Thornton

NAMING THE SPIRITS

"A powerful story . . . *Naming the Spirits* is a spiritual odyssey readers should not miss."

—*Chicago Tribune*

"Thornton's book resurrects the nameless dead, restoring their identities, their stories, and their dignity."

—*The New Yorker*

"The novel has a dreamy, elegiac quality. . . . It builds an atmosphere of quiet horror that eventually elicits a visceral response. . . . Thornton again demonstrates his ability to personalize the dimensions of political mass murder."

—*Publishers Weekly*

IMAGINING ARGENTINA

"Remarkable . . . deeply inventive . . . Thornton has imagined Argentina truly; his inspired fable troubles and feeds our own imagining."

—*Los Angeles Times*

"In a time when much North American fiction is contained by crabbed realism, Thornton takes for his material one of the bleaker recent instances of human cruelty, sees in it the enduring nobility of the human spirit and imagines a book that celebrates that spirit."

—*Washington Post Book World*

TALES

FROM

THE

Lawrence
Thornton

BLUE

ARCHIVES

Bantam Books

New York   Toronto   London   Sydney   Auckland

TALES FROM THE BLUE ARCHIVES

A Bantam Book / published by arrangement with
Doubleday

PUBLISHING HISTORY

Doubleday edition published November 1997
Bantam trade paperback edition / December 1998

Book design by Richard Oriolo.

ISBN 0-553-37798-1

Published simultaneously in the United States and Canada

Bantam Books are published by Bantam Books, a division of Bantam
Doubleday Dell Publishing Group, Inc. Its trademark, consisting of the words
"Bantam Books" and the portrayal of a rooster, is Registered in U.S. Patent and
Trademark Office and in other countries. Marca Registrada. Bantam Books,
1540 Broadway, New York, New York 10036.

*De puntillas se alzaban, ebrias en su fatalidad, y cada pisada
dejaba las huellas de un insomnio. Extrañamente, sus
pañuelos parecían ser alas o el sonido de la lluvia,
transmutado en neblinas, y así iban las brujas de la verdad,
deslizándose, inventando clarividencias ingenuas.*

They arose on tiptoe, intoxicated in their doom, and each
footstep left behind traces of insomnia. Strangely, their
kerchiefs seemed like wings or like the sound of falling rain
transmuted into mist, and this is how the witches of truth
went about, slipping away and inventing ingenuous visions.

—MARJORIE AGOSÍN

For Toni, as always

TALES

FROM

THE

BLUE

ARCHIVES

O N E

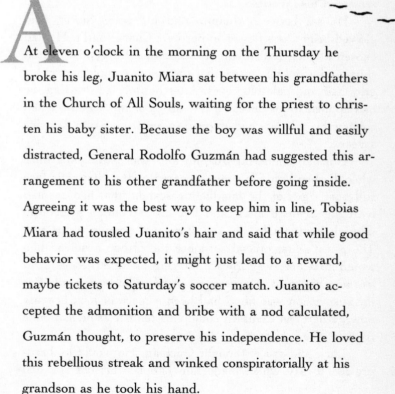

At eleven o'clock in the morning on the Thursday he broke his leg, Juanito Miara sat between his grandfathers in the Church of All Souls, waiting for the priest to christen his baby sister. Because the boy was willful and easily distracted, General Rodolfo Guzmán had suggested this arrangement to his other grandfather before going inside. Agreeing it was the best way to keep him in line, Tobias Miara had tousled Juanito's hair and said that while good behavior was expected, it might just lead to a reward, maybe tickets to Saturday's soccer match. Juanito accepted the admonition and bribe with a nod calculated, Guzmán thought, to preserve his independence. He loved this rebellious streak and winked conspiratorially at his grandson as he took his hand.

Inside, Guzmán breathed deeply of the flowers. He admired the ivory statue of the Virgin and the stained-glass images of saints looking down with a special benevolence, so it seemed, upon the people come to witness Marpessa's christening.

Like all soldiers, Guzmán had an abiding love of rituals, seeing in both the exalted and mundane a profound expression of human need for order and civility. The conviction extended to all matters involving his family, and as they followed him to the front-row pew he gave free rein to feelings about his bloodline that bordered on the mystical. Of all the Latin words he had learned in parochial school, paterfamilias remained his favorite.

He sat between Juanito and his wife, Gloria, who glowed bright as a flower in her new Chanel outfit. He had chosen a black Italian suit, a custom-made Egyptian cotton shirt, and a red tie, aware that the colors complemented his gray hair and pale blue eyes. After he finished dressing, he had applied to his cheeks a few drops of the lemon-scented cologne his mistress had shipped to her from Santiago twice a year.

Guzmán smiled at Juanito and was patting his knee when Father Von Claussen appeared at the altar. His face still bore signs of the humiliating scandal that had erupted with the Scilingo affair and left his reputation grievously injured. Fortunately, the sad story was coming to an end. The priest's first official act since the bishop absolved him would go a long way toward allaying his bitterness and refreshing his spirit. Marpessa's refusal to be born until after the suspension was lifted had been a piece of luck because now Father Von Claussen could christen her as he had done Alicia's other children.

Luck and grace, thought Guzmán. He would be hard-pressed to say which made him happier, his old spiritual adviser's rehabilitation, or Marpessa's embrace by the Church.

Gloria began sniffling with the first words the priest spoke in his gravelly voice. When Alicia glanced up and caught his eye, Guzmán felt like crying, too. Standing beside her husband, Hugo, who looked on proudly as the baby's forehead was anointed with holy water, she looked as beautiful as the Madonna.

Guzmán relished every word, every gesture of the rite, wishing it would go on and on, fill the day. It seemed as if the priest had only just begun when he delivered the benediction.

With a sigh, he turned to Juanito, winking to let him know how pleased he was with his behavior. Then he stepped into the aisle, genuflected, and made sure his grandson did the same.

Led by Father Von Claussen, the families went up the nave and emerged into a flawless summer day. Guzmán accepted Violeta's congratulations and made a date to go shooting later in the week, warning him that his new over-and-under would wreak devastation on the clay pigeons. He wandered from group to group before stopping to talk to Alicia about the party at her house that evening. He had ordered lavishly from the caterers. Did she think there would be enough food? What about place cards, punch bowls, chilled champagne?

"Oh, Daddy," she said, kissing him on the cheek. "Why do you worry so much? Everything will be fine."

"You know how he is," Gloria said with an affectionate laugh. "He always has to be in control. I'm going over to her house this afternoon to help," she told him. "Promise you won't tire yourself out. You'll want to stay up until everybody's gone."

Guzmán said he planned to go for a swim and then take a nap. Juanito came over and took his hand, complaining that there was no one his age to talk to. Guzmán gently reminded him of his promise and was about to suggest a walk around the church when he saw Father Von Claussen and told the boy he needed to speak to the priest. They could spend time together later.

He had been right about the effect of the christening; the priest was beaming as he clapped a hand on Guzmán's shoulder.

"You don't know how good I feel today."

"Oh, I think I do. You'll be there tonight?"

"I wouldn't miss it for the world."

Twenty minutes after he left the church, Guzmán stopped at his bank to cash a check. He put the bills into two envelopes he requested from the clerk, writing "Pablo" on one, "Guido" on the other. He had not felt so happy or fulfilled in a long time. With the christening over, he could still look forward to fine-tuning his arrangement with Sánchez-Macias and Berletti before the party.

Determined as he was to enjoy the afternoon and evening, it was impossible to ignore the irony that lay behind his need to milk the pleasures from a single unusually busy day. Of the things he missed since being cashiered from the army none was more painful to remember than his hectic, demanding schedule. He had thrived on juggling time and commitments, solving one problem while thinking about half a dozen others. The truth was that losing his place in the world of affairs had been more devastating than the trial or imprisonment. The humiliation had been terrible but finite, whereas the days of unstructured existence went on and on, one sliding into the other without differentiation.

His colleagues' talk about accepting the pleasures of forced retirement fell on deaf ears. With sufficient effort he could lose himself for a while in simple tasks. He always felt wonderful in the company of his grandchildren, but there were too many times when he found himself alone with nothing to do other than listen to the clock, the rush of traffic, sounds that had begun to seem like the not-so-distant trumpets of the grave. Well, today was not one of them, he reminded himself. Today he intended to savor every hour, squeeze out every ounce of satisfaction.

He swam for twenty minutes, long enough to loosen up. After he showered and changed into a fresh suit, he went down the hall to his study where his birds began singing as he opened the door.

He had started with a pair years ago. Now a dozen occupied a large cage set against one of the windows so they would have plenty of light. In a city whose citizens lavished unstinting affection on their birds, where the most devout *aficionados* considered cages *objets d'art*, his was one of the finest, fashioned from lacquered strips of speckled bamboo and further distinguished by three round doors fastened with ivory hasps.

Maya, his favorite, chirped impatiently from the topmost perch for the next hour while he studied the maps until he was satisfied there was nothing else he should tell Pablo and Guido.

After replacing the maps in the desk, he unscrewed the top of a jar of seeds, put one between his teeth, and opened the large middle door of the cage, slowly inserting his right hand, palm down.

"Maya," he said softly.

The canary, banded with a small gold earring on her left leg, jumped from the perch to his hand. The moment he raised her to his face she took the seed and swallowed.

"Now," he murmured, "a kiss for Daddy."

No sooner had she pecked his upper lip than the phone rang, frightening her into the air. Guzmán picked up the receiver and said, "Hello."

As he watched Maya circle the room, he heard sobbing, a pause for breath.

"Papa!" Alicia cried. "Juanito's broken his leg!"

Her frantic words contradicted the memory that came to him of his grandson genuflecting, another of him wandering around outside the church.

"What?"

"He fell out of a tree. The bone came through the skin!"

As Maya landed on the far side of the desk he saw the bone clearly in his mind's eye. It was jagged, sickeningly white.

In the background Gloria shouted, "The ambulance just arrived. Give it to me. Rodolfo? She told you? They think he might have internal injuries."

The trees Guzmán remembered behind Alicia's house seemed tall as skyscrapers. He imagined Juanito plummeting to the ground. Then he heard the boy cry out, a long, piercing scream of pain.

"I'll be there in twenty minutes."

"No. We're leaving for the hospital right now. Meet us there."

"Which one?"

"Central."

He swallowed hard. "Get hold of yourself. It's probably not as bad as you think."

She stifled a sob.

"Yes, it is. Maybe worse."

Panicked, his heart racing, he slammed the receiver onto its cradle. Let him be all right, he prayed. Please let him be all right.

The moment he reached for her, Maya hopped away from his extended hand.

In desperation he scooped some seeds from the jar and scattered them across the desk.

"Please," he implored.

She warily regarded the bounty, advanced a step, retreated. He tossed another handful closer to her. When she gave in and began to eat he closed his fingers around her struggling body. In the cage she flew back and forth, driving the other birds into a frenzy that reminded him of Juanito's scream.

He could be dying, he thought as he ran out of the house to his car. He could already be dead.

With a scream of rubber from the tires, he sped off down the street while Juanito's voice echoed in his head. A terrible vision of a funeral filled his mind. He saw a casket piled high with flowers surrounded by friends, by relatives from distant provinces, by veiled women crying. He jammed the accelerator to the floor.

Twenty minutes later, breathless from running all the way across the parking lot, he pushed the door open and entered the gleaming lobby. Corridors branched in four directions. He heard a muted two-tone bell, Muzak, a woman's voice on the intercom summoning a doctor.

"My grandson," he said to a nurse at the reception desk. "Juan Miara. Where is he?"

She flipped through a computer printout with agonizing slowness, put it aside, and looked at him with a puzzled expression.

"When was he admitted?"

"Tonight! His leg's broken. A compound fracture. He has internal injuries."

"Oh," she murmured sympathetically. He watched her pick up a clipboard with "Emergency" printed on a strip of tape.

"They took him directly to surgery. The waiting room's on the second floor. Take the elevator at the end of the hall."

Alicia was sitting between Hugo and her mother. When Gloria saw him she jumped up and embraced him. Alicia cried inconsolably.

"How is he?" he asked Hugo.

"They're setting his leg," Hugo answered shakily. "The

doctor isn't sure what else is wrong." He gave Guzmán a desperate, pleading look. "I told him not to climb that tree, but you know how headstrong he is. It's my fault."

"You can't keep your eye on him every minute," said Guzmán consolingly. "Not even if you wanted to."

"The girls are fine," Hugo said, clearly relieved that he wasn't being blamed. "They're with the housekeeper."

"Why tonight?" Alicia whimpered.

Guzmán's heart seemed to crack open at her pain. She had been preparing for the party for weeks. Now Juanito might be dying.

Ignoring the question, he whispered encouraging words and kissed her forehead.

The room was suffocating. He went out and paced in the hall, returning every ten or fifteen minutes to check the clock on the wall.

An hour passed. Then another.

"What's taking so long?" Alicia said. "Something must be wrong."

"There's nothing to worry about," he told her.

Minutes after he returned to the hall his heart froze. Their doctor was emerging from the surgery. Guzmán stood still, staring at him, searching his eyes in an effort to read what had happened and prepare himself if he had to. As the doctor approached he took a deep breath, held it, expelled it slowly. He felt old. His body seemed to weigh a thousand pounds.

"Well?"

"It was a nasty break. I had to pin the leg. Other than that and some bruises, he's okay, though he'll be in a cast for months."

Guzmán remained in the hall while the doctor went inside. He watched the agony fall away from their faces like masks, the tears of relief course down his daughter's cheeks, his wife's, Hugo's. He felt short of breath. His heart was pounding. He wanted to stay there until he was in control of himself but Hugo was motioning to him.

The doctor said Hugo and Alicia could spend the night in Juanito's room. He would have cots sent in. Gloria wanted Guzmán to drive her back to the house so she could see the girls.

The dining room table was piled high with untouched food and drink. Brightly wrapped presents were stacked on the sideboard.

"Everyone was so sorry," said the housekeeper. She put her hand on Catalina's shoulder. "This one was an angel. She helped me tell the guests about the accident."

"Is he okay?" Catalina asked.

"He's fine," Gloria told her. "Now I want you to get into your nightie. It's way past bedtime."

"I'm glad, but Daddy warned him."

"I won't have you finding fault with your brother," Gloria said sternly. "You know better."

With downcast eyes, Catalina took the housekeeper's hand and let herself be led away.

When they were gone Gloria looked steadily at Guzmán, her eyes unwavering, full of purpose, composed.

"We were so lucky," she said.

He had been prepared to console her but it was he who needed support. He was vibrating like a tuning fork from the brush with danger, the fear of loss. On the way from the hospital his mind had taken him back to the vision of Juanito falling, except this time it was as if he were one with the body, that they were both watching the ground rushing at them.

Embarrassed by his vulnerability, he poured warm

champagne into two fluted glasses, hoping the act would help him regain his composure. He did not care that it had gone flat. He wanted the alcohol.

"I'll stay a few days," Gloria said. "Alicia will have her hands full."

"Yes, of course," he replied, nodding stiffly. "That's the best thing. I'll go see him first thing in the morning."

On the drive home he gave vent to his emotions, weeping loudly and without shame, his chest heaving uncontrollably as he remembered Juanito sitting beside him in church, Alicia holding Marpessa, the trees stretching skyward. In all the world nothing was more precious to him than his grandson. He would die for him. He would gladly lay down his life for Juanito.

He heard the phone ringing as he unlocked the front door but the line was dead by the time he picked up the receiver. Pablo, he thought as he headed for his study, Pablo had probably been calling off and on all evening, angry that he had not been home to pay him.

There was an uncharacteristic silence when he entered the room, a heavy scent of night-blooming jasmine. He turned on the lights. The window was open. The middle door of the cage gaped wide. For the briefest of moments he thought a burglar had been there. Then he remembered his panic when he had returned Maya to the cage. He had forgotten to fasten the ivory hasp! With a groan he rushed to the window, thinking he heard a bird singing outside. When he looked out, he saw only the full moon hanging low in the sky.

TWO

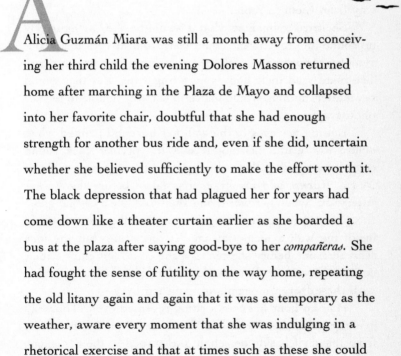

Alicia Guzmán Miara was still a month away from conceiving her third child the evening Dolores Masson returned home after marching in the Plaza de Mayo and collapsed into her favorite chair, doubtful that she had enough strength for another bus ride and, even if she did, uncertain whether she believed sufficiently to make the effort worth it. The black depression that had plagued her for years had come down like a theater curtain earlier as she boarded a bus at the plaza after saying good-bye to her *compañeras*. She had fought the sense of futility on the way home, repeating the old litany again and again that it was as temporary as the weather, aware every moment that she was indulging in a rhetorical exercise and that at times such as these she could only settle down and wait for hope to get the best of her.

Sometimes when the depression struck, she lost her sense of her own individuality. It had happened earlier. The moment she said good-bye to her *compañeras* her soul felt as if it were flowing out of her. That was one of the worst things, even more frightening than the images flitting through her mind, swift as night birds. Her only remedy was to go home as fast as possible, surround herself with the familiar, the long-known. Here the flowing out did not matter because she had lived in this house so long it was part of her, the repository of her history and her dreams. Every piece of furniture had belonged to her family and she could not re-member the last time any of them had been moved. If I ever lose my sight, she thought, I will have no trouble finding my way from room to room.

She tried to imagine what it would be like having to rely on sound and touch. She could learn to deal with the incon-veniences, become accustomed to feeling her way around. The blind read their houses with fingertips. But that would not matter, nothing would matter if she was unable to see her photographs.

Raising her eyes to the wall her husband painted white before his death, insisting it was the perfect background color for a family gallery, she regarded the studio portraits of Marta, Rubén, and her grandsons taken before the *Proceso*. Afterward, when her world had shattered like a crystal glass, she considered framing everything in the album so she could make the wall a memorial against forgetting, but the idea scarcely came before she realized she could not endure their constant presence. She needed control of her communion with these frozen moments of vanished lives.

Half an hour later, in a ritual repeated every Thursday evening when the clock chimed six, she removed the album from the shelf beside her chair and turned to the first page, to her son, Rubén, two days old. Beneath it and each photograph in the album a date and location were printed in white ink.

She looked at snapshots from his childhood, wedding pictures of him and Marta, their honeymoon in Europe, their first apartment, Marta holding Joaquín while Rubén stood beside her hospital bed, the whole family when Roger and Joaquín were two and three, Roger posing on a Christmas tricycle, Joaquín holding a plastic ball too large to circle with his arms. There were more photographs of picnics, Christmas dinners, the boys playing in the park, Rubén and Marta standing on a dock at twilight.

Always when she went through the album she counted the pages by touch, the fingers of her right hand on the edge of the pages telling her she was coming close to the middle. The end is the middle, her fingers said. It goes no further.

She turned to the last, the middle page, remembering the day she mounted the photograph of the boys in matching sailor suits and printed in white ink where and when it had been taken. It was in the upper left-hand corner, the only photograph on the page, stranded in a sea of black where others should have been.

Because this one stood alone she responded to it more reverently, more passionately, with more sorrow than to any of the others. She herself had taken it, snapped the shutter happily one bright August morning. It had been innocent when she mounted it—innocent, what it was, the thing itself, two little boys smiling. The image would always be innocent but not her seeing. A stranger would see only what was there, whereas she saw the boys with the knowledge of the future neither she nor they nor their parents had possessed that day. She had mounted it without the slightest qualm because there had been no reason to think it would never be followed by hundreds of others that ought to have swollen the album with a record of their lives. This photograph, especially this one but all the others too, was incomplete, could only be finished, made whole, by her knowledge of the future, which was now the past, a future aged thirteen years.

She leaned forward with her hands on her knees to see it better, knowing what was about to happen. Whenever she looked at it, it seemed as if she were in a theater watching a film that suddenly became stuck and caught fire, projecting a widening hole on the screen until nothing remained.

Always she had to remind herself that the space the boys disappeared into was an illusion, that they were alive somewhere in Argentina. She would track down the source of the burning circle. A time would come when she no longer had to fight to believe, go to the place she returned to week after week, month after month, because there and only there might she learn where they were. Not that the belief lifted the burden of sadness. Nothing could do that. But it was strong enough to let her see a little light, as it was doing now, give her strength to once again walk to the corner and catch the bus, endure the bumpy ride and stench of diesel fumes, determined as a pilgrim.

Because she had delayed and was running late, she ate dinner standing up in the kitchen, then grabbed a heavy sweater in case the evening turned cold, hurried out of the house, and reached the stop just as Horacio's bus arrived.

After waiting at this corner every Thursday for the last two years she was one of his "regulars." An unvarying routine had developed between them. As soon as she stepped on board he said, "Out on the town again?" "I'm old," she answered, "but I'm not dead yet." Once she deposited her fare and took the seat behind him, they chatted awhile about the day's news. "Are you ever going to tell me where you go?" She answered, good-naturedly as usual, "None of your business." She was not being coy. From the beginning it had seemed that the less said to Horacio the better.

She had long ago memorized every detail of the route,

knew how many stoplights there were in each neighborhood, the speed limits, where people waited who for reasons of their own rode this bus on Thursday evenings. She knew the names of the shops along the way and exactly how long it took to travel from her corner to a cobblestone walk where three old women sat gossiping on wooden chairs unless it was raining or very cold.

Familiar as everything was, she never lost interest in the world streaming by outside because she believed in signs, believed that even though she had never come upon one in all the time she had made this trip, it was always possible she might see something that would signal her long search was coming to an end. She would know it immediately. The moment she reached her destination she would describe it and they would tell her what to do.

Half an hour after she'd dropped her coins in the meter, Horacio reached her stop. The pneumatic doors hissed open.

"Don't be late," he called.

Dolores waved without speaking and set off down the street. She had walked these three blocks in rain, wind, summer heat, walked them when she was excited, discouraged, determined, miserable, her moods varied as the weather, her heart assailed by doubts when she recalled how often she had visited the old house and now the new one, how many years had come and gone, how many times after an hour or two of avid listening she had retraced her steps to the bus stop and gone home as ignorant as before.

Over the years she had become intimate with all the shapes of discouragement, had sensed, more than once, the approach of grief powerful as a high wind, had leaned her weight against it while thinking how easy it would be to give in, let go, be swept away, able to resist because it was never strong enough to kill her hope that someday she would see her grandsons once again.

The house came into view as she crossed the last intersection. Several of the cars parked on the street had been new when she first met their owners in front of the old house and they had all exchanged nervous glances under the street-light, knowing they had come for the same reason, embarrassed to be there but determined to grasp at any straw.

Everyone was older now, their bodies thicker, their hair graying above faces creased where once the skin was smooth, but their eyes had not changed. Desire burnished by time bound them together. By their eyes they would recognize each other immediately wherever in the world they chanced to meet, the brightness the sign of their shared story, indelible as the numbers tattooed on the arms of Jews.

At the old house on Calle Córdoba, a cobblestone walk had led directly from the street to the garden. She thought this arrangement must have been easier on Carlos and his family, though he had never seemed much concerned with ease. The gift he now shared with Teresa had made him intimate with places where comfort would never be at home.

She followed a couple up the stairs to the open front door and passed through the living room to the garden where a large ficus tree was festooned with dead lanterns. The tables were white instead of cobalt blue. There were fewer chairs, the attrition of hope over the years having thinned the number of supplicants. But the feel of the place was the same. The old spirit of hope dwelt here, too.

She sat in the second row between a woman she did not know and Maria Ritter, whom she had met during the first months of the war.

Maria nodded, forced a smile, and Dolores did the same. They exchanged a glance that never varied. Part encouragement, part sympathy, it acknowledged many things, not the least of which was their determination to return here week after week, drag themselves if necessary, arrive on crutches or in wheelchairs until they either found what they needed or had grown too old to care.

For the next twenty minutes visitors new and old took their seats. Dolores had learned to know when the last arrived, sensing a gathering of tension the way one does just before a cleric rises to have his say.

There was a changed silence and then, very faintly, a melody played on a guitar, each note as familiar as her name. She closed her eyes and listened, entering deeply into the music, aware that Maria was doing the same, that everyone, even the newcomers, instinctively understood that this was part of the transition to the place where the Disappeared might be found.

When the music ended with a chord played in the flamenco style, *rascudo*, the clash of fingernails against strings, each note clear and pure, she heard the patio door open with a smooth rush of bearings, footsteps on the flagstones as Carlos came out wearing his usual black shirt and trousers, his guitar slung on a strap over one shoulder, his fierce eyes gleaming. Not once in all the years she had known him had his expression been other than what she saw now, a mixture of anger and sorrow and determination. The only change was in the way his body moved with a certain fluid grace denied him until Teresa had returned.

He waited for her, held out his hand as she emerged, her face pale, ethereal, immune to time. She took Carlos' hand and glanced neither to the left nor to the right as they went out to the lawn where she took her place in the rattan chair and he moved off a little way, strumming chords.

Even in the dim light from the house Teresa's white dress glowed as she sat with her hands clasped, waiting for her mother to help her little brother into a chair. Cecilia gave him a cookie, then she stood up and went to the lawn. From a pocket in her full skirt she removed a box of wooden matches, struck one, lit the first lantern. While Cecilia circled the ficus tree, reaching up and setting fire to the candle wicks, Teresa closed her eyes, returning, Dolores thought, to the darkness, wherever she had been, already searching for signs of life.

The chords broke into the single notes of a plaintive melody as a yellow gleam reflected on the tables, brightened the faces of the visitors, wreathed the tree with light so that it looked as exotic as an Asian temple.

Every week it was the same. The moment Cecilia blew out the match after lighting the lantern above her daughter's head Teresa opened her eyes. Her gaze passed slowly over the crowd, lingered awhile on each person before shifting to the next.

Dolores had never gotten used to it, never would. Always when the girl held her eyes she felt an upswelling of hope that tonight would be her night, that all the years of failure had been preparation for what was about to come to pass. The feeling remained after Teresa looked away from her to Maria Ritter and then to the man who sat beside Maria and the two women at the end of the row of chairs.

"Tell me your stories," Teresa said softly, her voice just louder than a whisper. "Tell me the names. Who must be found?"

For years Dolores was often the first to speak, standing up and pronouncing the names of her grandsons in a firm voice she hoped would not break. She could not number the times their names had rolled off her tongue only to be greeted with silence. She had persisted because there was nothing else to do, because sometimes Carlos or Teresa would catch a glimpse of them. Once, only a few years ago, Carlos saw the Ponces driving through a mountain town with the boys, the scene clear and sharp as a photograph, he said, and she had felt her heart in her throat as he described the car, only to see it disappear in a cloud of dust beyond the last house on the narrow street.

That failure and many others had taught her patience.

Nothing was certain. Being in the garden was the important thing. Being available. Letting time do its work. Now she usually spoke only when a lull came upon the crowd. Sometimes she said nothing at all.

"My son, Paulo," said Maria Ritter. "He believed in freedom and for that was dragged into one of the cars while he was walking to the university. I ask the government. I ask the police. Their answers are always the same. No one knows his name."

Teresa kept her eyes on Maria Ritter as she waited for an answer, an image to fit the name, give it substance. Her eyelids fluttered and Dolores knew she had gone deep into herself and returned with nothing that could ease the pain of Maria Ritter.

"I'm sorry," she said. "I see nothing. He will not come tonight."

Maria Ritter breathed in deeply. She raised her left hand to her mouth while Dolores took her right and guided her down into her chair, whispering that she must remember this was how it worked.

"My wife, René," said Pablo Ortiz.

Hand in hand they listened to his familiar story, as familiar to them as theirs were to him, a story that began in happiness and ended when René called him the very afternoon she disappeared and explained what he should warm up for their dinner.

"My friends," cried Ana Epelbaum, who once had been an engineering student but had lost her heart for study. "Marco, Darla, Isabel, Saul, Elena, Victor, Alonzo."

She paused for a breath and went on to say they had all disappeared near the end of the war in less than two weeks. She asked only for news of one. "Surely," she pleaded, "surely that's not too much."

Teresa listened, strove to see, hear. She said she saw

nothing, heard nothing, and when she asked for more names there was silence.

Dolores understood their disappointment. She was intimate with the leaden feeling in heart and limbs that descended upon people on nights like this, the weight that was no lighter when Teresa apologized as she was doing now, saying in her still-girlish voice that she had no control over the things she was vouchsafed to see.

Again Teresa asked for names. Dolores looked around and saw no one prepared to speak. A man was already leaving. Two months had passed since she last told her story. During that time she had listened to newcomers and veterans, was delighted when Teresa found someone's granddaughter alive in Uruguay, grieved when the girl described where a man could find the bones of his sons.

"Try," Maria said, gripping her hand. "What have you got to lose?"

The question freed her tongue. She stood and faced Teresa.

"You know who I am and you know my story. I'll tell you again. First they took my family, all of them, even the baby. They put them in a clandestine prison and then they killed Marta, my daughter-in-law. Afterward, General Guzmán gave away my grandsons, Roger and Joaquín, to some people named Ponce. I have the proof, a copy of a note signed by the general. My son, Rubén, escaped with the baby, Félicité, but he was heartbroken when he learned what happened and fled the country. I want my grandsons. I want justice done to Eduardo Ponce, to his wife, Beatriz. None of us did anything to deserve this." She was shaking with rage. "None of us," she repeated, as if the words were bones caught in her throat.

Her eyes remained fixed on Teresa. For a long time, it seemed, they stared at each other. Dolores had a vision of the boys in their sailor suits, remembered other evenings when she had told her story and Teresa looked just as she did now, on the verge of something, only to lose it.

Finally, in a halting but firm voice, Teresa spoke.

"I know him. I saw this man Ponce when I was in the pampas, coming home from where I had been. It was the end of the day. He offered me a ride but when he saw me close there was fear in his eyes. He drove off fast. When he reached his house he told Beatriz they were leaving, they had to leave before it was too late."

Carlos had been weaving a melody behind her words, a soft accompaniment of single notes that ended abruptly when she described the Ponces' flight. He leaned his guitar against the tree and went to her, taking her hand in his.

"Where?" he asked intently. "Can you see the road?"

Teresa looked at Carlos before her gaze rose to the lanterns. Concentrating, her face bathed in yellow light, she pointed with her index finger.

"South. To the sea."

A compass point, a coastline, more than she had ever heard.

Dolores' legs felt weak and shaky and she had to force herself to stand there, facing Teresa, afraid the slightest movement would disturb the vision that had come upon her. This was the crucial point, the moment she had seen Teresa and Carlos reach when darkness fell, killed what they saw.

"South," Teresa said, repeating the word confidently, "beyond the cordillera in a town named after the sea there is a house with a tile roof and two chimneys. It is set apart a little from the others, at the end of the first road. She keeps it spotless as a shrine for her husband. She wears her betrayal like a necklace hidden beneath her clothes."

"Roger and Joaquín," said Carlos coaxingly. "What of Roger and Joaquín?"

Teresa searched the lanterns. When a man in the front row moved, Carlos held up his hand in warning.

"Day and night they hear the waves. At first, the sound kept them awake. Now it leads them into dreams. They love the town and the sea is in their blood."

Dolores stared at the tree of lights, looking for what Teresa saw, a fragment of coastline, a mountain ridge.

In a trembling voice she said, "The name. What is the name of the town?"

Teresa closed her eyes. Without opening them she said, "Mar Vista."

THREE

After his morning walk, Guzmán retired to his study with coffee and newspaper, anticipating the usual pleasant half hour of solitude. Comfortable as he was in the rambling house, he felt most at home in this room. He had intentionally kept his former office in the Casa Rosada as bare as a monk's cell, having discovered that pristine walls had a subtle intimidating factor that gave him a distinct advantage over visitors. Here he had indulged his sentimental nature, his Baroque imagination, by decorating his study with mementos of his career.

A dozen framed photographs of his family crowded a table beside the desk. The remaining space was reserved for him. His regiment's ceremonial flags were displayed on the wall behind his desk. The sword he received the day of his commissioning was fitted into brackets above the door. Letters of commendation hung beside photographs of him on bivouac with his first infantry company, his face smeared with camouflage paint; lying prone at a firing range; in his office looking pensive; with Massina at a party, their arms around each other's shoulders; grainy newspaper pictures of him in the streets with his pistol drawn.

The mementos were both a solace and a trial, for he could never regard them without thinking of what might have been. The last photograph to be put up showed him with Galtieri on a balcony the day the president declared war on the British, the crowd below half obscured by a sea of Argentine flags. Their ardent patriotism still brought a lump to his throat.

He let his eyes linger on the picture, studiously ignoring the blank space to the right where there should have been more pictures, capstones of a career cut short. When he felt the old bitterness take hold and remembered how a few spineless cowards brought calamity on them all, he spun around in his chair and faced the windows, determined not to spoil his sense of well-being.

He was smiling over a story in the sports section about a soccer star's exploits with three women as he folded the paper back to the front page and was dealt a ringing blow. An old acquaintance, Lieutenant Commander Adolfo Scilingo, had confessed to throwing prisoners out of a plane during the war. He had implicated others, even going so far as to say that Father Von Claussen had given him moral support.

As he read on, Guzmán could feel his belief that the past had been scattered on the winds of forgetfulness coming undone. Scilingo's words stopped the wind, perhaps reversed its direction if he were to accept the reporter's opinion. Fresh investigations of the regime were promised, even a new chapter in the country's life.

The memory of the trial raced back, the sentencing, the terror and humiliation of prison that had filled his waking hours and his dreams, until Menem conferred the amnesty demanded by the military. Safe as he was in the document's embrace, the memory of his cell raised a chill along his spine, as if he were falling through icy air to a world he thought was gone.

He remembered Scilingo's vaguely handsome face. The narrow eyes hovering before him as in a hologram would never be mistaken for those of a genius. On the other hand, it was impossible to believe he had been so stupid to speak out. He reread the paragraph where Adolfo said he had confessed because of guilt, dismissing the explanation out of hand. Something else had loosened his tongue: vengeance, or an urge for self-destruction. Conscience, however misguided, could not account for such an act.

He poured a drink from the decanter on his desk. After recovering a little from the shock, he called several old colleagues who had also seen the story and could make neither head nor tail of it.

"Why now," Massina fumed, "so many years later?"

Violeta reminded him that Scilingo was a devoted son of Argentina, outraged by the dissidents, the threat of communism. "It goes without saying that something drove him crazy."

At lunch the next day, Massina and Guzmán offered their condolences to Father Von Claussen. As soon as he walked into the restaurant, Guzmán saw that the priest was beside himself, the pretense of calm on the phone when he invited him earlier having taken flight.

Father Von Claussen sat down heavily.

"In case you're wondering," he said, his lips barely moving in the pale face sheltered beneath a wide forehead and bald skull, "I didn't know what the navy was doing until he told me."

"That should be known," Massina said. "The papers should be told."

"Too late," the priest responded. "The bishop has suspended me."

Yes, he went on without being asked, he had counseled Scilingo. At the time he was serving as military chaplain at the Naval Mechanics School. It was his job. As a priest, he would have been derelict in the sight of God had he not performed it.

"He came to see me the day after his first flight. His conscience was uneasy and he told me why, what they did with the people. He needed comfort and I provided it. I provided a Christian explanation."

Father Von Claussen glanced angrily out the window, the muscles of his jaw working beneath the slack skin.

"I told him they had died a Christian death because they were unconscious from the drugs and had not suffered. I reminded him that war was war, that they were enemies of the state, and because they were Communists, enemies of the Church as well. I reminded him of a passage in the Scriptures where we are told to eliminate weeds from our wheat fields."

He looked unrepentant as he downed his wine.

Guzmán thought of the accusations brought against him at the trial, some true, some malicious lies, all presented out of context. There were things the prosecutors had missed. Nothing as damning as what Scilingo did but damning nonetheless. The sense of vulnerability that visited Guzmán when he saw the headlines yesterday returned. He had a vision of his cell, the aluminum tray filled with slop he was forced to eat. The paper had promised new investigations. It was a blanket amnesty, he reminded himself, given in perpetuity. He was certain it applied to civil courts.

"What can we do for you?" asked Massina.

"Nothing. It will have to run its course."

"Have you seen Adolfo recently?" Guzmán asked.

"Not since the war."

"I assumed something must have happened between you, some kind of falling out. He had to know this would stir up a hornet's nest."

Father Von Claussen shook his head. "Conscience does strange things."

"Does that mean you think he believed what he said?" asked Massina.

The priest regarded them with a frank, almost meditative gaze, going on as if he had not heard Massina's question.

"Because it is such a powerful emotion, it can distort reason, create wrongs where none exist. Yes, Adolfo no doubt believed. We must ask why. In my opinion, it was because his conception of the past was twisted. There are times when fear masquerades as conscience. One learns this in the confessional. Fear of the consequences of his acts, brought on by God only knows what catalyst, could have made him speak, fear so strong it blinded him to the truth of history, made it impossible for him to see that his acts were part of something larger than himself. He could have forgotten that things had to be done, that war is war. Things had to be done," he repeated, "justifiable things to purify the country. You both know that as well as anyone."

He shook his head wearily. "I'm sick of this. It's all I've been able to think of since the story broke. Don't either of you have any good news?"

"Alicia's pregnant."

"Wonderful. Let's pray to God I'll be able to christen the child."

• • •

Guzmán remained skeptical after leaving the restaurant. Much as he respected him, the priest's explanation seemed too pat, an exercise in Jesuitical reasoning that brought him no closer to Scilingo's motive. For the moment, that was less important than his adviser's pain. Lacking the influence he once wielded, he would have to support his old friend willy-nilly, as best he could, find ways to make the humiliation a little easier for him to bear. While he could no longer think of the past as sealed, he felt in no personal jeopardy. Like the priest, he had nothing to do with the flights. As far as other events were concerned, he had carefully distanced himself with layers of deniability.

For the next several weeks the scandal dominated the news. Human rights groups were emboldened. The Mothers of the Plaza de Mayo demanded a full accounting of the Church's complicity with the regime.

And Scilingo continued talking. While reporters hung on his every word, he was hardly more interesting to them than the priest, whom they hounded unmercifully.

Guzmán advised him to deny any knowledge of Scilingo and refuse further comment. The last time Father Von Claussen appeared at the door of his residence, he spoke scornfully to them, saying, "I don't give replies, clarifications, denials, anything. You should all be ashamed of yourselves."

The same afternoon he told Guzmán that his superiors were maintaining a stony silence regarding his future.

"Of course they have to because it's political but there's no doubt I'm being made a scapegoat."

Despite the attention of Guzmán and other sympathizers, he seemed to be withdrawing into himself. Guzmán smelled wine on his breath even in the mornings. Massina, Violeta, and Guzmán tendered invitations for dinner he refused, saying he no longer felt like going out.

Guzmán expected the same response when he invited the priest to accompany him and his grandchildren on a visit to the *estancia* of Pedro Moncalvillo. To his surprise, the priest gladly accepted, saying that was just what he needed to escape from the glare of publicity.

On the way he talked nostalgically about the freedom of the pampas. When the children complained about how long it was taking, he took their entertainment upon himself, inventing a game on the spot about saints' names.

Juanito and Catalina jumped out of the car as soon as Guzmán parked in the circular driveway, insisting on a ride before they did anything else. He could never resist them and they knew it. After the priest, Gloria, Alicia, and the Moncalvillos had settled down with drinks on the veranda, he and an old gaucho saddled the ponies and led them out of the corral where Guzmán cupped his hands and helped the children mount.

They were following the white-railed fence when the wind suddenly came up and blew off Juanito's hat. Guzmán retrieved it and put it back on the boy's head, cinching the drawstring tight.

"There," he said, "you look just like a gaucho."

He handed the reins back to Juanito, whose smile rekindled Guzmán's love. He was basking in the emotion, thinking pleasantly about the boy's future—he would of course be enrolled in military college—when he remembered the Ponces.

"Grandpa," said Catalina, laughing. "You look funny."

"It's nothing. Go on. I'll be right behind you."

Catalina dug her heels into the pony's flanks and trotted ahead. He watched the girl, concerned that she was not very steady in the saddle. Why was he suddenly worried about the Ponces? They were living in perfect anonymity hundreds of miles from Buenos Aires, safe from prying eyes. Then he realized that it led straight back to Scilingo. His commitment to the Ponces, a long personal crusade, rested on loyalty, and it was precisely loyalty, everything the word suggested, that Scilingo had violated. Eduardo had served him well in difficult times. Guzmán alone knew what enormous personal sacrifices the man had made to keep his family intact. Unlikely as it was, the tempest created by Scilingo could put them in jeopardy. The old women's ire was up, having gone beyond rage at the Church to fresh demands for information about the Disappeared. And the government seemed to be responding.

For the next half hour, until the children were tired and wanted to go back for something to eat, Guzmán brooded about the situation. No matter how he approached it, it was indisputable that the Ponces could be at risk.

On the veranda Father Von Claussen and Moncalvillo sat at a table by themselves, working up their blood.

"What's your opinion of Scilingo? Why did he spill his guts about tossing people out of planes?"

"Please," Guzmán said with a quick glance at Juanito and Catalina, "lower your voice."

"They're too young to understand."

"You never know."

The priest, who always became morose when he drank, regarded Guzmán miserably.

"I was just telling Pedro it wouldn't have caused such a stir if he hadn't implicated me."

"Try not to worry," Guzmán said distractedly. "Things like this blow over."

"A small martyrdom," said Pedro. You will endure it."

Before long, their talk turned sentimental. Things had changed in Argentina. The war had failed for several reasons, but the beginning of the end was Galtieri's idiotic invasion of the Malvinas. A disaster from start to finish.

Guzmán half-listened to their postmortems. Neither had anything fresh to say. He was intimate with every argument, understood better than they did the reasons behind Galtieri's ill-conceived strategy. It was not so much boredom as an ache for what might have been that made the talk unpleasant.

By the time the sun was close to the horizon, turning the fields gold, Guzmán realized there was only one thing to do. He would have to pay the Ponces a visit in Mar Vista. That way he could assure himself everything was fine and put this uneasiness to rest.

FOUR

Toward the end of the following week Guzmán looked down on Mar Vista from the road edging the cordillera. Its few square blocks of weather-racked houses, mostly cinder block, galvanized steel buildings fronting the dock, the haphazard scatter of narrow streets appeared even smaller than he remembered, less a town than an outpost wedged between mountains and sea. Eduardo had paid a fearful price for fatherhood. He himself could not survive more than a week in this place and that certainly increased his respect for Ponce. As he descended the mountain face, he was more determined than ever to let nothing interfere with his old friend's hard-won repose. He would tell Eduardo of his misgivings, the feeling that was not quite anxiety, and Eduardo would no doubt put him at ease.

The road skirted a bay whose waters were the darkest blue he had ever seen, an opaque mass unrelieved by other colors. Further on, he noticed purple streamers of kelp drifting lazily on the swells, tangled driftwood, bleached white from salt and sun, rimming the tide line. The men working on the dock, the boats anchored together like a school of sleeping pelicans, emphasized the sense of desolation and his feeling that this inhospitable spot was more suitable for a penal colony than a fishing village.

As he parked in the driveway of their house on Calle de la Ventana, Beatriz came out on the porch and waved, the inherent sadness of her wan smile still intact, as if it had not left her face since he last came here seven years ago. She bore little resemblance to the contented woman he had known in Buenos Aires. As he stepped out of the Mercedes, he thought her life must be an agony of loneliness on this wind-swept plateau.

She welcomed him brightly.

"Eduardo wanted so much to be here but he and the boys won't be home until dark."

He kissed her on the cheek, saying they would celebrate later. Her determined cheerfulness seemed forced, contradicting the look deep in her eyes. He wondered how she spent her time while they were at sea. It was hard to envision Beatriz with other women.

"There's tea but you probably want to rest. I cleaned up Manfredo's room."

"It was a long drive. A little nap, then we can talk. There's a lot of catching up to do."

The shelves overflowed with fishing equipment. Photographs of soccer stars lined the walls. Manfredo and Tomás had been children the last time he saw them. Now they were young men. He was curious about how they had changed, how life had marked them so far.

Giving in to fatigue, he lay down and closed his eyes.

The seemingly endless road south from Buenos Aires re-played its windings in his mind. He remembered the pretty waitress at Garibaldi's Inn, where he had spent last night. Suddenly a vision came to him of the bare overhead bulb that had lighted Beatriz' face the night his aides thrust the boys into the backseat of Eduardo's car. A familiar happiness had blazed out of her eyes. What did it remind him of? Gloria! Her expression had been identical to Gloria's the day she gave birth to his daughter.

A knock wakened him.

"They're home," Beatriz called.

It was dark outside. He fumbled for the lamp and slipped on his shoes.

Opening the door, he saw Eduardo and the boys sitting at the table, all sun-burned, dark as Indians.

Eduardo's face had been smooth the last time Guzmán saw him. Now it was crosshatched with the lines and creases of unforgiving work.

Manfredo and Tomás stood up self-consciously as he came out, tall, wiry youths with thick wavy hair and thin faces. He had a vague recollection of seeing their father but the cell had been too dark for him to know if he too had been tall.

"Eduardo!" he called.

Eduardo's face lit up with a wide smile. Stepping around Tomás, he warmly embraced Guzmán.

"It's been a long time," he said affectionately.

Guzmán held him at arm's length, looked him up and down.

"Too long. You look good, *amigo*. Fit. The work agrees with you."

Eduardo laughed and shook his head.

"In Mar Vista you have to be strong or die. We've made a life. What can I say?"

Guzmán turned to the boys.

"You don't look the way you used to."

They smiled awkwardly, unsure of themselves.

"I don't think they remember you," Beatriz said apologetically.

"No reason to. You were just kids when I was here before. But sailors now," he added emphatically.

"I guess," said Tomás. "Dad taught us everything."

"Come out with us sometime," Eduardo said proudly. "See what they can do. Sit down. Beatriz, would you bring the brandy?"

She returned with a brand Guzmán had never seen.

"What about us?" Manfredo asked as Eduardo filled the glasses.

"Juice till you're old enough," he said. He touched his glass to Guzmán's. *"Salut."*

The boys downed their juice, obviously wishing it was something stronger. Guzmán smiled, remembering his own youth and how frustrating it was waiting to be a man.

"How was the trip?" asked Eduardo.

"Not bad in the Mercedes."

"It's terrific," Manfredo said. "How fast can it go?"

"Two-fifty."

"Have you ever done it?"

"A few times, when I was in a hurry." Guzmán laughed as he glanced at Eduardo. "I have a feeling a ride's in order."

Eduardo looked sternly at his son.

"That's all right," Guzmán told him. "It was like that for me when I was a kid. I loved cars. Can you drive?" he asked Manfredo.

"A little."

"Maybe we'll find a decent stretch of road and you can give it a try."

"I'd like that."

Guzmán emptied his glass. He was feeling avuncular.

"I wanted to be a race driver at your age. Like Fangio. He was the most amazing man in the world. I saw him once, near the end of his career. He was still fearless. He took great chances but it didn't matter because he was such a fine technician. The problem was his lungs. They'd gone bad from inhaling so much exhaust. He had to wear a white scarf over his nose and mouth. It was spotted with blood."

Guzmán accepted another brandy. The boys were fascinated, especially Manfredo, who seemed to have more spunk than his brother.

"I've always thought of that scarf as a sign of courage," he went on, "the sign of a man who did what was necessary. But many professions are dangerous. Fishermen have the weather to contend with. Soldiers worry about being shot."

"Did you?" Tomás asked.

"I came close a few times. I've heard bullets whiz by my head. It's not a sound you forget."

"When?" Manfredo asked.

"During the *Proceso*."

Eduardo glanced at Guzmán, who smiled as if to say there was nothing to worry about.

"Some *montoneros* took exception to my looks."

"Have you ever shot anyone?" asked Manfredo.

"Beatriz!" Eduardo called. "Are we ever going to eat?"

"Ten minutes."

With a glance Eduardo made it clear to Manfredo that the conversation was over.

Guzmán commented on how good things smelled.

"Mom's the best cook in town," said Manfredo.

"In Argentina," Tomás corrected him.

"That's what happens when you spoil children," Beatriz said.

Eduardo wanted news from Buenos Aires.

"Alicia's pregnant, just when I'd given up hope of a third grandchild. Catalina's excited but I'm not so sure about Juanito."

After dinner, when they were alone, Guzmán remarked that Beatriz still seemed on edge.

"She hasn't been the same since we left Santa Rosalita. All the moving was harder on her than I thought. And worrying about someone finding the boys. That wears you down, I can tell you."

"Listen. Has anything suspicious happened recently?"

"Like what?"

"Strangers showing up, cars, boats you don't recognize."

Eduardo shook his head.

"I wouldn't be here."

"I suppose you've heard about Scilingo?"

"The one in the air force?"

"He spilled his guts about the flights. You know the ones. He said his conscience just suddenly jumped up and bit him on the ass. I don't believe it. Probably nothing will come of it but you never know. The point is there's been an uproar in the press. The old women are livid, so are the human rights people. The government's caving in to demands for more inquiries. I came to make sure everything's all right."

He put his glass down.

"I assume you have a plan in case something develops."

Eduardo regarded him with a half-smile. When he spoke, his voice had an ironic edge.

"You seem to have forgotten all the years I was on the run. I'm always ready. Those old western movies from America, the ones where an Indian puts his ear to the rails? It's such a habit I even listen in my sleep."

"Running's one thing," Guzmán said flatly. "A plan is another. You have money set aside for emergencies?"

"A little."

"I can help, if it comes to that, but it'd be a good idea to put away as much as you can."

Eduardo looked at him seriously.

"Is there something you haven't told me?"

"No. I've always been a great believer in taking precautions."

"This is the end of the world," Eduardo said confidently, "in case you haven't noticed. Not many people know how to get here."

"Nevertheless."

"I understand. I appreciate your concern. Now, what about some cards? I'm feeling lucky."

A sliver of light from the hall fell across Beatriz. Sleeping soundly, her breath slow and even, her hands resting, palm up, on the pillow, she looked younger, though hardly carefree. A shadow of the strain in her face remained, a memory in her flesh, Eduardo thought, of days and nights on the road, crisscrossing the country in search of peace. After all these years she still refused to discuss the past. What was done was done, she said. Talking would only rekindle feelings she wanted to forget. He undressed, wondering if something he did not know about lay at the heart of her sadness with other womanish knowledge, sealed against his venturing.

His head spun from the brandy as he crawled in beside her. He was bone-weary from a long day's fishing but filled with pleasure. The friendship with Guzmán was strong as ever, strong as steel. Few men could count on such ties. With a contented sigh, he moved close to Beatriz and buried his face in her hair.

He dreamed of his boat rocking on a swell, a street in Buenos Aires, the pampas seen from his house in Santa Rosalita, stretching to the horizon. The sun weakened, night came on. There was a drone trapped in its darkness. Headlights appeared, then the sound of a car growing louder by the moment, roaring like a freight train. Brakes squealed as the car skidded to a halt. Old women got out, shapeless crones in baggy dresses, their hair covered by white scarves whose ends tailed out like wings. The sound of their shoes on the porch was drumlike. The house shook. A gust of wind followed them inside, their faces set, eyes unblinking, chanting "blood is blood." As they walked past him toward the boys' room, one removed some clothes from a bag. Another was bent under the weight of a huge old-fashioned pen dripping ink on the floor. With gleaming eyes, she looked at him triumphantly. He asked why she had brought the pen. She stood there smiling as ink pooled on the floor and rose to her knees. She dipped the gleaming point into the ink. When she spoke he could not hear her over the wind. Seeing his distress, she shouted, "To cross out the names you gave them."

He shouted. He was sitting up, the night-light on, Beatriz' hand on his shoulder.

"A dream," she said. "You were dreaming."

The crones disappeared into the lamp's yellow glow. He took a deep breath. He had not dreamed of them in years.

"What was it?"

"The old women."

He licked his lips, swallowed, the fear still with him

along with the cold touch of wind. He lay down and pulled the blankets up to his chin.

"Rodolfo was talking about them."

She wanted to know why.

He told her about the confession, the uproar it had caused.

She remembered hearing about what Scilingo had done during the height of the war. There had been something terrible, a detail she could not recall that had made the story even worse.

There was nothing to worry about, he said. He had no connection to Scilingo. She listened as he went on about the dream.

After he had worked it out of his system, he kissed her neck. He wanted her.

She was slipping her nightgown over her head when it came to her.

"They were naked," she whispered.

"Who?"

"Scilingo's people."

In the afternoon Guzmán took the boys for a ride, letting each drive a little before he took over.

"You're still game?" he asked. "It's now or never. I'm leaving tomorrow morning."

"Sure," Manfredo said bravely.

Guzmán drove back onto the road. He approved of the boys. Naturally at this age they were unfinished but Eduardo had done a good job raising them. It would be interesting to see what kind of fiber they had deep down, what they were made of.

"Listen to the engine. You'll hear when it starts to reach its strength. The gearing's high. That's why there's no sense of strain."

The boys watched the speedometer climb past 180, 190, 200.

"Can it really go faster?" Manfredo asked nervously.

"This is enough for me," Tomás said from the backseat.

Guzmán glanced at him in the rearview mirror and floored the accelerator. There was a smooth surge of power. The land blurred. Telephone poles whipped by, the rush of wind increasing the sense of speed. Manfredo looked ahead resolutely. Tomás gripped the back of the passenger seat, his face drained of color.

The engine developed a subtle roar as the speedometer reached 250 and the needle settled snugly against its retaining peg. Guzmán was in his element. Maximum speed, maximum danger, balanced by sure hands and eyes that carefully searched the road ahead.

"Please," Tomás said.

"It's not as bad as high seas, is it?"

"Yes," said the boy.

"You have to look ahead and up close at the same time," Guzmán explained. "Your eyes have to be moving constantly. A rock on the road can throw the car out of balance. A pothole will break an axle."

Ahead the road curved left. Neither boy spoke but they both stiffened when Guzmán did not slow down.

"One test of a car is the speed it can maintain on curves. There are tremendous forces at work. The car wants to go ahead but the tires want to break loose of the pavement, disengage from the rims. These are the best, P6's, but there's a limit."

He kept the pedal on the floor as they entered the curve. The tires moaned, a low sound that quickly developed into a squeal.

"The steering's superb at these speeds," he told them, "perfectly engineered." He lifted his left hand from the wheel. "See? You can drive with one hand."

Manfredo gripped the handhold.

"Oh God," said Tomás.

As they exited the curve, the squealing subsided and Guzmán returned his hand to the wheel. The boys were still upset even though he had slowed down. Guzmán looked at Tomás in the rearview mirror, then at Manfredo, who was staring straight ahead, trying to regain his composure.

"Did you enjoy it?"

"Yes," Manfredo answered shakily.

Tomás said nothing.

Guzmán parked in the driveway and turned in his seat so he could see both of them.

"The test of a car is in the curves, straightaways are nothing. The test of a man is how he endures the unexpected. You don't get much of that here, I know, but you will, later in life."

In his room, Tomás looked at his brother.

"I thought he was going to kill us."

"It wasn't so bad."

Manfredo was reluctant to admit he had been scared. He liked Guzmán and admired the certainty he had about himself. The sense of authority that emanated from him was of a different kind than his father's, crisper, more embracing.

"He was going pretty fast," he admitted sheepishly.

"Why?"

Manfredo shrugged. "I don't know. What he said in the driveway."

"I don't believe it. Even if it were true, what gave him the right? And why did he come all the way down here?"

"He and Papa are old friends. They worked in the same building, remember? Papa did things for him. He lends Papa money sometimes."

"Why? What are we to him?"

Frustrated, Manfredo looked at his brother.

"You ask the stupidest questions."

"There's something we don't know," Tomás insisted. "I can feel it."

Manfredo laughed. "You feel yourself. I can hear your bedsprings at night."

"Go to hell," Tomás answered as he got up and went over to the window. His father and Guzmán were standing by the car. He watched them shake hands. Guzmán embraced his mother.

"Do you think they'd tell us?" he said without looking away.

"What?"

"What he means to them?"

"Why don't you ask?"

"Maybe I will," he said.

Something was wrong, he thought. He had little experience to measure the world against but he knew a streak of cruelty ran through Guzmán like a vein in a mine. The ride was proof.

His parents waved as Guzmán drove off down Calle de la Ventana.

"There's something else," he said, turning to Manfredo. "Why isn't he still in the army?"

FIVE

Ecstatic, impatient, Dolores boarded the bus and paid her fare without a word to Horacio. Free of the need to sit near other passengers as was usually the case after leaving the Ruedas' garden empty-handed, her heart as hollow as a dried gourd, she took a seat in the back, repeating to herself the two words Teresa had given her, sacred words more charged for her than holy writ, caressing them, admiring their shapes in her mind's eye, remembering their sound as they rolled off Teresa's tongue alive but delicate, even chimerical until she transferred their magic to letters on a map.

Horacio's shifting was glacial, the movements of a half-dead man. He waited for ages at every traffic light. She closed her eyes to make time pass faster. Mar Vista. The name. Mar Vista. Teresa was never wrong.

She walked quickly from the bus stop to her house, pushed the door open, and switched on the lights without breaking stride as she headed to the bookcase.

The atlas lay on the top shelf. She blew dust off the gold edging. Opening it on the table, she ran a trembling finger down the index until she found Mar Vista. It was there, in Argentina, just as Teresa said.

She flipped through the glossy pages, each taking her further south, closer. The region was rimmed by mountains, colored from beige to green, cartographer's code that meant nothing to her.

Inches from the bottom the coast turned ragged, formed a bay. There was a star just above the town's name, close as Venus to the moon. It had been waiting all those years, within reach of her chair! The way of the world, she thought, but no longer. They were there, that was all that mattered, more than enough to ease the bitterness of having waited longer than half their lifetimes. They were there. She would see them soon.

She studied the map, memorized topography, roads, rivers, towns along the way.

Her eyes blurred. She rested them and went on, reading every line about the region, drawn to descriptions of flora and fauna, aching to see the fan-shaped leaves of a certain plant, volcanic rock, the flukes of whales because this was what they saw every day, the familiar shapes that greeted her grandsons' eyes. Already she felt as if she were traveling, that her spirit was wrestling with her body, urging it toward the door.

When she finished reading she raised her eyes to the portraits of Rubén and Marta. She had never stopped talking to them. No matter how deep her discouragement, she spoke in response to something she could not quite name but knew was there, a beneficence, a presence, a trace of life that showed so brightly in their innocent eyes.

"We will have them back. We will have them back in this house where they belong. Tomorrow I go to the police."

She looked a long time at their faces, promising she would not fail, that failure was behind them now, an impossibility.

On her way down the hall to her bedroom she leaned against the wall, suddenly overcome by the inexplicable. She had always hoped for this night but she had not fully believed, she realized, not as she thought she had. The revelation frightened her and made all the more wonderful the vision of Teresa beneath the lanterns, tapping the crystal of reality until it broke.

Midway through the night a dream came to her. The boys were in a boat. She stood in surf up to her waist, buffeted by waves as she called, begged them to respond. Her voice was strong enough to carry over the crashing water. Why did they ignore her? Because they knew themselves by names that were not their own! "Silvio!" she shouted. "Luigi, Marco, Pablo," desperately crying every name she could think of. The moment she discovered the ones given them by the thieves they would turn and look and recognize her. Together, they could begin to unravel the lies binding them to a story they did not belong in.

Her voice grew hoarse, her throat painful. Her lips bled. When she could no longer speak, she retreated to the beach, wrote more names with her finger in the sand, the letters so large Roger and Joaquín could not fail to see them. Sooner or later she would find the right combination of letters and accents. Once she did, she would bathe their false names in acid, curse them as they boiled away to nothingness.

• • •

In the morning, for the first time in more than a decade, she put on a dress that was not black. Not an act of faith, she thought, but of certitude. Get thee behind me, blackness, she admonished her dresses. Then she strode out the door to the bus stop.

A sergeant at the police station explained that Captain Sorano handled all inquiries concerning the Disappeared.

"Your name?" he asked.

"Dolores Masson."

"You have met with him before?"

"Today is the first time I have needed to."

"A moment," he said and left the room. When he returned he held the door open.

"The last office on the left."

Sorano was a small, balding man, compact of body, with dark steady eyes. No sooner did she sit down than he asked the purpose of her visit.

The story spilled out like wine running down an overfilled glass. Crucial information about her grandsons had come into her hands last night. Since their disappearance she had marched hundreds of miles with other women in the Plaza de Mayo, enough to have walked from Buenos Aires to Tierra del Fuego. From time to time, clues to their whereabouts emerged only to prove worthless. She had been on a treadmill going nowhere until last night when she learned where the Ponces lived. Her source was impeccable. Her source knew Ponce. There was a precise description of his house in Mar Vista. All she lacked was an address.

"They're my flesh and blood. I want them back."

Sorano leaned forward, resting his chin on the tips of his fingers and looking as if he understood her urgency.

"The facts in these cases vary," he said sadly, "but the stories are all the same. We almost never find the kidnappers. It's worse than looking for a needle in a haystack. They change their names, run away at the drop of a hat, take new jobs. I don't have to tell you how lucky you are but we'll need evidence they're your grandsons, enough for a warrant. What do you have?"

Dolores removed two envelopes from her purse, opened one and unfolded a sheet of paper.

"This note fell into the hands of a friend a few months after the war. How it survived their fires and shreddings I'll never know but Ponce's name is on it, and an indication that my grandsons were given to him. It's signed by General Guzmán."

She handed the paper to Sorano, who read it quickly.

"It's the first time I've heard he was involved with this kind of thing."

"They were all involved," she said angrily. "Every one of them."

"Do you have any idea why it was Ponce?"

"Does it matter?"

Without waiting for him to respond she opened the second envelope, spread photographs of the boys over his desk as if she were dealing cards.

"They were very young then but you can trace adolescents' features in pictures like these. Everyone knows that. All you have to do is hold them up beside their faces."

"Tangential," Sorano said as he glanced through them. "What else?"

"Roger has a birthmark on his left shoulder the size of a cherry."

"Good. Excellent."

"Is that enough?"

"For now."

"How long will it take?"

He gazed at her, seemingly intent upon judging her strength.

"As far as time is concerned, we can start in a few days.

Assuming your information is accurate, finding them will be easy. But you need to prepare yourself for the aftermath."

"Why is that?" she asked impatiently.

"You've thought about these people a long time. If you're like everyone else, it's been one-sided, from your point of view only. Try it from theirs. As soon as they got the boys they made certain adjustments in their morality, demonized the real parents, imagined themselves as the children's saviors. They're almost always childless couples. They become doting parents, the children are the center of their lives, more so than in regular families. Years of loving attention is the rule. Roger and Joaquín think the Ponces are their parents and I can assure you they've been steeped in love. They'll have a much different view of this than you do."

Sorano took a bottle from his desk. His movements were precise, almost ritualistic as he filled the glasses. Without having to think about it, she knew this was something he had learned to do with others like herself, a delay calculated to let what he said sink in.

Given his warning, she almost felt guilty for feeling so alive, so excited, as if there were too much happiness in her heart. Of course the sun would rise and fall with the Ponces. The boys would have no memory of her, Rubén, Marta, Félicité. When they saw her she would be a stranger. But she was happy despite this because Sorano had overlooked the most telling fact of all.

She finished her drink in one swallow. The brandy warmed her throat. She looked at him candidly.

"But it's a lie," she said. "Everything from start to finish is predicated on a lie. The Ponces aren't who they say they are. Roger and Joaquín aren't who they think they are."

She recounted her dream of the night before.

"You see," she said when she finished. "I've already been preparing. I know it will be difficult but hardly more than having to look at two little boys, all that's left of your family, surrounded by fire. I've seen that image as long as they've been gone, every day, and I've survived. The lie they're living in is like the fire. I can hold my hand to it, walk on it with bare feet."

Sorano looked at her frankly without bothering to hide his skepticism. She liked his openness. Here was a man after her own heart, one she could deal with.

"I don't question your knowledge about these things, but believe me, señor, I am prepared for anything. Let me tell you a story.

"Years ago, before the *Proceso,* I read about a junk dealer in Eastern Europe who came into possession of a strange machine. Since he was in the salvage business, naturally he dismantled it with the hope of finding something to sell. Beneath lead panels he discovered material that glowed in the dark. He was so enchanted by the blue color that he took the substance home and put it on a table for his family to marvel at. Neighbors were summoned, bottles uncorked. It was radioactive. Of all the people who sat drinking in the room that night, one survived.

"For a long time it was just a terrible story, one of hundreds you come across. But the instant my family disappeared that blue glow came to life in my mind. It has become the color of memory, shedding unwavering light on everything that happened, every emotion I've felt from the day they were taken. It is the light of my archives, of everyone intimate with the word 'Disappeared.' If my skull were dug up a hundred years from now, the blue would still be there, fierce as ever. What could be worse than what I've already lived through?"

A silence fell between them.

Moved, eyes glistening, Sorano cleared his throat.

"Would you describe the color for me?"

"The blue of Argentina's flag."

• • •

She stayed up late studying the atlas. The cartographic details were vivid beneath the magnifying glass, irregular swirls and eddies denoting the shapes of the land, elevation. Of necessity, the terrain was depicted as though seen from high above in the eye of a satellite. She made the planes shift, restructured the map in her mind so that everything lay directly ahead of her. She saw the cordillera looming, saw the narrow road rise through it. From the peak she saw Mar Vista, light upon the sea, the boys in a boat approaching shore.

SIX

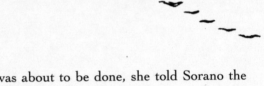

Sweet justice was about to be done, she told Sorano the morning they left Buenos Aires. The chickens were finally coming home to roost.

Justice was rarely so simple, he cautioned, and often carried within itself bitter seeds of irony. For her own sake, so she would not be disappointed, she needed to remember what he had said in his office.

"They believe the lie. To them it's the truth."

She presented her hand, palm out, for his inspection.

"And you need to remember what I said about the fire. The blisters are invisible but they're there, inside. There's nothing more the Ponces can do. My grandsons will weep. Then they will begin to understand."

The countryside engulfed them, isolating their car in

green valleys and barren plateaus. She had studied the route in her atlas until the smallest details were imprinted on her memory. If Sorano asked, she could tell him what lay around every curve, over every rise. She knew exactly where they were, the next benchmark, the one after that.

With her eyes on the road she thought ahead to the next day. How would she feel the moment she saw them? Ecstatic. Transported. But what she allowed herself to say depended on Roger and Joaquín. She had to be very careful to avoid confusing them, pushing them beyond their capacities, had to remember that regardless of what happened the death of the nightmare was only a matter of time. They would overcome whatever obstacles lay in their path. All it required was patience and she had plenty of that. If patience were the virtue people claimed it was, she had already stored up enough to be sanctified.

At nightfall they took rooms at Garibaldi's Inn.

After dinner Sorano insisted on going over the procedures. "If you forget them when we get there, that could mean trouble." This was a legal matter. She must let him and the local authorities do their job.

She appreciated his thoroughness. He exuded the self-sufficiency of a man who had mastered his trade, a godsend, really, who made her feel secure in the embrace of his competence. The law, debased so long, was resurrected in men like Sorano, a flash of steel against darkness.

She listened politely, out of respect, but she could not focus on the sequence of events, the fog of legalities. All she cared about was sunlight.

On the road descending the cordillera late the following afternoon she surveyed Mar Vista, hating its ugly utilitarian sprawl of corrugated metal, squat houses, the yard with fishing boats supported on wooden frames, hulls pale from sandblasting. She wanted to destroy everything, scorch the earth so thoroughly no one would ever know a town had been there.

The bay looked cold and threatening. The faces of workmen at the dock were craggy, their skin eroded by salt and wind.

"Give me the directions again," Sorano said. "We'd better make sure about the house."

She repeated Teresa's words.

"You never told me who your friend is."

"A young woman."

"And if we need her in court?"

"She'll come."

Two girls on bikes stared at them as they turned onto Calle de la Ventana. The houses were identical on the first two blocks. Those on the third looked the same. Halfway down the fifth the road curved left. At the end, abutting a field, stood the house with a tile roof and two chimneys. PONCE was painted in childish letters on the mailbox. Clothes fluttered on a line, the drying shirts, trousers, dresses, signs of a history in which she had played no part.

"How do you feel?" Sorano asked.

"Like I'm coming back to life."

"It would be best for me to see the magistrate alone."

"Yes," she whispered, looking at the name on the mailbox. She thought they must have still been quite young when they painted it.

Hernando Mendoza, the sole officer of the law in Mar Vista, was stunned when he read the warrant. It was impossible. His colleague must be mistaken.

Sorano shook his head. There was ample proof the Ponces had taken the boys. He asked Mendoza if he knew them. He did. They were friends of his son. Then, said Sorano, he might want to examine some photographs.

He laid them on the counter. Mendoza picked up each one, held it to the light.

"It's interesting," Sorano said, "how features really don't change much from childhood. Their grandmother believes she will recognize them instantly. What do you think?"

Sorano pursed his lips and waited while Mendoza studied the photographs. Finally the magistrate shook his head.

"This is devastating."

"It always is," Sorano answered as he returned the photographs to the folder.

"It's hard to believe."

"That's always the case too."

Mendoza looked at him.

"Let me break the news."

"Whatever's easiest," said Sorano. He glanced at his watch. "I'd like to start back by mid-afternoon."

"What about Eduardo and Beatriz?"

"If the DNA tests show a match between the boys and Señora Masson, they'll be summoned."

"Prison?"

"What do you think?"

Dolores tried to imagine the conversation going on inside, her confidence in Sorano giving way to fear that the magistrate would refuse to help. Any delay meant the Ponces might learn she was there. She was ready to go inside when the door opened and Sorano's eyes told her everything was fine.

She shook Mendoza's hand, saying she was grateful for his help. He told her he was sorry, it was horrible.

"Yes, but it's all about to change, isn't it?"

She was almost lighthearted when they set out. A few minutes after they started, following Mendoza's car, she could not get enough air. Gripping the crank tightly with her gnarled fingers, she rolled the window down, breathing deeply as she wept for Rubén and Marta, especially Marta, whom she prayed had lost her life before she knew she had lost her sons.

When they pulled into the Ponces' driveway behind Mendoza, a neighbor working in his garden paused and leaned on his hoe.

Two doors down, a woman with a bandanna over her hair came out on her porch and impatiently called to someone inside.

"We have an audience," Dolores said. "The more the better."

Sorano looked at her.

"This is going to be very ugly. I think you should wait here until they've gotten over the shock."

Dolores shifted her attention to the house, interrogating its shape. In a steady, slow-paced voice, she said, "When I wasn't thinking about this place I dreamed about it. For years."

She paused, caught up in memory, reliving the time when there was no mailbox, no clothes, only the barest hope.

"You're a good man, Sorano, decent, intelligent. What makes you think anything could stop me from walking through that door?"

The Ponces were having lunch. Eduardo was in the middle of a joke when the knock came and he quickly delivered the punch line before getting up. The boys laughed, and he was still chuckling to himself as he opened the door and saw the misery in Mendoza's eyes. He glanced at the other officer, then the old woman who regarded him with what seemed a bizarre mixture of rage and delight.

"We were just having lunch," he said uncertainly.

His voice was nothing like what Dolores had heard in her dreams, or imagined, endlessly, during her waking hours. That voice was gruff, low, evilly inflected, whereas this one sounded like an ordinary man's who was beginning to suspect something was wrong. She was disappointed; a thief of children should not sound so common. The timbre of his speech should give him away. Some law, natural or moral, should force his voice to match the blackness inside his heart. She wanted to curse him, wanted to deliver one of the impassioned speeches she had composed over the years when she had thought about this moment.

"You bastard!" she said venomously. "Where are my grandsons?"

Her words pinned Eduardo like a butterfly in a velvet case. The horizon behind her tilted. The sparkle of the sea slid away. His throat was tightening with panic when Beatriz called, "Who is it?" and the innocent tone of his wife's query, her ignorance, entered his heart like a knife. With the scrape of her chair against the floor his mind reeled sickeningly into the past, to a vision of the dream cars.

Beatriz came up behind him and slipped her arm through his.

"Hernando?" she said, inflecting his name into a question.

Mendoza stared at his feet.

"Señora Ponce, I am Captain Oswaldo Sorano. I have a warrant to take custody of Roger and Joaquín Masson."

"And I am their grandmother."

Beatriz raised a hand to her mouth.

"You're mistaken," Eduardo said in a strangled voice. "Our sons are Tomás and Manfredo."

Beatriz was glaring at Dolores when she heard the boys getting up. Whirling, she shouted, "Go to your rooms. This has nothing to do with you."

"Roger!" called Dolores. "Joaquín!"

She tried to slip between the Ponces, who blocked her way.

"Do as I say!" Beatriz shrieked over her shoulder.

The boys could not see Dolores or Sorano. Confused, they stood by the table a moment before Manfredo gestured with his head toward his room.

As soon as they went in, Beatriz grabbed the door with both hands and tried to slam it.

"Get out!" she sobbed.

Sorano leaned against it with his forearm.

"We must speak to them."

"Never!" cried Beatriz.

As Sorano stepped across the threshold, Eduardo threw a punch that grazed his cheek. Sorano was wrestling him to the floor when the boys came running from the room, looking exactly as Dolores knew they would: thin-cheeked, almond-eyed.

Terrified, Tomás shouted, "What are you doing?"

"Cuff him," Sorano told Mendoza. To the boys he said, "This is a matter of law."

"What law?" Manfredo demanded.

"It's a mistake," Beatriz said as she put her arms around him. "I love you more than my life. And you," she told Tomás.

Eduardo had been lying face down on the rug but at the sound of the boys' voices he struggled to his knees.

"Don't believe anything they say!" he gasped.

They looked from him to Sorano.

"Please," the captain said, "sit down. You too," he told Beatriz.

Weeping, she collapsed on the sofa and embraced the boys.

"They're ours," she insisted. "They always have been."

"Always," said Eduardo. "This is insane."

Dolores wanted to embrace them, tell them she would heal this wound, but it was too soon. She was a stranger they looked at hatefully. This was part of what had to happen, the prelude she had no choice but to endure.

"This is going to come as a shock," Sorano said.

"More lies," said Eduardo.

"I want you to prepare yourselves."

"We have birth certificates," Beatriz said in a quavering voice. "I'll show you."

"Something terrible happened during the war. The Ponces are not your parents. You are Roger and Joaquín Masson. This woman," he added, pointing to Dolores, "is your grandmother. We will make positive identification with a blood test but there is other proof."

Beatriz moaned. In the face of the old woman she saw her betrayal come to gloat and laugh. Had she been a good wife, they would be safe in Santa Rosalita.

"My mother," she managed to say, "*my* mother was your grandmother. Look at her. You can see nothing between her and you."

"Roger," Dolores said to the younger boy. "You have a birthmark on your left shoulder."

He looked bewilderedly at her.

"How do you know?"

"She's guessing," Beatriz said quickly. "A lucky guess."

Manfredo looked at Mendoza.

"What makes them think we aren't who we are?"

"Bitch!" Eduardo shouted. "They're my sons."

"They're my *blood*," she answered, her voice rising. "Blood is blood, no matter what you say."

Eduardo made a sound deep in his throat. As the words hammered inside his skull, he looked at Beatriz in a way she had not seen in years.

The boys had no idea what to make of her, Dolores thought. She could see it in their eyes. And because they were young and untried, it was easier for them to deny what they had heard, deny and challenge.

"I have photographs," she said, removing the folder from her bag.

"Of impostors," Beatriz said. "They could be pictures of anyone."

"Would you care to look?" Dolores asked. "What about you?" she said to Eduardo.

"Go to hell," he answered. "I wouldn't waste my time."

Dolores showed one to Roger.

"That's you, on the right."

Joaquín gazed over his brother's shoulder while Dolores went through the stack, holding each picture carefully by the edges so as not to mar the finish.

"This is your mother and father."

"They know who their parents are," Beatriz said. "I don't care. Show them a thousand."

Her smile, like a broken bone emerging from the skin, tightened when the boys looked at her, their eyes aglow with doubt.

"What happened?" asked Joaquín.

"Your mother died in the war."

"And him?" Roger asked, pointing at Rubén.

"After you were given to these people he left Argentina with your little sister. He thought you were dead and couldn't stand to live here."

She wondered if they remembered being handed over to the Ponces. The blankness in their eyes told her they did not. Joaquín adamantly refused to believe. She feared it would be the same with Roger. The resistance hardened in his face.

Then, suddenly, his eyes flickered. He was trying to ignore whatever had occurred to him even as it took hold more strongly. He glanced uneasily at Eduardo, a look that seemed part anger, part apology. "Who by?"

"A fairy," Beatriz interrupted bitterly. "Or maybe a goblin."

"A general he worked for," she said, nodding in Eduardo's direction.

Roger and Joaquín exchanged a shocked, knowing glance. The disbelief that had armored them only moments ago was crumbling. It was not sourced in anything she said but in something they knew. Roger silently interrogated his brother. Slowly, he turned to Dolores, his voice shaking.

"His name?"

"This will be good," Beatriz said. "I can't wait. Humpty-Dumpty? Rumpelstiltskin?"

"Guzmán. General Rodolfo Guzmán."

"I worked for him," Eduardo said disparagingly. "You know that. Many people know it. It proves nothing."

But it did. Dolores had seen the effect while the name was still fresh on her tongue.

Roger's eyes shifted to Beatriz.

"Mother?"

She moistened her lips. Dolores saw the desire for death in her face, a need so great Dolores almost pitied her. She watched Beatriz sit up, her eyes bright with purpose, and waited for the expected words, readied herself to counter them but they did not come. Beatriz' eyes lost their brightness the second she realized that it was too late for denial. She leaned against Eduardo and began to cry.

"I don't care," Roger said shakily.

"Neither do I," Joaquín added. "They're our family. We won't leave them."

"I'm afraid it's not that simple," Sorano told him. "As minors, you don't have a choice."

Eduardo glared at Dolores. "They'll never accept you."

"They'll hate you," Beatriz sobbed.

Sorano said, "You will very likely be charged with kidnapping and using forged documents. As of now the boys are no longer in your care. Until the hearing, they will remain in Señora Masson's custody. You may visit them under supervision."

Dolores leaned against the wall, suddenly aware of how tired she was, how weak, how there was so much more to say than she could give voice to now. She would have to tell them they were entering the hardest time in their lives, that to go on they had to go back, erasing as they did what they believed was truth, that they were victims of the war no less than those who disappeared. And that would only be the beginning.

When Sorano told the boys to pack, Eduardo weakly said he refused to allow it.

"You have no authority," Sorano said. "Everything has changed."

"Nothing has changed!" Beatriz yelled. "They'll always love us! We'll get them back! Wait and see."

Mendoza was the first one out of the house. Sorano and Dolores followed the boys down the walk while Beatriz screamed their names. Sorano had to hold her off until the boys were in the backseat of the car.

Beatriz slapped the windows with the flat of her hands. As the car headed up Calle de la Ventana she broke free of Eduardo's embrace and ran after it all the way to the intersection. She was kneeling in the street by the time Eduardo reached her. She looked at him stark-eyed as a crow.

"I hope their mother was on Scilingo's plane. I hope she was afraid of water."

SEVEN

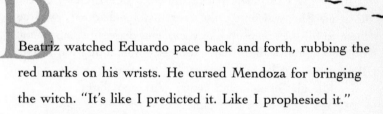

Beatriz watched Eduardo pace back and forth, rubbing the red marks on his wrists. He cursed Mendoza for bringing the witch. "It's like I predicted it. Like I prophesied it."

He stared distractedly at her. Whether he wanted confirmation or denial was unclear.

"But that's ridiculous. It was a dream, pure and simple. Something happened. Something made it possible."

She turned her head, sickened by his suspicion. A good wife would console him, agree, question, whatever he needed but she feared giving herself away. It was crucial to put him off the scent, yet she could think of nothing, not the slightest ruse. Perhaps she had used them up. Even if an idea came to mind she had no energy left to pursue it, having exhausted her emotions in screaming her desire for their mother to have died at sea. The nakedness that appalled her last night now seemed the last perfect touch of revenge. She remembered hearing about the flights from the wife of a naval officer. Every Wednesday they had made them, every Wednesday for two years. The subversives had been drugged by a navy officer. What if they woke between plane and sea? Would they think it was a dream or realize they were falling? The rush of air would be deafening but maybe no louder than a whisper. How would it feel, the air against bare skin? She wished she knew. She could have told the old woman.

She sank back onto the sofa and stared out the window at the sea. As Eduardo paced, the sun inched closer to the horizon. She welcomed the lengthening shadows, wanted them to fill the room up like water and drown his suspicion. But it was more than that. He knew. Something happened. That was what he said. Something had happened.

"I'll call Guzmán," Eduardo said over dinner.

"Yes," she answered dully.

"We'll have them back before you know it."

"Yes," she said again, too consumed with guilt to find her way to other words.

He ate slowly, thinking out loud about what they had to do, interrupting himself from time to time with questions. How could they have been discovered after all these years? He must have let down his guard, missed something. He had always read warnings in commonplace events. His intuition sent them fleeing in the middle of the night, sometimes with only the clothes on their backs. His sixth sense had failed, deserted him. How else account for this calamity?

Beatriz cleared the table. The dishes felt heavy as lead, the water she washed them in viscous. Every night, without being asked, the boys helped her clean up. She looked at her reflection in the kitchen window. Through it she saw their shocked, dazed eyes, the disbelief edging toward belief.

Eduardo was drinking when she joined him in the living room. Before the wine took hold, he repeated his conviction that they would find a way to get the boys back. She watched his eyes redden, heard his speech turn thick. Before long, he had retreated into himself like water going down a drain, lost in speculation and surmise. She stayed with him until he was ready to stagger into bed.

She slept a few hours, woke wide-eyed. Slipping on a robe, she wandered through the house, her body heavy, a separate weight pressing on her heart.

At first, she denied she had to do it. Nothing but pain would come from confessing. An hour passed and her arguments were in tatters. She had to tell him. It was impossible to live another day with the betrayal hidden in her breast. Quietly retrieving a blanket from the hall closet, she fell asleep on the sofa and woke with the first light of dawn.

After making tea and leaving the pot to steep, she went into their bedroom. There was a sour smell of wine. She switched on the lamp and jostled his shoulder.

He woke, startled. In a cottony voice he asked what time it was.

"Early. I couldn't let you sleep any longer."

"Why?"

He sat up and rubbed his eyes.

She felt old and heavy. She felt defeated and ashamed.

"Well?" he said.

Every moment of every day since they had left Santa Rosalita returned. She saw herself in the old kitchen, the secret latent in her eyes, heard it compromise her voice, her laugh. Years of deception spun round and round, like the boys' tether ball circling its pole.

"Eduardo," she said, her eyes filling with tears, "it was me."

"What are you talking about? Since you woke me up, at least bring some tea."

She fled to the kitchen, telling herself that he deserved better than this. Now that she had tried and failed to speak she was afraid her confession might stick in her throat, that she would choke on it like a piece of bone.

The cup and saucer clattered as she put them on the nightstand. Tea sloshed over the side.

"It'll be all right," he said. "There are things we can do. You can't go to pieces. Get some tea. You'll feel better."

She shook her head. "It was me," she insisted. "I brought it on us."

"Nonsense," he said, patting the bed. "I'm to blame if anyone is. We'll figure out what happened. We'll get them back."

She would have to show him, lead him through it step by step. *First the earring, then its story.*

She rummaged through the upper shelf of their closet for the strongbox whose cold metal chilled her fingers. She had not touched it since the day they'd arrived in Mar Vista, had hated seeing it whenever she opened the closet. Years ago she put a stack of clothes in front of it but she still saw it in her mind's eye.

After retrieving the key from her dresser, she put the strongbox on the bed and unlocked it. She was aware of him watching as she removed a square of paper and unfolded it with trembling hands.

Nestled in the white crepe, the earring looked even smaller than she remembered, thinner, more delicate.

"Because of this," she said, holding the earring in her palm for him to see. "They're gone because of this."

Eduardo stared. He recognized the earring but was ignorant of its meaning.

When she unwrapped it she had believed it had freed her voice, that she could blurt out the story and wait stoically for the retribution it would bring. But she could not speak. She could only stare at the gold circle glinting in the morning light. Suddenly, she threw it against the wall.

"It ruined us!" she sobbed. "It's cursed."

The earring spun on the floor, wobbled, fell. With the story gagging her, she picked up the earring and rushed into the kitchen, put it on the counter. She was raising the cleaver when Eduardo grabbed her arm.

"What's gotten into you?"

Looking into his eyes, she thought he could not be such a fool. *He had to know.* He was consciously drawing out her anguish to satisfy himself. It was part of his revenge.

"Do you want me to use it on myself? Would that suit you better?"

Eduardo pried her fingers from the cleaver. Slowly, deliberately, letting silence intrude between each word, he said, "We will get them back. I promise."

Half-astonished, she said, "You don't hate me?"

He looked for the source of the question in her eyes.

"Why should I?"

Everything she was about to say hovered before her like scenes in a film. She wished she could simply open her skull and reveal its contents.

"You remember the day the boys found it, the day in the pampas?"

"Of course."

"And how you worried about what it was doing out there, how you told them not to talk about it?"

"That's ancient history," he said uncomfortably. "What does it have to do with anything?"

"Because it wasn't the same with me. After you told me why it was there, that they'd stumbled on a killing field, I started thinking about the woman it belonged to. I started feeling her mother's grief in not knowing what had become of her daughter. I started thinking about how I'd feel if I lost the boys. I started taking the earring out of the strongbox after you'd leave for work, looking at it, feeling worse all the time."

What she wanted to see in his eyes was not there. She had hoped the meaning would strike him before she had to explain but there was only consternation.

"Why? You knew she had to be a terrorist."

"It didn't matter. Knowing and feeling aren't the same. I thought of her mother sitting alone in a room, wringing her hands. It got worse. After a while that was all I could think about."

She paused, sat down on the edge of their bed.

"One day I took it out of the strongbox and walked into town. I knew what you'd think. I knew I was betraying you but it didn't matter. All that mattered was that woman and her daughter's bones."

He was attentive now, wary, but still innocent.

"You know where I was going?"

He shook his head.

"To the police."

Without taking her eyes from his she remembered how the station looked, saw again the way Fernando de la Hoya reacted as she explained the origin of the earring. The surprise that had bloomed in the captain's face was nothing compared with what was coming upon Eduardo's.

"That's what brought the authorities to Santa Rosalita. That's how they found the site, why they started digging. They would never have known about it if I hadn't gone to De la Hoya. You wouldn't have become afraid and insisted that we move. We'd still be there with the boys."

Eduardo remembered the procession of trucks moving through town, their doors bearing the insignia of the Ezekiel squad.

He remembered his moonlight visit to the site so carefully prepared for excavation and the chill that had come upon him, the sense of danger closing in from all sides.

He remembered fleeing south the next morning, the endless hours of driving, his first sight of Mar Vista, all so vivid and shorn of time that he had to struggle back to the present as if he were surfacing from a dive.

She was waiting, searching his eyes.

"You fool," he said. "You fucking idiot."

Light and unburdened, she waited for him to go on. Light and unburdened but not free because she had only exchanged the weight of her betrayal for the floating sensation of guilt. The weight had held her down. Now the wind seemed to rush through her hair as she followed him into the living room aware of the silence, the absence left by the boys as if it were imprinted on the air.

"I told you," she pleaded. "I didn't have to. I confessed. Doesn't that count for something?"

He stood rigid, looking out the window.

The sun's glare on the sea made her dizzy. There was so much space and he was a dark silhouette in the middle of it where something terrible was beginning to happen. Her crying became laughter, laughter and silence weaving in and out. "I'm falling," she said, "falling."

When he turned she was weeping. He left, returned minutes later. She had not stopped.

"Get hold of yourself!"

She tried. With all her strength she tried but the tears ran of their own accord. They seemed to have nothing to do with her. The laughter parted her lips against her will.

He could stand it no longer and called the doctor.

"I don't know," she heard him say, "but you better come and take a look."

He glared at her with what seemed the purest anger she

had ever seen. She turned her face to the wall. In a while she heard him talking to Guzmán.

Eduardo spoke in quick disjoined phrases, his voice full of rage and some emotion Guzmán could not identify. The moment he started talking about Beatriz' grief he knew she was at the center of it. Something had happened to her that had thrown Ponce off balance, he was sure of it. There were two stories, the one of the abduction, another that Ponce was withholding, whether from embarrassment over some domestic trifle or because it was too private to share.

"All right. Don't worry. We know where they are. It'll take a while to arrange for the tests."

"I dreamed about this," Eduardo said softly. "It scares me."

"Dreams don't mean shit," Guzmán replied impatiently. "What you need to do right now is take care of your wife. Give me some time to mull this over. I'll call in a few days."

Guzmán felt less sanguine about the turn of events than he led Ponce to believe. He was worried about how they had been found. Eduardo was too careful to let anything slip. Unsound as she was, it seemed unlikely that Beatriz would have compromised them. His mind dwelled uneasily on a connection with Scilingo but it made no sense. Regardless of what angle he approached it from, he could see no relationship between the events. It was merely chance, he decided, one thing had nothing to do with the other. What mattered was not why it had happened but how it could be corrected.

He put on his swimming trunks, then glanced at the floor-length bedroom mirror. At sixty-four, he still had good definition in his chest from swimming a thousand meters every day, rain or shine. Gloria appreciated the way he looked. So did Anna.

Recalling his mistress put a spring in his step as he strode out to the pool and dove, immediately establishing his rhythm. He glided from end to end with his goggled eyes focused on the strip painted on the bottom. This was where he thought better than anywhere else. With only the sound of his breathing and the disciplined movement of his body, his mind was capable of subtleties denied him out of the water, quickly breaking down problems into their constituent parts. He considered his affection for Ponce, the boys, the fact that he had created a family with a simple command. The restitution of the boys to the grandmother was an affront to him as well, a belated defeat. What he could do would be complicated, even dangerous, but satisfying. A challenge.

With a quick thrust, his arms rose into the butterfly and sent the water flying.

EIGHT

Dolores glanced at her watch. No one had spoken since they'd left Mar Vista an hour ago, not a word. She was not surprised. Like her, Sorano and the boys were still reeling from the confrontations, the tone of accusations and denials spoken and shouted that had reverberated among the timbers of the Ponces' house like the clapping of great struck bells. The distorted expressions by themselves were more than enough to silence anyone but that was not where the silence came from. The silence was Beatriz' work, the legacy of the curse hurled like the knife as they drove away. Unlike herself and Sorano, the boys had no idea what it meant but the hate must have been clear to them. The obscenity of Beatriz' desire had sucked the air necessary for speech from the car, leaving them in a vacuum as they climbed the cordillera.

In place of speech there was the laboring engine and the squeal of tires when Sorano negotiated switchbacks. In its own way it was as eloquent as music in a film, the theme of success, though it signified something else to the boys — defeat, fate, a combination of ideas and emotions she was not privy to. She knew them better in memory than in the flesh, as they used to be, not as who they were. All she could be certain of was that the silence was a refuge for them, a shelter in which they were trying to confront what they could scarcely believe. She wanted to leave them there but it was impossible. The longer it continued, the more reluctant they would be to speak. She, too, was responsible for the silence. Had it not begun the night she carried home the name of the town from Carlos' garden? It had, and it was her duty to end it.

Yet she felt dumb as she turned in her seat to face the boys. Their eyes and mouths were eloquent chronicles of the day. She saw their love for the Ponces, and embedded in it, like a thorn, the suspicion of their origins. She wished they were older and more steeped in the ways of the world, capable of hiding their feelings as adults learned to do. With her eyes she tried to show them that she understood how they felt.

"Of course you're suffering," she said after taking a deep breath. "It would be stupid to think otherwise. But the only way to deal with this is for us to talk."

Joaquín averted his face and stared out the window. Roger regarded her with a mixture of confusion and anger before glancing down at his hands.

"I know you don't want it to be true. I'd feel the same if I were you. I'd try to convince myself it was a dream and that I'd wake up soon and everything would be the way it was."

Roger looked up long enough to give her a hateful look.

"But it's not a dream. My blood runs in your veins. I'm your grandmother but also a stranger who's turned your lives upside down. I will have to earn your friendship, your respect, just like anyone else. We have to learn who we are together, fill in all those missing years. My question is: How can it happen if we don't talk? The only resolution is in words."

The engine strained as Sorano shifted to a lower gear.

Joaquín looked at Roger before glancing at her. In a flat, deadened voice he said, "We have nothing to say."

They had recoiled from the sound of her voice, as if she had raised her hand and threatened to strike them. All new words—hers and Sorano's—would seem tainted. They wanted only the old ones, those they had heard and spoken before they knew she existed. She understood why they chose silence. Speech might loosen their grip on who they wanted to believe they were.

What the Ponces had done was even worse than she had imagined, what she had to do in response more difficult than she had ever dreamed.

Their faces seemed to loom out of the mountainside, large as boulders, granite-like, unrepentant. She searched the stone eyes for an explanation, so deeply engrossed in her reverie that it took a moment to realize Sorano was speaking.

"She's right," he was telling them as he glanced in the rearview mirror. "I've seen this before. It'll hurt less the sooner you accept it, believe me. Things get better when you talk them out."

"Things were fine," Roger answered bitterly.

Grateful as she was for Sorano's intervention, she was uncertain how he could respond to Roger. She was afraid the boy had silenced him.

"There's something you ought to know about your grandmother," he went on, "something that might let you see things a little more clearly. Will you listen, or are you going to act like children?"

Dolores stiffened. Her instinct to protect the boys was sharp and precise. "There's no need to insult them," she said crisply.

"I don't care what he says," Roger told her.

Sorano turned the wheel, braked, accelerated.

"You aren't the only kids who were stolen during the war. She's not the only grandmother who waited years for some word about where you were. Long before you were taken, a group of women began demonstrating in the Plaza de Mayo. They marched every Thursday, rain or shine, in front of the Casa Rosada, demanding an accounting from the government about the whereabouts of their children and grandchildren. Why do you think they did it?"

"How should we know?" Joaquín answered. "You know so much, you tell us."

"Because they had to. Dangerous as it was, they had to march and carry posters with your names and pictures because to go on living they had to refuse to accept your disappearance."

He paused to look at Dolores. When he continued, his voice was softer, lacking the sarcastic edge she had heard before.

"It was a form of hope, of love. Neither she nor any of the others can ever tell you how much it cost."

Despite their petulance, the boys could not ignore Sorano's words. They looked at him, reluctantly waiting for him to continue. He downshifted and braked almost to a stop, whipped the steering wheel.

"The military, the police, ordinary citizens thought they were fools. Traitors. They called them the 'crazy ones.' Some people still feel that way. But there are a lot of us who've always thought they were among the bravest of the brave."

Dolores felt acutely self-conscious. She had never

thought of herself in such terms, nor had any of her colleagues.

"We did what was necessary," she said quietly. "Brav-
ery had nothing to do with it. He's right, though, about why
we were there."

The years of marching in the plaza regardless of how
she felt, crawling out of bed on the days she was ill, enduring
heat, rain, and worst of all the constant threat of despair, the
danger of giving up, were all compressed in her mind, like a
medieval tapestry depicting wars that had lasted decades.
She wondered if the Crusaders had felt the same compulsion
she and her colleagues shared, the belief that odds were of no
consequence when the stakes were so high. She had no desire to talk about herself but her memories had led to something they had to know.

"I understand how you feel about Eduardo and Beatriz.
Love doesn't die with the truth. It doesn't get lost, either, no
matter how many years pass. My *compañeras* Señor Sorano
told you about never lost it. Neither did I. There were times
when I was almost overcome by despair but I never lost the
love behind it. I needed it the way I did air to breathe, food
to eat. It's what kept me alive."

She had addressed them slowly, careful to avoid sound-
ing shrill, wondering whether she should hold off talking
about it until they were more used to her, afraid they might
take her words as a challenge rather than a gift, that in putting her love on the table, showing all her cards, they would
feel overwhelmed, confused. Impossible to know, she
thought. She was ignorant of the workings of their minds
and hearts. She had to force herself to see only what was
there, accept the reality of the moment. They were not ready
for the gift. But through the confusion and pain glittering in
their eyes it seemed as though she could see a softening, that
they looked at her a little differently, as a person and not
merely a force to reckon with.

At the summit the road straightened out and began a gentle downward glide toward the valley where the horizon was already obscured by afternoon haze. A hawk flew low, wheeled, and glided upward until it lost its momentum and hung suspended in the sky.

She wanted to embrace Roger and Joaquín, say that they were already passing through the most difficult stage, and that soon everything would be better. She wanted to make that all there was to see, like the hawk dominating the sky.

"I meant it when I said my love for you kept me alive all those years. It was so strong I used to think that if this day ever came it would seal off the past like a boulder blocking a road. I was wrong. The past lives inside us like a virus. The only treatment is time, love, understanding."

Whether her words made sense to them she could not tell. Exhausted, her mind depleted, she realized that she had done all she could for now.

She settled back and watched dusk come down. It was almost dark when they stopped at the wayside inn where she and Sorano had spent the previous night.

In the lobby she asked if they wanted separate rooms.

Without consulting his brother, Joaquín shook his head. "We'll share," he answered.

"I'm starved," Sorano said. "Why don't you get us a table in the dining room? I'll bring in the luggage."

The housemaid who doubled as the inn's waitress had brought a carafe of wine and a basket of bread by the time Sorano joined them. After pouring wine for Dolores and himself, he reached across the table for Joaquín's glass. The boy quickly put his hand over it.

"We aren't allowed to drink."

Dolores stiffened. It was nothing, a simple habitual response, one of hundreds of prescriptions for living learned from the Ponces she would have to deal with. But understanding where it came from made it no easier to bear. Joaquín's comment and all the others like it that would follow would be a constant presence in her life, symptoms of the past. They would come without warning and take her unprepared. All she could do was be aware such things were going to happen and hope she could find a way to keep the pain they caused at bay.

She called to the waitress for some water.

The woman returned with two bottles and waited for their orders.

Sorano and Dolores chose steak.

"And you?" the waitress asked the boys.

Dolores saw them exchange a glance.

"Order anything you want," she said encouragingly.

"The same," Joaquín said.

Dolores began eating as soon as their plates arrived, then noticed that the boys had not touched their food.

"Is there something wrong with it?" she asked, putting down her knife and fork. "Would you like something else?"

Joaquín shook his head.

"We aren't hungry," Roger said.

She stared hard at them, felt the blood rising in her face. They were trying to appear disinterested in the food but their wolfish expressions gave them away. It was not the test that angered her so much as what lay behind it. Better to deal with it now, she thought, make her feelings known from the outset.

"You have rules to live by," she said sharply. "So do I. I will not tolerate lying."

They looked at her, clearly surprised. She wished that the first words she spoke to them with the authority of a relative had been other than these. Words of love, encouragement, were what she wanted to offer, words to soothe.

"Think what you want to about what's happened, ask

all the questions you need. I'll always listen to the truth, no matter how painful, but don't ever lie to me."

Roger seemed embarrassed. Joaquín looked as though he were prepared to speak, then thought better of it.

"This is important to me but it goes beyond the personal. You're here, I'm here, because of lies that began in the highest places and spread like a sickness across the country."

They understood she was angry. They did not know why. Their history was blank, she realized, an unopened book whose pages might as well be pure white, unnumbered. A memory of standing in the office of a bureaucrat returned, of the boredom in his voice when she said there were no records of Rubén and Marta. Another of an official statement in the papers denying that anyone had disappeared. They were not ready for such things. Someday, yes, but the weight of that knowledge was too great for them to bear.

"I know you're hungry," she said calmly. "If you won't eat as a protest, have the courtesy to say so. I can accept that. Or take the food to your room, if that'll make it easier."

She began to eat, glad to have drawn the line even though it had been harder for her than they knew. She kept her eyes on her plate and did not look at them when they picked up their knives and forks.

Whether they ate because of hunger or because she had shamed them, it was obvious when they finished that they considered dinner a defeat.

"Listen," she said, aware that staying at the table with her and Sorano any longer would only make it worse, "it's been a very long day. Why don't you go up to your room?"

Joaquín searched her face with surprising earnestness. So far as she could remember, it was the first time he had looked at her without anger. He nodded curtly, perhaps in grudging acknowledgment of her frankness, perhaps only from gratitude at being released. There were so many things to learn, a whole invisible network of signs and signals that made them who they were.

She watched them go up the stairs. Though their minds were foreign to her, their lean and supple bodies were familiar, the way they walked like Rubén with the same unconscious grace that had lain dormant in their blood and now had flowered. She was consoled by the thought that some things about them were too deep for Eduardo and Beatriz to have touched.

Sorano ordered coffee and cognac. In a while he said, "We should go to bed. I'd like to get an early start. The sooner we're back in Buenos Aires the better for everyone."

She wished she could approach the coming night as only another night, that nothing in its long hours would be any different from the past. But she had begun to feel apprehensive the moment she lost sight of them on the stairs. A vision came to her of them repacking their suitcases, whispering, making plans. She could almost hear their voices—

"I'm sleeping down here."

He cocked his head to one side, regarded her quizzically.

"Why?"

"Do I have to spell it out?"

She was afraid he misunderstood and that she was going to have to explain something she preferred to keep inside. To her relief he frowned.

"You're afraid they'll try to get away."

She nodded.

"Aren't you?"

"I suppose," he said, looking at her uncertainly. "Do whatever you want to. I just think . . ."

"That she's an exhausted old woman. It doesn't matter."

"The doors can be locked from the outside."

"Absolutely not!"

"What's the difference?" he asked dryly.

"How do you think they'd feel if they realized we'd locked them in? I won't put them through that. If they try to leave I can talk to them, reason with them. I don't mean to be difficult but that's how it is."

Sorano ran two fingers over his mustache. "I'll be happy to do it."

She shook her head and put her hand on his arm. "They're my responsibility."

She was happy he had the good grace not to argue.

"If you need me," he said as he got up.

"I know."

After he left she listened to footsteps, doors closing, the sounds of people settling down for the night. From the kitchen came the clattering of pots and pans, tired voices raised in complaint.

The waitress appeared, surprised to find her stretched out on the sofa.

"Is something wrong with your room?"

"No. This is fine."

The woman looked at her curiously, shrugged. She went into the back and returned with two blankets.

"It gets cold here at night."

"Thank you," Dolores said. There was already a chill in the air. She wrapped one blanket around her shoulders and spread the other over her legs. "You're very kind."

The waitress smiled and turned off the lights.

In a while Dolores' eyes adjusted to the dark. A bird sang and was answered by another; small, plaintive sounds that pleased her. Soon from their faint music an image of the boys emerged, their easy, lanky grace as they climbed the stairs.

She drew the blanket up to her chin, conscious of an emotion so long absent from her life that it took a moment to realize it was happiness. And why not? Last night the boys had been ignorant of her and of who they were. Now they were upstairs. Ten hours, twelve hours on the road tomorrow and she would lead them up the walk to the house where she had given birth to Rubén, unlock the door, watch them step across the threshold and reenter the world where they belonged.

But the story of happiness was matched by another, the story of the past pulling at them like an undertow, dragging them down, a story that could begin with a creak on the stairs.

She imagined switching on the lamp beside the sofa. Trapped in its yellow light, surprised, uncertain, frightened, Roger and Joaquín would stare, wondering what she was going to do, waiting for her to act.

It was possible. If it happened, could she order them upstairs like a prison guard, find words to convince them that everything had changed when she knew they had the right to follow their hearts? Because they must be free to choose. Must be. Otherwise, they could not live together as a family. But if she believed that, why hadn't she offered them the choice in Mar Vista? Was she supposed to go to their room now and confess her fear that they might run away, that to prevent it she had taken up a post in the lobby? Was she supposed to tell them her desire was tainted with selfishness and that they were free to choose, that she would not stand in their way? And if she could not do it, did that mean she was a hypocrite, that the love she described to them yesterday was inward-turning, one-sided? Did she have to be a saint?

The questions re-formed without her bidding. Words changed places, implications shifted. The consequences of speech or silence grew strong and waned. But even as the debate raged she knew the outcome. For every argument that would lead her up the stairs and force a knock on the door there was the memory of their absence, the photographs of them in their sailor suits, the great gaping wound

in her heart. She could not do it. They were too young, too
new in the world. She had to protect them with her knowledge.

The birds were closer, their singing stronger. She wondered if they were perched in the tree outside her window.
She remembered the bird market where hundreds of them
sang to passersby strolling up and down the aisles. Was it
merely for pleasure, for the feeling in the throat, the sound of
the melody, or were they asking to be released?

She dreamed of Rubén walking along a narrow street
with Félicité. Wet cobblestones glistened under streetlights.
In the distance a shadowy figure played a hand organ while a
monkey dressed in a flowing gown scampered at his feet.
The music was strange and sad, a lament of the sea.

Rubén and Félicité vanished with the organ grinder.
The light grew stronger until the cobblestones moved like
water and the monkey pointed to a bay. The boat was there,
the boys were on it. She recognized them even though they
were a long way out.

The monkey chattered and ran out the length of his
chain. He looked at her with red eyes and pointed urgently
toward the boat. Now she understood. It was adrift, dragging its painter. She had been certain there were oars, had
heard the hollow sound of wood against metal in oarlocks.
But it was only a sound the monkey made. They were adrift
without oars, borne by the tide toward a black rock. Not a
rock. It was Eduardo with the painter over his shoulder.
Tiny fish clung to the rope like jewels. Up to his chest in
water, buffeted by swells, he moved steadily southward, pulling the boat behind him as the sun set and his skin turned
blue, the boat turned blue. The boys stood, holding each
other for balance. Their legs were blue. The color rose like
water as the monkey screamed.

NINE

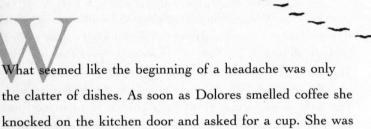

What seemed like the beginning of a headache was only the clatter of dishes. As soon as Dolores smelled coffee she knocked on the kitchen door and asked for a cup. She was drinking it by the window when Sorano appeared wearing a heavy jacket and gloves.

Casually, but with an edge to his voice, he said, "Did they try?"

"No, thank God."

"Good. And you're all right?"

As he searched her eyes she felt no overwhelming need to explain her change of heart. Even if she did, this was hardly the time to explore the idea.

She smiled. "I'm happy. I'm clearer in my mind than I was last night."

He seemed poised to ask her why and she was wondering if she had given away the conflict with a gesture, a word, when he glanced out the window.

"I always walk in the morning. Want to go along?"

"Thank you but no. My hips."

He was heading for the door when the boys came downstairs. Their eyes were red-rimmed, their faces puffy. They watched Sorano turn up the collar of his jacket as he went out.

Roger looked at her apprehensively.

"Are we leaving?"

"He's off for a walk."

Through the window she saw Sorano reach the road and turn left.

"Let's have breakfast," she suggested. "I don't know about you but I'm starved."

Joaquín gave her a suspicious look, as if anticipating a comment about the scene at dinner.

"Last night was last night," she said. "I don't hold grudges. Come on. The coffee's good. Hot and strong."

They ate voraciously, mopping their plates with bread before she was half-finished.

They watched her uneasily. While she was having her coffee earlier she had wondered what difference the night might have made in them, whether their resistance would soften or grow harder, but there seemed to be no change. So far as she could tell, yesterday's sullenness remained intact.

Suddenly her appetite was gone. She took another bite and put down her fork while they looked at her blankly, revealing nothing.

"Sometimes things happen we don't understand at first, things we'd never expected. I know you're in pain but try to remember I'm not the cause of it. The three of us, we're all victims, we're all innocent. Maybe that's hard to accept but it's the truth."

Roger had glanced down at his plate as soon as she began speaking. With a sudden toss of his head he confronted her.

"Did you ever think how we'd feel when you came? What it would be like for us?"

"I thought only of making the world whole again."

"And that's supposed to make it all right?" Joaquín said.

"That is the work of the truth."

"What if it doesn't?"

"It must," she answered. "Otherwise, we're all lost."

She brushed a wisp of hair out of her eyes. They regarded her skeptically, already resisting what she might say next.

"Listen. Until I walked into that house I thought only of how it would feel to get you back. All the way from Buenos Aires I imagined how you looked, how you'd feel when I hugged you, what your voices sounded like. I was greedy for you, greedy as someone starving is for food. But nothing's ever as simple as it seems. I meant it when I said love can't be forgotten, can't be forced. But I resisted what follows — that people who love each other must be free. I spent last night in the lobby because I was afraid you'd leave. I realized I couldn't stop you, had no right to stand in your way. Even with the law on my side I was denying your freedom, taking away your right to decide."

She did not say she had been certain they would try to escape, that she was still surprised they had not. Her candor seemed to have left them off-balance. For a moment she thought that was why they seemed hesitant. Then it came to her. They did not believe the story she and Sorano told but they did not disbelieve either. They were trapped between those stories and the Ponces'.

"What can I do to make you feel better? If I were you, there'd be all kinds of things I'd want to know."

Joaquín shifted in his chair. His heavy eyelids gave him a brooding look. He was less predictable than Roger, with moods that seemed to run deeper. He was the mercurial one, like Rubén. Roger had his mother's disposition.

She watched him lean forward and clasp his hands on the table.

"All right. How did you find us?"

There was no answer he could understand.

"Luck," she said slowly. "Luck and persistence. There were rumors over the years about where you were but the trail always turned cold."

"What did you do?" Roger asked.

"I marched every Thursday in the Plaza de Mayo with a sign bearing your pictures and a question: 'Where are Joaquín and Roger Masson?' All the signs had questions like that. They were double-edged, ironic. The answer could be either alive or dead, a place where someone lived or was buried. After a while one name stood for all names."

They listened attentively, not against their will as they had yesterday in the car.

"I told my story everywhere I went, to anyone who would listen. I told it over and over to a young woman and her father. She is the one who told me where you were."

"How did she find out?" Joaquín asked.

"That's something I'll never know."

She paused and thought about how to proceed. They had no idea what she was talking about.

"All I can say is that she realized where you were."

"You mean she guessed?"

"There are people who would say so. Others would say it was more than that. What they think depends on what they need to believe. In the end, it doesn't matter if she guessed or had a vision. She was right."

They regarded her skeptically. She waited for their skepticism to harden or break into protest. When neither happened she knew it was because of the way she had entered their lives. Her sudden advent yesterday, their presence at this table this morning, rather than the one in the Ponces' house, must make her explanation seem unexceptional.

Roger looked at her, cleared his throat.

"You say we're your grandsons. This test. What do they do?"

"Just draw a little blood," she answered. "It's nothing to worry about."

"And then?"

All she knew about the procedure was that it was complex and time-consuming. She recalled a newspaper photograph of a technician in a lab introducing a dark substance into a solution.

"They'll look for a match. DNA is like a fingerprint. They'll search for things we have in common, what they call markers."

Joaquín put his hand on Roger's arm. A warning? A gesture of support? She was afraid they might deny that the test could prove anything. Yet if that were the case, she would sense it. Their discomfort, their tension had another source.

"You said Guzmán gave us to them," Roger said. "You know that for a fact?"

She nodded. Roger spoke as though "gave" was the beginning and the end. For him it was, for Joaquín. For her it was only the first term in an equation of misery. *And took,* she wanted to say. He gave you away and they took you, *stole* you like a thief does jewels in the night.

"And that made it worse for me," she said. "I knew who did it, who was responsible. I knew where it happened. I went there once. That was all I had to do. It's as clear in my mind today as it was years ago. None of my *compañeras* from the plaza had such knowledge. Their grief was born in darkness, lived in darkness. Mine was in the light. Who can say which is harder to bear. He gave you. He made a present of you to them."

"I told you," Roger said. He took a deep breath and spoke to her in a shaky voice. "We know him. He came to Mar Vista not long ago."

"We thought he was just a family friend," Joaquín added. "That's what they said."

The words seemed to bypass her mind and enter directly into her heart. There was something obscene in the knowledge he had been with them, looked into their eyes as she was doing now, perhaps touched them. That he might have put his hands on them, clapped them on the shoulders, was more appalling than the feeling of entrapment in some deceit she did not yet understand.

Confused and alarmed by what they had admitted, they looked at her with more questions on their lips, sought comfort she was too stunned to give.

"When?" she managed to ask.

"About a month ago," Roger answered.

"Did he say why? Did they?"

"It was just to see how we were. It had been years. We hardly remembered him."

So they had crossed paths. Unlikely as it seemed, in an obscure corner of Argentina she had put her feet down in the same places Guzmán had. Day after day, month after month, year after year hatred of him had filled her heart the moment she awoke. In her life he had become the first mover, creator of a world of anguish, a godhead attended by angels cruising the city in green Falcons.

She still hated him but she did not feel the old intensity. Hatred had been replaced by a profound sense of disorder, the workings of chance as visible as the ribs of an emaciated animal. She could have arrived a month earlier, he could have come a month later. And if they had met in the Ponces' house, would she have vomited at the sight of him? Fainted? Would she have gone for a knife and plunged it into his chest up to the hilt, twisted the blade until she felt it enter his heart and heard his gasp and saw his eyes go blank?

"Why did he do it?" Joaquín asked.

She heard him perfectly well, even the almost imperceptible flutter of disbelief like the single note of a bird. But to answer she had to return from the moment that would have been, release her grip on the knife she buried with all her strength, let go of the words in her mind she would have screamed as he died.

"Because he could," she answered stiffly, haltingly. Because it was within his power."

"Why them?"

"Because they were colleagues. Because Eduardo and Beatriz could have no children of their own."

They wanted everything she said to be a lie. Yet as she watched them she saw belief creeping into their eyes, putting down roots. There was nothing she could say to help them, nothing she could do. The pain belonged to them. It was the birthright of their second birth. As she looked from one to the other and they returned her gaze, she saw the next question already forming, rising like an ocean swell, one they had to ask as surely as the wave had to fall.

She wanted to blurt out the answer, save them from having to ask. But they had to do it. One of them, both of them, had to drag the words out and hurl them across the table. It was their question, not hers.

She thought it would be Joaquín but it was Roger.

"They knew where we came from?"

She closed her eyes, opened them. She wanted to make her love palpable, surround him with it and soften the blow.

"Yes."

He swallowed. She watched the muscles working in his neck.

Joaquín's face sagged with despair. The answer to the question she knew he was about to ask gleamed like a knife blade in his eyes.

"And they knew what happened to . . . Marta?"

He could not say mother, could not bring himself to name what she was.

"Eduardo worked for Guzmán from the beginning of the war. He was his trusted civilian aide. He knew what went on inside the building you came from. It would have been impossible not to."

"I still love them," Joaquín whispered. "What are we supposed to do?"

She remembered yesterday's words. Facts could not interdict love but for her they could abrade it, flay it raw. Guilt for their pain rode on the incontrovertible fact of their love for the Ponces.

The door banged. As Sorano came in he waved, peeled off his gloves, and started toward them. His appearance vexed her. She had thought it would take weeks of patient coaxing to bring the boys to this place, the verge of looking the thing itself in the eye, the primal evil moment. But now the opportunity to enter it and go beyond it was past. Perhaps it was for the best. It was possible they had reached the point too soon. To define the evil, to answer Joaquín's question now, less than a day after they had been torn away from what they believed was their reality, could overwhelm them. She looked at Joaquín, then Roger. It was in their eyes, like water rising in a glass too fast.

If Sorano could see it too he kept his knowledge to himself. From the moment he came inside he had affected a resolute good humor.

"It's freezing out there but it woke me up. A walk first thing gets your blood circulating. Maybe I should have invited you along."

His presence was putting them at ease. Clearly they

were glad he had returned. Roger daubed self-consciously at his eyes, grateful that Sorano was occupied with his menu.

"What about the two of you?" Sorano asked. "You look athletic."

"We swim a lot," Joaquín said flatly. "At least we used to."

"I swam in school," Sorano told him, ignoring the jibe. "The hundred-meter free-style. For three years running I was district champion."

As soon as he began describing his exploits she knew what he was up to. Having intuited a crisis, he was leading them away to a neutral place. She thought of men she knew. The boys would need male friends, old and young. Her place in their lives would be different, with another purpose. She remembered the statue in a park not far from her house, a mythological woman girded for battle, sword raised against an invisible enemy. Her bronze flesh and flowing robe had long ago turned green but the corrosion had not touched her spirit. Night and day she stood her ground, eyes fierce with determination.

TEN

Time had been frozen. The hands on clocks moved, the trees shed leaves, sprouted fresh new buds, the city's bricks went slowly darker, stains ran like vines down necks and chests of statues, mementos of bygone storms, but all the work of time was done outside her, beyond her heart and mind. Over and over she relived two days, the day of disappearance, the day she learned the boys were given away.

Dolores had been so used to immobility that she missed the first sign of thaw. There would have been something lovely and just if she had returned to time the moment she saw the boys, something she would not forget. But it was nowhere in her mind. Nor did she sense the crack of ice, the dripping of unfreezing water on the drive north from Mar Vista, discovery and journey seeming to have occurred within a bubble, a transparent enclosure where she could see the world float by outside that had yet to rediscover her, yet to set the clock of her life ticking once again.

It was the kind of thing poets thought of, the stuff of refrains and rhymes. For her, the place where the ice broke and the first tick sounded was lost, gone forever. All she knew was that time had been moving when she entered her house, that it was speeding the next morning, and had kept the pace throughout that day and the next and the one after that. The hours that had weighed upon her like stones in the old days sailed now, moved with the speed of hawks. Tomorrow they would go to the clinic. The word had always sounded threatening, denoting the site of pain, of doctors shaking their heads and saying nothing more could be done. No longer. As she closed the album and turned out the light the word seemed numinous, the name of an altar where her blood and theirs would be taken, the signs it hid decoded and made to speak.

In the dream she lay on the sofa in the inn listening to the birds calling back and forth. Suddenly all the lights came on. A man in a black three-piece suit said the clinic was closing. If her blood was to be drawn it had to be done within minutes. Otherwise, her claim to the boys would be null and void, forever forfeited.

With the threat echoing in her ears, she rushed into a bright corridor, positive she had seen doors but as she went on she found none, only pristine white walls. From somewhere came the sound of a clock. The hall led to a dead end. She headed back toward the entrance, looking left and right for a door, running her hands over the surfaces of the walls for hinges, knobs, latches. She was trapped inside a white box where the ticking grew louder by the moment.

"Dolores Masson," she said nervously to the receptionist at the counter. "I have an appointment."

The woman offered a vague smile and ran a finger down the ledger that lay open in front of her. Her nails were glossy red, perfect. It must have taken ages to do them, Dolores thought, aware it was odd to focus on something so trivial this morning. But wasn't that how people dulled anxiety, managed it? She identified the color: crimson, softened by a hint of pink. It clashed slightly with her lipstick. So much attention to her nails and then to miss that little dissonance.

"Three of you?" the receptionist asked in a slightly curious voice.

Dolores said, "Yes," grateful to escape the rag-ends of her thoughts.

The receptionist reached for a clipboard, slipped three forms under the clasp, and handed it to Dolores.

"You'll need to fill these out. And if I can have your doctor's address."

"No one's sick. We're giving blood for the Bank of Genetic Data."

"Oh," the receptionist murmured, her face softening as she glanced into the clinic's waiting room. From her expression Dolores knew that she had singled out Roger and Joaquín, whom she had left with Sorano.

"May I borrow a pen? I didn't know."

"Forms," said the receptionist with a sympathetic laugh. "You can't get away from them these days."

"No," Dolores answered briskly, impatient to get this over with.

The receptionist handed her a pen.

"I don't mean to pry, but aren't you one of the grand-mothers from the plaza?"

"One of them."

"I thought I recognized you. There was a picture in the paper—all of you protesting at the diocese about the priest."

"I didn't see it."

"It was a few weeks ago."

"You have a good memory."

"It's not that," she said earnestly. "Since the story about Scilingo came out I've read everything I can get my hands on, trying to understand. It was terrible, unbelievable. For a priest to have counseled him, to have said it was forgivable . . ."

Dolores put the clipboard on the counter.

"Von Claussen's collusion surprises you?"

"Didn't it you?"

She felt the anger rising in her throat, coating it with the taste of bile.

"No. From the first the Church backed the regime, re-member? They were complicit. They said they were protect-ing the faith from godless Communists. Von Claussen's one of them. Priests have various desires. Some dedicate them-selves to goodness. Some bugger altar boys. Others need something more exciting."

The receptionist stared, wide-eyed.

"I'm sorry if this offends you but you're the one who brought it up. My feeling about priests changed after they climbed into bed with the generals. I suppose there might be some good ones. If you don't mind, I'd rather not talk about it."

"I understand. It must be hard."

"You've met others in my situation?"

"Yes. Everyone comes here for the test."

"You've looked at them? At their eyes?"

The woman nodded.

"Then you already know. It's the same for all of us, hard, but nothing like what came before."

A man approached the counter. While the receptionist attended to him Dolores turned her attention to the registration forms. There were spaces for names, addresses, phone numbers, dates of birth, each with its own numbered box. She filled in the information about herself, then printed Joaquín's name in capitals. As she added "Masson" she remembered the last time she had written his name, in a police station the day after she learned they had been taken.

Hysterical, half out of her mind, she had rushed in begging for help. An officer listened indifferently. When she finished telling him her story he advised her to write down their names. His voice came back, a slightly bored drawl whose calm had survived intact all these years. Even then, ignorant as she was of what lay in store for her, innocent, she had known his intonation meant nothing would be done.

The glare from the fluorescent lights in the ceiling had cast the shadow of her hand across their names. Like the officer's voice, the shadow told her that the letters had no meaning, signified absence rather than presence, that she was inscribing mere shapes of the alphabet divorced from flesh and blood. She had been so afraid the sense of loss would return that until today she had never written their names. The freedom to look at them had been stolen by the Ponces.

What seemed a mere formality was really an act of restoration. She printed Roger's name in large letters, bearing down on the pen so the lines were dark, thick strokes of assertion. She signed with a flourish at the bottom and handed the clipboard to the receptionist.

"How long do you think?"

"Awhile, I'm afraid."

A woman glanced up from her magazine as Dolores crossed the room. Someone coughed. Sitting a few feet away from Sorano, the boys studied her with solemn, troubled eyes, obviously aware they were about to give up more than a vial of blood, relinquish to science who they thought they were.

Joaquín looked at her when she sat down on the bench. "What were you writing?"

"Nothing important," she answered in a reassuring voice. "Just registration forms."

He was unconvinced. Everything in his life was alien, threatening; even her house, which he had entered three days ago, where nothing was familiar, not even the portraits of Rubén and Marta she had put back on the wall the night before leaving for Mar Vista. Home, what should have been home, was foreign, the world outside it worse.

She had persuaded them to take two bus rides in the hope that a few geography lessons might help them feel more at ease. The first was short, fifteen minutes around the neighborhood. The second took them deep into the city. They sat opposite her gazing out the windows at avenues, storefronts, the wild variety of architecture, the rush of people and the glitter of things. She had thought they were bored or resentful. Not until they got off and were walking back to the house did she understand that Buenos Aires frightened them.

"Names, addresses, birthdays," she explained.

She wanted to tell Joaquín how much it had meant to write his name, what had been put to rest by that simple act. Someday, when things were better, she would. She would tell him about that and much, much more. Her mind was crowded with things they needed to hear. Encyclopedic.

"Listen," Sorano said. "Let's go out for lunch when this is over. I know a place where soccer players hang out. Madragora's been there."

"You don't have to bribe us," Roger told him. "We aren't kids."

"Did I say you were? The invitation stands if you change your mind."

The boys tried to appear confident but the clinic's atmosphere muffled their bravado. Cool, efficient-looking, with a faint antiseptic odor, it possessed an unmistakable air of authority. The other patients huddled within themselves, concentrating on their maladies. One by one they were summoned by a nurse who stood at the door leading to the examination rooms, propping it open with one hand as she read the names from a chart.

Dolores glanced at her watch, stared at the wall. She had to stay calm, that was the important thing. She had to mask her anxiety with a detachment she did not feel, think of being elsewhere.

Her thoughts drifted to the Ponces and a wave of anger struck, a physical sensation in the pit of her stomach. As an antidote, she tried to imagine the pain in their faces, the emptiness they must feel. Though she was entitled to vengeance it was a useless emotion. What she could get from it was infinitesimal compared with the cause, a grain of sand, not even that. To feel vengeance in a way that would satisfy her would endanger her soul. So it had to be resisted. She had to allow them to drift toward whatever was in store for them, Guzmán too. But he was not so easy to let loose. She wondered again what had drawn him to Mar Vista. Why, after so many years, did he make that journey south?

The door opened and she saw a man come out. The nurse looked at her chart.

"Dolores Masson. Roger Masson. Joaquín Masson."

Dolores took a deep breath and stood up.

Sorano patted Roger on the back. "It'll be all right," he said reassuringly. "I'll see you in a little while."

Roger flinched and turned away from Sorano's hand.

"Down the hall," said the nurse, "third room on the right."

The nurse stepped aside and Dolores followed the boys through the door, determined to keep her attention focused on them. Since making the appointment she had rehearsed this walk half a dozen times. The best course was to keep her eyes on Roger and Joaquín, the set of their shoulders, the way their hair hung long in the back. *This is not a dream. This is real.* She gazed hard at the boys, remembering the panic, the terrible knowledge that there were no doors. This hall was lined with them, all gaping, inviting.

A nurse in a white dress ushered them into the room. As they entered, Dolores noted her name on the plastic tag pinned to her chest: Rosa Cattini.

"This is Dr. Vicario," the nurse said, nodding toward a thin man with wavy hair and rimless glasses. He stepped forward and offered his hand to each of them.

"Please," he said, indicating the chairs. "Sit down."

The boys were all angles and awkwardness as they slipped into the chairs.

Dr. Vicario looked at them. "There's nothing to this. I just draw a vial of blood and that's that. Who wants to go first?"

"I do," Joaquín told him.

"Please roll up your sleeve and make a fist."

His arm was surprisingly thin, almost like a child's. She saw the muscles contract when he closed his hand.

"Good," Dr. Vicario said as he ran his finger along the upper part of Joaquín's forearm. "You have nice fat veins."

Rosa Cattini handed him one of the syringes laid out on a white cloth and he quickly inserted the needle. Blood gushed into the barrel faster than Dolores thought possible. Joaquín revealed neither pain nor queasiness as he watched it fill. His eyes were dull, dull and lusterless and so sad she

had to avert her own. If the sample were not absolutely essential she would have stopped the procedure then and
there, pressed her finger on the point of entry, removed the
needle.

"That's it," said the doctor.

The nurse taped a round of cotton over the tiny hole.

"Roger?" Dr. Vicario said.

Again the rush of blood, the helpless look.

When it was her turn, Dolores extended her arm. Dr.
Vicario tapped the inside of it to encourage a vein. She
glanced at the boys as he inserted the needle, aware that they
were hoping for a miracle, hoping the blood draining from
her arm lacked the necessary markers, that failing a match
she would have to return them to the Ponces.

It would be a miracle if they did not think of such a
thing. It was all they had. She wanted to tell them she understood, that bitter as the knowledge was, her own heart had
beat in the same way. She remembered how she had fed on
hope all those years, traveled with it on the bus to Carlos'
garden, and how battered and misshapen it was when neither he nor Teresa could help, how it survived because it had
to.

She watched the doctor remove the needle from her arm
and hand the full syringe to Rosa Cattini.

"It will take a while to do the tests," he said. "The lab
people will let you know as soon as possible."

She was pulling on her sweater when the doctor swiveled in his chair to face the boys.

"Nobody likes having blood drawn," he said. "When it's
done to me I can't look. Other people's blood I don't mind.
My own's another story."

They were not sure what to make of his comment, nor
was she.

"Where did you live?" he asked.

"Mar Vista," Joaquín said.

"Ah," Dr. Vicario said, nodding. "It's nice in that part of the country. All that space. Unfortunately for me I could never be anything but a *porteño*. I know the city's big and noisy but there are plenty of distractions. You'll like it here."

Roger looked sharply at him.

"Nothing's proven yet," he said.

Dolores understood what Dr. Vicario was doing, gilding the city to help them accept their new estate, see it in a positive light. Roger was trying to salvage the time between now and when the tests were finished. She could not blame him. It mirrored her endless visits to the Ruedas, took as much strength for him to hold on to hope against all odds.

"That's true," Dr. Vicario said.

Joaquín watched Rosa Cattini label the vials with strips of tape. When she placed them in a plastic bag, he turned to the doctor.

"The sea's in our blood. Why don't you test for that?"

"Forgive him," Dolores said. "He's just upset."

Roger stood up and rolled down his sleeve, looking calmly at Dr. Vicario, as if his outburst had satisfied his need to protest, assert himself. But when he shifted his gaze to Dolores she realized he was not finished.

"What Joaquín said is true. It always will be, no matter what happens. We learned to be fishermen and that's not something you forget. The old guys who hung around the docks envied us when we went out on the boat. They still wanted to. The sea's better than any city."

"In time," Dolores said.

"It's more than just being on a boat," Joaquín explained. "It's the air, the birds, the way the land looks when you come back at the end of the day."

"And the whales," Roger added. "Whales migrate near the mouth of the bay. When we were kids, Dad . . . Eduardo wouldn't let us get close to them in the boat because it was too dangerous. We had to watch from the beach."

She imagined them standing there. It was neither nostalgia nor history they were indulging in but part of who they were.

"We'd count the spouts," Roger went on, "and how many times they breached. If it was sunny when they came up, the underside of their flukes looked like gold."

"I made fun of him," Joaquín added, "said it was just the reflection of the sun."

"I didn't believe him. To me, their flukes looked just like an earring Mom kept in her strongbox."

As quickly as they began they abandoned their recollections. The effect on Dolores was like stepping off an escalator. One moment she was being moved briskly along, the next she had no momentum. Their faces told her nothing. She was not certain what she felt. On one hand was her ambivalence and the pain of hearing the Ponces' names, on the other her awareness that this story of the sea had revealed things she had not known. In her mind's eye she saw a golden fluke raised from the sea, saw an earring and wondered why there was only one.

Dr. Vicario stood up and thrust his hands into the pockets of his lab coat.

"The last thing I wanted to do was offend you. I'm sorry."

"I had to say what was on my mind," Roger told him.

"I'm glad you did."

It was over. Dolores thanked Dr. Vicario and followed the boys out. The hall loomed long and wide, filled with airy light. She increased her pace, and when she caught up with them she slid her arms into theirs.

• • •

In the café she said, "It's all right to think about the sea. You should remember the good things, the ones that gave you pleasure."

"It was all good," said Roger.

"It still is," his brother added.

Joaquín looked at her a long time. She could hardly bear the sadness in his eyes.

He said, "It takes more than blood."

"That's where it begins."

"I don't even remember you. I look at the pictures of Rubén and Marta and I don't remember them."

"The Ponces do. Guzmán does."

Sorano put his hand on Roger's arm, nodding toward the door. "That's Madragora."

The star and half a dozen retainers took a table across the room.

"I don't care about him."

"You want to be home."

"Yes."

"Home wasn't there," Dolores said. "It was an illusion, a trick. It was only home because your mother was executed."

"*They* didn't do it."

"They knew."

Late that night she heard them whispering in their room. She heard Roger's voice break, his brother's consolation, silence. She hoped he dreamed of golden flukes.

ELEVEN

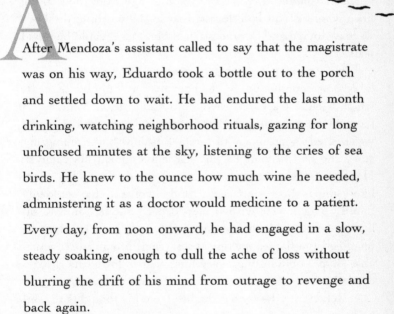

After Mendoza's assistant called to say that the magistrate was on his way, Eduardo took a bottle out to the porch and settled down to wait. He had endured the last month drinking, watching neighborhood rituals, gazing for long unfocused minutes at the sky, listening to the cries of sea birds. He knew to the ounce how much wine he needed, administering it as a doctor would medicine to a patient. Every day, from noon onward, he had engaged in a slow, steady soaking, enough to dull the ache of loss without blurring the drift of his mind from outrage to revenge and back again.

He would have preferred spending his time at sea, would be there now if he could work the boat alone, or had money to hire a crew. Everybody wanted too much, even the old salts who hung out at the dockside bar claimed they were worth more than he could pay. From the way their tongues hung out while they nursed their drinks and watched crews preparing to sail, he had assumed they would jump at his offer. He consoled himself with the thought that even if he had been able to hire two of them they'd have been too stiff-jointed to pull their weight. The hard work would have fallen on his shoulders. He would have been lucky to break even.

Not that their refusal mattered now. It was a minor annoyance, something to pass the time fretting about while he waited for the future to clarify its intentions declared when the phone rang, freeing the message from the sagging lines where it had lain dormant since the morning the boys were abducted and Sorano warned him there would be blood tests.

He was just beginning to imagine some procedure in a laboratory conducted by technicians in long white coats when Mendoza's car turned onto Calle de la Ventana. A moment later he heard Beatriz moving around inside and was visited by an image of Santa Rosalita. Since telling her story she had become its physical embodiment, its catalyst. Hearing her was enough to make it break out in his mind, like pampas fires supposedly under control that suddenly flared up again. He wished there'd been one in Santa Rosalita. It was a weirdly pleasant idea, and for a moment he imagined the flames melting the earring into an unrecognizable shape, obliterating everything that followed its discovery.

Reluctantly he forced the fire from his thoughts to concentrate his attention on Mendoza's car. He had envisioned this day for a month, worked it over in his mind, studying possible scenarios that all ended in defeat. No other outcome was conceivable once Mendoza delivered the summons. Still, he had found some pleasure in thinking about how difficult he could make it for the magistrate, how the little volition that was left to him might be used most damagingly.

He was wondering whether the magistrate intended to come right out with it, or if he would have to stumble around while he worked up his courage when he heard the sound of breaking glass. Besides sending Beatriz into a black depression, the tragedy had made her ham-handed. She seemed never to be in the kitchen more than five minutes before she dropped something, punctuating his days with little explosions that only renewed his anger.

Mendoza's cruiser, a ten-year-old Chevrolet Caprice, crawled along the street. Usually, he drove his own car but today he was hiding behind his badge, just as he had hidden behind his assistant, too ashamed to make the call himself. What could be expected from a man who betrayed a friend? It would take more *cojones* than Mendoza ever had to deliver the summons without his official trappings. A sudden vision of the boys flared in his mind. He longed to put his arms around them, hear them laugh. With a groan he made himself think about the here and now. It was not over. It was only beginning. As he watched Mendoza coming, he repeated the words over and over, investing the hope they enshrined with inevitability.

The car slowed down, seemed to float in slow motion past the mailbox where the boys had insisted on painting his name. It finally came to a halt in the driveway where it settled like a fat old woman.

Usually the cruiser was dusty, its fender wells mudspattered. Eduardo smiled at its cleanliness. The paint gleamed. Even the tires were immaculate. Mendoza had washed it for the occasion.

The magistrate patted his jacket over his chest before he stepped out, closed the door, and faced the house. Eduardo's eyes moved from left to right, tracking Mendoza's approach while he kept his body absolutely still, his hands flat on the arms of the chair, an imperious position, exactly the right posture to receive the son of a bitch and maximize his discomfort. It was the sort of thing Guzmán used to talk about in the old days, ways to increase your advantage.

When Mendoza reached the foot of the stairs Eduardo could tell that being watched increased his uneasiness. His eyes drooped like those of a dog caught misbehaving. Pathetic, really. He wants to be forgiven. No sooner did the magistrate open his mouth than his words made Eduardo feel like a prophet.

"I know what you're thinking but I was only doing my duty. I didn't have a choice."

In a minute or two the power would shift from him to Mendoza, officer of the law, bringer of bad news. In the meantime Eduardo intended to make him pay.

"I'm coming up."

Eduardo blinked in response, stared while Mendoza mounted the stairs and stopped a few feet away. The magistrate was looking down on him but Eduardo still had the advantage. The knowledge was exhilarating, seemed to lessen the pain of what was coming, prelude to God knew what added difficulties.

Mendoza looked away as he reached inside his jacket and removed a fat envelope, an oddly modest gesture, Eduardo thought, the kind of thing that might happen in a gym if Mendoza had inadvertently glanced at his cock. The idea made him want to laugh.

Mendoza held the envelope.

"I'm sorry."

"You bastard."

Mendoza closed his eyes, opened them.

"You probably know it's a summons."

Eduardo silently accepted the envelope without taking

his eyes off the magistrate. The power was shifting, the dynamic changing, but his reserves were not depleted.

"For Christ's sake," Mendoza pleaded. "I have to."

Delighted that his guilt was holding up, Eduardo smiled coldly and waited.

"Am I supposed to say I'm sorry? I'm sorry. What more do you want?"

His silence had a stronger effect than he had thought; Mendoza was positively squirming but the opportunity to answer his question was too tempting to pass up.

"Loyalty," Eduardo said. "A friend would have stopped them. Not even a friend. Just someone with a little decency."

"It was my *job*."

"I know. That's what friendship is all about."

Eduardo saw that he had struck a nerve. He knows, he thought. He knows everything I've said is true.

"We've been friends for ten years. Our kids went to school together. *They* were friends. Does your son know what you did?"

Mendoza flinched, recovered. In a heavy voice he said, "Their blood matches. You and Beatriz will have to go to Buenos Aires for a hearing."

Eduardo kept his eyes on him.

"You should have told me," Mendoza said pleadingly. "A long time ago."

Eduardo cocked his head. "Why?"

"Maybe if I'd known in advance . . ."

Eduardo's cheerless laugh cut him off.

"You'd have acted like a friend?"

Mendoza sighed. "Don't do this, Eduardo."

"I know I shouldn't have said a word," Eduardo replied. "You want to know why? Because I know you'd have betrayed me the minute you found out."

He leaned back, expecting either protest or apology.

"Well? What do you have to say for yourself?"

"Think what you want," Mendoza said, clearly exasperated. "I was going to say that I could have advised you, helped you avoid that . . . scene. What you did was wrong, a crime."

Eduardo's anger seemed to gather in his throat. He felt as if he were choking. Gripping the chair so hard the wood dug into his palms, he thrust himself up.

"Get the fuck out of here!" he said through clenched teeth.

Mendoza looked at him uncertainly.

"Now, you bastard!"

Eduardo felt the pleasure of the curse, savored it as Mendoza retreated down the steps. He watched the magistrate a few moments, then leapt from the porch to the yard. Advancing on the car, he yelled, "Out of my sight!" He followed the car as Mendoza backed into the street. He had run him off. It was a tiny but satisfying victory. That was something. For now it took the edge off the feeling that he was the victim of a conspiracy.

When he turned back to the house he saw Beatriz standing in front of the window, the curtain bunched in her hand, staring at him with dull, lusterless eyes. *Because of her,* because of her mouth idiotically yammering to De la Hoya, he was standing there with Mendoza's present gripped in his hand. He had lived with a stranger since coming to Mar Vista, an impostor who smothered him with devotion to hide her stupidity, deceived him into thinking all the fear and uncertainty were behind him, buried in the pampas. He waited until she blinked and dropped the curtain.

Stoop-shouldered, more like a beggar than anything else he could think of, she waited in the middle of the room. He glared.

"What did he want?"

He slowly raised the envelope. With her pinched face,

her eyes brightening, she stared at it as if it were an exotic bird.

"The summons," he said bitterly as he tossed the envelope on the table. "Their blood matches. We're going to take another trip, Beatriz, to Buenos Aires this time. There will be a hearing."

He watched her cover her mouth with both hands, an old gesture of pain for which he felt nothing now.

"What did you expect? A bouquet? A miracle? There aren't any. Only stupid things people do."

He was ready to go on, wanted to rain down curses on her until he was too tired to speak. But she stopped him with that weird expression he had noticed daily since her confession, the purest look of guilt he had ever seen. It made him sick. He loathed it, never more completely than he did now.

"I'm going out. Read it. I want you to think about what you told me, that we'd still be in Santa Rosalita if it weren't for you. In Santa Rosalita with the boys."

He ignored everyone at the bar and found a seat at the end, away from where the regulars had congregated around the television.

Rather than insulating him from his predicament, the drinks only darkened his mood. He could not stop thinking about the boys. Soon it was all he could do to keep from crying and making a fool of himself. He was like a character in a movie he'd seen a long time ago. The title escaped him but the last scene of a man being lowered in a cage into a pit remained vivid in his mind. He remembered the grandmother and spat out her name in his mind. He remembered the dream that had haunted him, telling himself it was pure chance, coincidence that she had come.

He needed to get hold of himself, devise a plan. He

would have to take to the road again but this time he would leave Argentina. He was not going to take a chance of this ever happening again. Then he thought about how things had changed, how the roots he had put down had already been pulled up and were even now rotting in the sea air.

The house was dark when he returned. He switched on a lamp. Beatriz was lying on the sofa with the summons spread across her chest.

"I've been waiting," she said.

"That's wonderful," he muttered. "That's just fascinating."

"I have to tell you something."

He leaned heavily against the wall. Without looking at him, her eyes focused on the ceiling, she said over and over, in a childlike voice, that it was her fault.

"I never denied it. I accept all responsibility. I'll do anything you ask, but I can't live if you shut me out like this."

She spoke without a trace of the whine that had started getting on his nerves recently, spoke almost as if she had found another voice, quiet and calm. For some reason it frightened him. Half-drunk as he was, he could still think clearly. He decided to soften his ways.

"Make some coffee."

He drank two cups and ate some sausage before he spoke again.

"This is going to be hard," he said. "Complicated. Do you understand? We need a plan. I've been thinking about it. I want you to promise you'll do everything I say."

Her hunger to please him blazed in her eyes.

"I promise."

"How long have we got?"

"A month."

Mechanically, hollow-voiced but obedient, she recited the date and the time they were to appear in court. He calculated what had to be done between now and then, cursing softly under his breath. He would need a lot of luck.

"We're leaving."

"Where?"

"I don't know yet. Maybe Mexico."

Beatriz was truer to her word than he ever imagined possible. Since the boys were stolen she had been lost in herself, wrapped up in some impregnable reverie except when she felt compelled to beat her breast, say she never thought what she had done could lead to this, never, not once. She had regularly begged his forgiveness. The day following his ultimatum she was so attentive, so tractable to his every whim and desire, that her previous submissiveness seemed like open rebellion in comparison.

There was another, totally unforeseen development. She became passionate, shameless in the ways she aroused him. He would lie beside her afterward, fighting off sleep in order to understand her sensuousness. It was not a resurrection of youthful desire, for she got nothing from it, offered herself as if she were a commodity, a receptacle. Then it came to him. She was pleasuring him out of guilt, paying with her body for her betrayal.

At first he was angry. The night after discovering the key to her new sensuality he felt demeaned in his manhood, as if he were taking advantage of a drunk, but as soon as they began he thought about what she had done, the ruin she had brought into their lives, and the memories freed him to take his pleasure like a satyr. There was something exciting in this kind of sex, in knowing it was all for him, a combination of revenge and forbidden fruit. Always he came before he wanted to, unable to stop the spasm.

One morning he told her that money was the first thing,

the second thing, the only thing. Getting the boys from the old woman was only the beginning. To escape from Argentina required every cent they could lay their hands on.

She listened as attentively as a schoolgirl. With her hair up in a bun carelessly pinned at the nape of her neck, her stodgy print dress, it was hard to believe she was the same woman who had so expertly led him to the brink of exhaustion.

After breakfast he drove down to the docks. Swallowing his pride, he went from boat to boat until he found work as a common deckhand. When he came home that night stinking of fish, he put the money he had earned in the strongbox.

He had always listened to the radio at night, and read a little in the week-old papers from Buenos Aires, before he started drinking.

Now he had one glass of wine and went straight to bed. He had lost all interest in the world's affairs: everything that mattered was lodged within his heart. When he and Beatriz finished coupling, he rolled away from her and thought of Mexico.

On Friday of that week he went to see the shipyard owner after work and offered his boat for sale. Though the man quoted an insultingly low price, Eduardo accepted it. After signing over the deed, he returned to the boat under the glare of bare bulbs set on spindly posts. He removed all his personal items, as well as the boys' sweaters and foul-weather gear, stuffed everything into a box and retreated to the dock where he stood looking at the boat. Already it was no longer his. He remembered how the boys used to move around the deck. With a groan he turned away.

The moment he entered the house he told Beatriz to sit down, there was something he had to tell her. She complied, as usual, without a word. The memory from the dock was still fresh. He had given up his domain. Now she had to give up hers.

"I sold the boat. We have to get rid of everything that won't fit in the truck."

"All the furniture?"

"Every last stick."

Her chin trembled. He wanted her to cry. Tears would even things out a little. Just as he thought the first would spill, she got up without a word and quickly went into the kitchen. He felt cheated and his impulse was to follow, stand in the doorway until she turned and he could see them. He was not sure why he stayed where he was.

Beatriz woke to the sound of hammering. Without bothering to slip on a robe, she went out to the living room and opened the front door. Eduardo was on his hands and knees, pounding a nail into a sign that said, FURNITURE FOR SALE.

He glanced up. There was just enough breeze to make her nightgown cling. It was odd that someone so modest would stand there in full view of the neighborhood. He thought about telling her to cover up, then realized he didn't care what they saw. She could do what she wanted.

Once the sign was finished, he stuck it in the ground beside the mailbox, hopped into the truck, and went into town to put up fliers in places people would be likely to see them.

By the end of the day Eduardo was selling things to neighbors and strangers. Beatriz listened dispiritedly as he negotiated, watched silently as the pieces they had accumulated over the years were carried out the door like coffins going to unknown fields.

Night by night, as the lamps were sold off, the house grew darker. Its emptiness seemed to yawn as chairs and tables and sofa went. She nearly broke under the strain of hearing Eduardo wheedle the last cent out of a stranger for her dresser, whose carved drawers and sprays of wooden flowers always made her happy. When the deal was struck, Eduardo and the man picked it up. As they approached the door she saw her reflection in the mirror jiggling unsteadily from side to side.

She retreated to the kitchen and started washing dishes, going about the task even more methodically than usual. As she rinsed a plate, beneath the running water, on the white surface, Dolores' face appeared. She saw the car going off down the street, remembered without remorse the curse she had hurled after it. When the boys looked at her out of the rear window she dropped a serving dish, bent to pick up the scattered pieces, and sank to the floor. Her body felt like lead. She drew her legs up to her chest, put her arms around them, and stared at the wall.

The boys burned like twin candles in Eduardo's mind. It was their light that gave him strength to haul in the fishing nets, endure the long hours on the stinking boat for meager wages.

As the month drew to a close, he spent the evenings thinking of the flight to Mexico. With maps spread out on the remaining table in the living room, he settled down to study all the possible routes, weighed the advantages of major roads against the greater safety of minor ones, considered access to towns for gas and lodging, places where a truck might be hidden if that were necessary.

Years of running had made him wily, sharpened his instincts. This time he had the advantage of being able to plan what he would do, rather than fleeing in the middle of the night with no clear idea of where he was going. What better poetic justice could there be than to turn this upheaval on its head by rescuing Tomás and Manfredo and escaping from the country? In Mexico they would disappear like the sun descending into the sea, gleaming one moment, gone the next. In Mexico, they would be free.

He worked three more days on the fishing boat.

On the fourth morning he rose early and was drinking tea when Beatriz came in.

"What are you doing here?"

"I quit. Today's for packing. We leave first thing tomorrow."

"Good," she said emphatically.

He was skeptical about her enthusiasm until he noticed the way she surveyed the denuded room.

"I meant it. There's nothing here. You can smell the emptiness, hear it. What should I do?"

"Pack the clothes. I'll get started on the truck."

He went outside before she could ask for help, if that was what she'd wanted. He had been looking forward to the work, the heft of objects, the satisfaction of tying them down, but her voice had sounded as if it were coming through a wall, the way she looked around the room had taken the edge off his pleasure. His inclination toward sympathy turned to resentment as he imagined her giving the earring to De la Hoya. He put his pistol in the cab. As he started loading boxes he doubted that he could ever forgive her.

Eduardo said nothing when they left the next morning but she could read the code of his gestures and expressions. The set of his jaw, the ripple of muscles in his thin arms as he steered and shifted, the way he worked his eyes spoke in the eloquent language of familiarity perfected over years of marriage. It was her fault, his jaw said. His arms accused her of betrayal.

Staring at the road, shuddering inwardly as memories of

midnight flights unraveled in her mind, she remembered Tomás and Manfredo huddled together in the backseat, confused and frightened. It had always been Eduardo's choice to run. Though it was his decision leading them up the cordillera, she was the cause this time. She had created the danger. As the mountains rose up, their towering shapes seemed like her past toppling down to crush her.

They spent the night in the cheapest room at Garibaldi's Inn. Two hours after leaving the next morning the left front wheel developed an ominous whining sound.

"God damn it!" said Eduardo, slamming his hands on the steering wheel.

"What is it?"

"A bearing."

The wheel was smoking by the time they reached a town with a garage. The mechanic had a replacement. When he quoted a price, Eduardo exploded.

"That's what I charge," the man said. "Take it or leave it."

Eduardo was reluctant to part with his cash. There was no telling when he would really need it. "I've got some jewelry. Are you interested?"

"I might be."

"Get the box," he told Beatriz.

He laid out a few pieces on the counter. The mechanic said he would take the silver necklace, the one her mother gave her. As Eduardo handed it over she rushed outside, looking blindly through her tears at the dilapidated buildings lining the street.

When she returned he was helping the mechanic. He glanced at her. She could not tell if he had forgotten or did not care.

It was dark by the time they reached the outskirts of Buenos Aires. Eduardo watched the distant glow becoming

brighter, larger, a great dome of light encompassing the horizon. While it fragmented into street lamps, windows in
houses and apartments and factories, blazing neon signs, he
recalled the nights in Mar Vista where there were not
enough lights to hold back the heavy darkness. Step outside,
and you were confronted with blackness peppered with the
most amazing array of stars. Drive, and your headlights were
lonely probes nibbling at the edges of the universe. He had
forgotten how the city sparkled.

"Go by our house," Beatriz said when they reached the
suburbs. "It'll only take a few minutes."

"Don't be a fool."

He continued toward a district of cheap hotels, glad the
breakdown had occurred because the loss of time made it
possible to enter Buenos Aires when only its skeleton was
visible, its bare bones strung with lights. It was better than
having to look on everything he left behind in the sun's stark
glow.

He threaded the truck into the maze of streets as though
he were making his way through the freshest memories. In
the heart of the city the thoroughfares were so brightly lit he
could see Beatriz as clearly as if it were day.

Half an hour passed before the lights became more
widely spaced, the streets narrow and potholed. Laughter
and music rose from the doorway of a seedy bar as he parked
in front of the Hotel Bolívar. A red neon sign missing a letter
welcomed them with a gap-toothed smile. Above it, rates
were posted by the hour, day, and month.

Beatriz looked glumly at the uninviting facade. "Would
you ask for a room with a bath?"

The night clerk, a heavy man whose belly strained his
suspenders, said rooms with private baths were half again as
much as those without. Eduardo paid a month's rent in advance on a cheaper one. As he handed over the money, a

man approached and asked for a room at the hourly rate. A red-haired woman wearing a skimpy dress waited beside him. When the man turned around and dangled the key she smiled crookedly, revealing bad teeth. Eduardo watched them go up the stairs. A few hours with a strange woman. Out of curiosity he asked how much. The clerk quoted a price.

Eduardo stood in the door and motioned to Beatriz. When she got out he said, "We'll have to take the things up. You can't leave anything in a neighborhood like this."

"Did you get a bath?"

"They're too expensive."

The lobby was in far better condition than the rest of the hotel. The stairway carpets were dirty, worn through to the wood in places. An unmistakable odor of mold permeated their room. When he opened the windows to let in some fresh air, noise from the street rose up, a tangle of voices and music mixed with smells of exhaust and food. It was definitely not the glittering Calle Florida they had passed through. Then he thought: It doesn't matter. He was here, that was the important thing. He decided to call Guzmán first thing in the morning.

He pulled off his clothes and crawled into bed beside Beatriz. Enough light came through the blinds so he could make out her features. With a little thrill of guilt, he recalled the *rubio's* crooked smile, wondering what it would be like with her, how much different.

When he asked the day clerk if he could use the phone he was told it was out of order but there was a public one in the bar across the street.

The housekeeper said Guzmán was swimming the first time he called at eight o'clock, advising him to try again in an hour.

Eduardo borrowed the phone book from the clerk. Upstairs, while Beatriz made breakfast on the portable burner, he jotted down names and addresses of pawnshops.

"There's no other way?"

With a sigh, Eduardo put down his pen. The question irritated him. He had already explained why they had to sell her jewelry. Still, the way she asked touched him. Her voice was full of resignation. He put his arm around her waist and in the patient tone one would use with a child, said, "Let's eat, then I'll try Guzmán again."

The answering machine started its recorded message before the housekeeper picked up, interrupting Guzmán's voice in mid-sentence. He had come in, she said. If he would wait just a minute.

Traffic clogged the street, people the sidewalks, but it was quiet in the bar. A derelict wandered in carrying a mesh bag over his shoulder. When he asked for money the bartender said, "Get the fuck out of here!" Eduardo leaned against the wall, wondering if he would get another glimpse of the whore. Then he remembered they had only taken a room for an hour.

"Yes?" Guzmán said.

"It's Ponce. We got in late last night."

"Where are you?"

"A fleabag called the Bolívar," Eduardo said with a laugh. "You wouldn't have heard of it."

Birds were squawking in the background.

"How are you?" Guzmán said.

"Better than I expected."

"You sounded bad the last time."

"I felt worse. But things are getting clearer. I've been working on an idea."

"And?"

"Can you help me get the boys out of her house?"

"That shouldn't be a problem. Where are you going?"

"Mexico. Somewhere by the ocean, maybe Acapulco. I've come up with some routes and alternates. Maybe you could tell me what you think?"

"You might be jumping the gun. It's possible the hearing will go your way."

"Their blood matched."

"It all depends on whom you get for a judge. A few are still around who understand what happened. Even the ones Menem appointed are leery of this kind of thing. From what I hear, they tend to sympathize with the people who've had custody. They listen to what the kids want."

"Does that mean you think there's a chance?"

"There's always a chance. How is Beatriz?"

"The same. You're coming to the hearing?"

"I've been keeping a low profile since this Scilingo business."

"It's rubbed off?"

"Nothing connects me. I wasn't involved. But it reminds people and there's a stink. The padre's caught in the middle of it."

"More trouble?"

"More of the same. The diocese decided he shouldn't say mass for a while. I think they're just waiting for it to blow over but right now the shit's pretty thick. Is there anything else?"

"I'll need money."

"You're all right for now?"

"For now."

"I'll see what I can do. Be strong, Eduardo."

"Yes," he said, then hung up.

Eduardo did not like what he saw when he entered the room. Beatriz was dressed, ready to go, but the posture of her body said she hated what they had to do. The jewelry was part of her. Her face had the look of a new amputee. It would be useless to explain once again why it was necessary. The best thing to do was to act businesslike.

"It was a good conversation."

"He'll help?" she asked.

"Of course. Why wouldn't he?"

"I'm worried. Sometimes . . ."

"We have to rely on him." He picked up the list and stuffed it in his pocket. "Come on. This'll probably take all day."

He had organized their foray geographically, starting with pawnshops nearest the Hotel Bolívar. There were check marks on the map, street numbers, but he needed neither map nor markings to find his way. Buenos Aires was a second skin, his birthplace, his spiritual home, repository of the best life had offered him, the equal, he thought, of her jewelry. Driving through it, walking, even gazing out the window of their room filled him with a sense of intimacy, for he knew this place the way he knew his own mind and body. But the pleasure of returning last night was muted by his feelings this morning. His return had become elegiac. Each neighborhood, park, monument bid him to look long and hard and lovingly because soon the city would be lost to him forever.

He told the clerk in the first shop that he was not interested in selling individual pieces. That was fine, she replied. She preferred buying whole lots.

He watched her examine each piece with a jeweler's glass and was encouraged when she occasionally said, "Good," or "This is nice."

When she slipped the glass up on her head it disappeared into her gray hair.

"I like them but you understand I have a big inventory."

She pursed her lips and made an offer.

"That's not even funny," he said incredulously.

He made a counter-offer for more than he was prepared to accept.

"Señor," she said, "everybody comes in that door thinking they'll get ten times what I can pay. This is a pawnshop. I help people out when what they offer will help me. It's the best I can do."

"The pearls alone are worth that," Beatriz said angrily.

"Maybe, but not here."

Eduardo swept the pieces into the jewelry box.

"You won't do better anywhere else."

"We'll see," he said.

The offers at the next three stores were essentially the same, one a little higher, two a little lower.

At lunch they were so discouraged they hardly spoke. Eduardo had calculated the cost of each day on the road to Mexico, pared expenses to the bone. The shortfall between what had been offered so far and what he needed was alarming. He was smart enough to know the amount was likely to be the same wherever they went. He was tired of the haggling. The best thing to do, he told Beatriz, was to take the first offer that was higher than the last.

"They're criminals," she said.

"And we have to deal with them."

The next shop on the list was twenty minutes from the café. The area was a step above the others, possessed of clothing stores, a stationer's, a newsstand, and a better-looking café than where they had eaten. And the people were more presentable. He glanced irritably at Beatriz' styleless flower-print dress. Her washed-out expression bothered him.

"Pull yourself together. Looks count in a place like this." He smoothed the front of his shirt and buttoned his jacket. "Remember, we don't plead. We don't act like we need the money."

A bell on the door tinkled with an old-fashioned sound. Looking around, he saw this was a different kind of establishment. The floor was not littered with merchandise. Everything was displayed in glass cases whose surfaces gleamed. The jewelry in them was substantial, expensive. He felt a surge of confidence. Surely they would do better here.

A middle-aged man wearing a shirt and tie came through a beaded curtain and surveyed them over the top of half-glasses.

"May I help you?"

"I'd like to have some things appraised," Eduardo said. Motioning for Beatriz to hand him the box, he laid the pieces out on a velvet cloth. They looked much better than they had in the other places.

The clerk picked up Beatriz' pearl necklace. He examined some of the pieces through a jeweler's glass, others with his naked eye, jotting down figures on a pad. When he finished he tore off the sheet and handed it to Eduardo. The total was slightly higher than the morning's best offer.

"They're worth more."

"I know," the clerk said steadily, "but this is a bad time for pawn. Everybody's selling. The economy. You can see," he added, gesturing at the filled display cases.

Eduardo had wanted to keep the earring to barter with on the way north but cash in hand seemed more important. He removed it from the box and handed it over.

"How much for this?"

The earring caught the light from the window as the clerk held it up. He nodded appreciatively.

"You don't come across much of this anymore. May I see the other one?"

"There's just this."

"That's too bad."

Beatriz' face paled. She closed her eyes.

"How much?" Eduardo asked.

When the clerk quoted a price Eduardo said, "For Christ's sake, it's gold!"

"Do you mind telling me what I can do with one earring?" the clerk said crisply. "I'd have to sell it to a dealer to be melted down. That cuts the price. If you had the pair . . ."

A moan escaped Beatriz' lips, a sound so sorrowful both men turned to her at the same time. With the back of her hand pressed against her mouth, she looked at Eduardo and fled outside. She leaned against a lamppost and raised her head as if inspecting the sky. Eduardo felt the blood rise in his face. He had felt lousy looking at the damned thing, too, having to handle it, talk about it, but to act like this in public, embarrassed him.

The clerk cleared his throat.

"It happens all the time," he said, "usually with women, but not always. Heirlooms are harder to part with than people think. I can tell when they come in. A few days ago . . ."

Eduardo interrupted with a laugh. He glared at the clerk, enjoying the man's confusion and taking what bitter pleasure he could from the misunderstanding.

"You'd better sharpen your eye," he said as he pocketed the earring. "You can have the rest."

Eduardo watched carefully as he counted out the bills. The denominations were small, the pathetic stack hardly half an inch thick. He picked it up and left without a word, slamming the door so hard the bell rattled before it rang.

Beatriz waited with her hands pressed together, her eyes brimming. As he glared at her, ready to tell her never to embarrass him like that again, she raised her face, a meaningless gesture, another of her oddities. Then he understood. She was prepared for him to strike her. He had wanted to, ever since she told him. As his imagination offered a vision of mayhem, she closed her eyes long enough for him to see the tiny veins on her lids. When she opened them a surrendering seemed to well up from deep inside her, a stark, utterly re-signed acquiescence. The earring, the bargaining, the inadvertent question had broken her down. Her helplessness made him fearful.

Awkwardly, his voice still pinched with anger, he said, "They haven't forgotten us. They're waiting for us to come and get them."

She nodded weakly, as though her head and neck had received only a partial message from her brain.

He took it as a sign of belief and guided her toward the car, wondering how he could possibly manage their flight with so little money in reserve.

Beatriz glanced at him, knowing how her eyes looked, grateful that his attention was elsewhere so that he had no time to read the question she knew was there, plain to see.

TWELVE

After Dolores picked up the telephone and heard Dr. Vicario say their blood had matched, "No doubts, no ambiguities," she laughed and cried and made a fool of herself, releasing emotions that had been tamped down like pipe tobacco, compressed like a spring. Her feet seemed not to touch the floor. Her voice soared. Because she had never worried about what the tests would reveal, the news should have been anticlimactic but to her it was a vindication. Behind it all the power of the law was gathered, the majesty of the law, the sweet embrace of the blindfolded woman. Dolores imagined dancing with her, swirling around the room, never missing a beat of the music playing in her head, the coda that sang all was well.

When she told the boys they were neither surprised

nor dismayed. They knew what the truth was, perhaps as early as the moment she entered the Ponces' house. Because of that they did not hate her, though love, the idea of it as well as the emotion, confused them. Sometimes the three of them stayed up late, drinking hot chocolate and discussing what it was. In the soft pooled light from the living room lamps they asked her how they should feel. She answered that what they felt was what they should feel, neither more nor less. Love was what it was at the moment. It changed with knowledge, took on new shapes but always slowly, never without doubts and regrets. She was lucky. Her love for them, for Rubén and Marta and Félicité, had been as steady as starlight. Theirs for the Ponces was like a photograph slowly fading, going backward through the development process. A glimmer of what they felt would always remain. Years from now the faint gray-and-white negative would still be there. They should honor it because even though it was based on a falsehood it had seemed real. What they had felt had been real. She told them about her archives. Their love for Eduardo and Beatriz would stay in their minds as her memories did in hers.

The information passed from clinic to ministry to court and then weeks went by without a development of any kind. She was beginning to think that justice moved on crutches when the date for the hearing was announced. Roger wished it was not so far off, Joaquín years away. Afraid that her hatred of the Ponces would creep into her voice and stain it with sounds she never wanted them to hear, she said she understood that the day circled on the kitchen calendar was momentous, a watershed, but it was still only another day in their lives. They would wake that morning and go to court and then it would be over. They would grieve and feel despair, such emotions were to be expected, but in time they would begin to fit into the world where they belonged.

The day Sorano told her the summons had been delivered she tried to imagine how they looked when it came, a petty act, she knew, yet one she reveled in, allowed to stay in her mind until it faded of its own accord.

Memory was as close to them as she wished to get. She had no desire to see them again, shuddered at the thought of being in the same courtroom and breathing air they had breathed, hearing the same words they heard. Yet she could not think of them as blighted souls, not after coming face to face with them and seeing what was in their eyes, hearing their anguished voices. They felt exactly as she had felt all those empty years. The darkness she had known would be passed to them, the rage and despair and the sense that time had stopped. In her hatred, against her will, she perceived a spark of pity and wondered how that could be.

She woke the morning of the hearing with a nagging sense of fear settled deep in the center of her mind.

When Sorano came for the boys she queried him again. Was he sure everything would be all right? Might something have been overlooked? A legal technicality?

"I told you it's an open and shut case," he answered. "Don't worry."

"I don't like the idea of them seeing the judge alone. Who knows what he might put in their heads?"

"You've been deposed. So have the Ponces. De León always talks to the children the day of a hearing. It's his job to look after their interests."

"Who's going to know?"

Sorano gave her an impatient look.

"Listen," he said as he glanced at his watch. "I have to go. There are things I need to do after I drop them at the courthouse."

She was acting like an ingrate. Sorano had volunteered to take the boys, sparing her and them an exquisitely unpleasant bus ride.

"I'm sorry. I'm a wreck."

"Really?" he said, raising his eyebrows in mock astonishment. "I'd never have guessed."

He leaned over and kissed her cheek.

"Remember that De León had found for the grandparents at the other hearings."

Roger and Joaquín came in, looking at her with closed, guarded expressions. She had expected that would happen, had tried to prepare for it, but she knew too well what they felt and that nothing she could say would change it.

Sorano asked if they were ready.

Joaquín nodded.

"I'll be there in a few hours," Dolores said.

Roger's tie was crooked but she resisted the urge to straighten it. Until the hearing was over she could not touch him.

They looked like stone plinths in the backseat of Sorano's car, as if they had been there a thousand years. She watched until they disappeared in traffic. When she closed the door she flinched at the sound that echoed in the living room.

She thought of the other women whose stories were identical to hers—grandchildren stolen, years of misery, unexpected discovery. Sorano's words had been intended to ease her doubts but they had exactly the opposite effect. She believed in odds and those successes increased the possibility of failure. That the judge had twice awarded custody to grandparents lessened the possibility of him finding in her favor. A vision of a spinning wheel, rimmed with out-of-sequence numbers in different colors, was projected onto her mind. A white ball tumbled crazily from notch to notch.

Three out of three was a perfection in which she had little confidence.

She had worried beforehand about the two hours she would have to deal with until she caught the bus downtown. They had yawned wide and threateningly and she had approached them like a chess player plotting her moves, deciding all she could do was to pack so much into the time she would have no idle moments. She had done this sort of thing all her life, finding relief in the work of her hands, the simple, reassuring skills of the house.

She attacked the furniture in the living room with her favorite dust cloth, imagining motes where there were none to see.

In the kitchen, she ran the water until it was blistering hot and washed the breakfast dishes as though she had declared war on germs.

With hands still red and tingling, she laid out the clothes she planned to wear, filled the tub, sprinkled in bath salts, and watched the bubbles rise. She loved to lie submerged up to her chin in the water and let the warmth leech away the pain of arthritis. No sooner did she ease herself into the tub than she wondered what the judge was asking them, what he was insinuating, what he might want to hear them say. One minute, she said to herself. Then she closed her eyes and began counting seconds.

She dried and combed her hair in front of the bathroom mirror. She looked old. Well, she was. Except for occasional aches and pains, age was not as bad as she once thought it would be. When she finished she dressed quickly, tied a white scarf over her head, and went down to the corner.

It was warm on the bus. Through her reflection in the window she gazed at familiar buildings, storefronts, traffic, attuned to the compressed energy and thrust of city life that died long after she fell asleep and renewed itself before dawn. She wanted to see its multitude of colors and shapes as party favors scattered in celebration of the day, a sweet idea, living in the moment, all pastels and flowers. But she had spent too many years straddling past and future while her present was only the silence between the ticking of a clock to change the way she lived in time. Hers could not be divided that way. Perhaps for the woman on the sidewalk pushing a stroller, the couple walking behind her, hand in hand, lost in each other's eyes—perhaps for them the moment was complete in itself. For her, what was happening now, what was soon to happen, was inseparable from the past, as though present and future were being swept along on the current of memory, her life turning, tumbling, going under, snagging on shards of what had come before. Had the Ponces, in unguarded moments, considered how they had deformed her sense of time, made it collapse so that her history flooded the present like a river out of its banks? She could not believe it.

She looked hard at pedestrians' faces, signs flowing by that advertised a thousand things, an old man walking three dogs. She could concentrate on none of it, had lost the ability to be absorbed in things.

The driver turned onto a wide, tree-lined avenue. The courthouse was only a few blocks away, obscured for the moment by thick leaves that somehow managed to survive in the polluted air.

The pneumatic brakes hissed. A passenger got on.

As the bus pulled into traffic she caught a glimpse through the treetops of the courthouse roof bristling with aerials. It vanished behind a tree, reappeared, was gone again. With each meter the bus traveled, larger sections of the building appeared in the gaps, planes of prefabricated concrete pierced with rows of windows reflecting many suns. It was one of the least attractive structures in Buenos Aires, pure modernist function, graceless as a shovel, but so long as what occurred inside was true to the spirit of the place its shell was immaterial. Its ugliness could even be thought of positively, as a symbol of justice solid and incorruptible as those gray slabs.

Sorano would not have said the hearing was a formality if he didn't believe it. Not once in the time she had known him had he glossed over a difficulty. The tests matched their blood, *prima facie* evidence. There was more, all bound together, a juggernaut of proof. But the judge was adept with language, trained to discover hidden meanings, a manipulator of ideas and precedents, who even now might be questioning the boys.

A kiosk papered with advertisements floated by. The moment it passed from her line of sight she saw their white scarves against a background of concrete, glass, polished steel, so many *compañeras*. She was not surprised. They had looked after each other for years, borne the weight of each other's sorrow. Of course they would come. Today was a triumph for them all.

As she got off the bus, reporters edged toward the curb. Uncomfortable as it was being on display, she felt a grim satisfaction in knowing that everything they wrote, every picture they took, would give new life to the past, that people would once again be forced to consider what they had tried to forget, sweep under the rug, deny had happened.

Hermione refused to give up her place by the bus door. She looked irritably at a young woman wearing a black blouse and pants who squeezed in front of her brandishing a spiral notebook.

"I'm sorry. They got here before we did."

"It's all right," Dolores replied, touching her arm. "Remember how we used to complain when they wouldn't come to the plaza?"

"But today?"

"Especially today."

"Julia Fuentes," said the woman. *"La Opinión.* How

long were your grandsons missing? We've heard conflicting reports."

She would have been ten or eleven during the war, Dolores thought, too young to have understood. She was cheered by the idea that her generation were still interested. A flashbulb went off and Julia momentarily vanished in its afterglow, reappearing ringed by a bright aura.

"Thirteen years. Thirteen years, seven months, and eighteen days."

"How did you keep track of the time? With a calendar?"

Dolores shook her head. "I didn't have to."

"How, then?"

"In my heart."

Julia Fuentes jotted in her notebook without taking her eyes off Dolores.

"How did you feel during that time?"

"Like I was paralyzed in life."

"Did you ever lose hope?"

"I couldn't afford to."

Two men pushed their way to the front.

"You must have known the odds were against finding them," said the younger one. "What kept you going?"

"Did you find comfort in religion?" the older one asked.

"I knew they were alive. I knew the Ponces would make a mistake someday."

"What was it?" Julia asked.

"I think being who they were."

The young reporter said, "Have you followed the stories about Scilingo?"

"Every word."

"Do you have an opinion about him?"

"A man capable of such things is not human."

"Which means you would like to see the government bring him to trial?"

"I would love it."

"And what about the priest, Father Von Claussen?"

"He aided and abetted. He comforted Scilingo after his first flight. If he hadn't, perhaps Scilingo would have refused to go on the second, perhaps more people would not have died. Why should he be immune?"

"You feel strongly about him."

"About the man I've only seen poking his nose out of the door at the diocese, no. About his church, yes. His church was involved. Everybody knows that."

"Pardon me," said the older reporter. "You didn't answer my question about religion."

"That was because it no longer occupies me. It has not occupied me for a long time."

Julia interrupted.

"Can we go back to where we were a minute ago? Do you mind?"

"Ask whatever you want."

"What was it like without your grandsons? How did you spend your time?"

"Enough!" Hermione said angrily.

"But—" protested Julia.

"No buts. Enough is enough."

Dolores allowed herself to be guided by the strong pressure of Hermione's hand. It had been a natural question to ask, inevitable, the kind of thing she herself would be interested in reading if the story were about someone else. Still, she was glad she had not answered. It would have been like tearing a bandage off a wound.

"Like vultures," Hermione fumed.

"She had to ask."

"All the same."

They were walking parallel to the building, away from the reporters, when out of the corner of her eye Dolores saw a truck pull over to the curb. She stopped in her tracks, amazed that the look of it had remained intact in her memory.

"What is it?" Hermione asked.

She nodded in the direction of the truck. "It's them."

Since the date had been set she had been storing up in her mind dozens of moments she would have to deal with today, each charged like thunderheads with unpredictable energy. She had wanted to know them in advance so she could prepare for assaults of images and words, anticipate her responses and have time to decide how best to amend or strengthen them.

This one above all the others had taken hold of her, invaded her dreams. It had danced on the windowsill while she stood at the kitchen sink, washing dishes. When she first saw them she had thought no one could maintain such rage and hatred but they had. Their expressions were the same as she had seen in Mar Vista.

As she watched them getting out and saw their faces highlighted by sun streaming through the branches, the reality was not what she feared. She had expected evil to radiate from them like the heat lines of a mirage. Except for the anger, they appeared startlingly ordinary. Eduardo looked smaller, less compactly built than she remembered. The confidence of his glance at the crowd seemed forced. And something was wrong with Beatriz. The face that had been so mobile in its rages was as pale as the scarves Dolores' *compañeras* wore, her eyes as expressionless as a doll's.

She watched Beatriz pass behind the back of the truck and join Eduardo on the sidewalk. There was a certain awkwardness in the way they stood together, resentment in the way Eduardo spoke to her that made her think they were not as allied as they were. They know they're going to lose. What else could account for such grimness? But there was more than a foreshadowing of loss. Something uninterpretable lay behind Eduardo's eyes. She was privy only to the bass notes of his thinking, unable to hear the melody in the treble.

"Shall we go the other way?" asked Hermione.

"No."

The envisioned moment was supposed to culminate in an exchange of glances. Whenever she had imagined it she felt half crazy not knowing whether she could meet their eyes. All the lost years would be there, every moment she could have spent with Roger and Joaquín. She had invented things to say, dramatic gestures, a whole repertoire that was wasted effort, for no sooner did they notice the reporters converging on them than Eduardo grabbed Beatriz by the arm and rushed her inside.

Dolores let out her breath.

"All right," she said. "Let's go in."

Marble floors, brass fixtures, muted lighting, everything in the long foyer done in various hues of brown. She should have come in advance of today, as she had considered doing, to put herself at ease. It had been a lifetime habit to get a sense of atmosphere beforehand. She had visited the chapel where she was married, the church where Rubén and Marta were married, the hospital where Marta gave birth to the boys, the cemetery where her husband was laid to rest, but this place had frightened her too much because she did not know the outcome in advance. Now she was paying for her weakness. The more she looked, the more alien and dangerous it appeared, a great vaulting structure dedicated to neutrality of judgment, the weighing of facts that could destroy her.

Why was she taking such a risk? She should have bought plane tickets and spirited the boys out of the country. What was the law to her? A source of grief, lies, evasions.

She imagined looking through the narrow window of a plane as it taxied to the runway, the Ponces running after

her, the judge's robes flying in the wind, all too late as the
engines roared and they were thrust back in their seats.

She followed Hermione through the double doors into
the courtroom. Rather than the dark place she had expected,
it was light, almost airy, the bright blond wood paneling
catching the sunlight.

She saw the boys seated at a long table in front of the
judge's bench, conferring with a man in a dark suit. The
Ponces had stopped halfway down the middle aisle. Eduardo
was talking to a policeman while Beatriz stood rigid beside
him, staring at Roger and Joaquín, her face pale as it had
been outside while her eyes blazed like burning coals, a look
full of loss and longing. The story in them, for there was
one—Dolores would have had to be blind not to see it—was
rooted too deeply for her to understand, a text in a language
other than her own.

Sorano sat in the front row near two officers posted by
a gate separating the spectators' seats from the bench. He
smiled and raised his hand to greet Dolores when Beatriz
suddenly turned away from her husband. Eduardo reached
for her.

"No!" she shouted as she slipped his grip and broke
into a run.

At the sound of her voice Roger and Joaquín swiveled
in their chairs, their hands still on the table, bodies poised in
a less fraught moment while their eyes grew wide with confusion as Beatriz reached the gate. The startled policemen
held it closed while she pushed with both hands.

"It's my fault," she said in an anguished voice. "Forgive
me."

Eduardo caught hold of her, shook her, anger flaring in
his eyes as he spoke. Dolores heard "trouble" and "patience," but could not make out their context. The lawyer put
his hands on the boys' shoulders, spoke to them briefly before joining the officers. As he did, Beatriz went limp, lean-

ing so heavily against Eduardo that Dolores thought she might faint. When an officer pointed to seats on the far side of the room Eduardo roughly pulled Beatriz away. She looked back over her shoulder at the boys until they reached the seats and he made her sit. Eduardo said something. She buried her face in her hands.

The lawyer returned to the table where Roger sat ramrod straight, his face tight as a drumhead. Joaquín was trying to hold his emotions in check but his eyes gave him away. Confusion, Dolores thought, perhaps embarrassment, then she quickly realized it was neither. He was afraid.

"What do you think that was about?" Sorano asked.

"I wish I knew."

Beatriz' outburst had destroyed the equilibrium Dolores had regained after seeing them outside. She ventured a glance in their direction and saw Eduardo still haranguing Beatriz while she kept her eyes on him like a dog that has displeased its master. Dolores wondered if Eduardo's anger sprang from Beatriz' unseemly dash down the aisle or was a reaction to what she said. Had a secret been revealed? She repeated Beatriz' words to herself. They were meaningless. Like walking in on the middle of a film, the meaning of her utterance depended on something that had come before.

Eduardo spoke briefly, then fell silent. Beatriz responded by nodding her head. When she turned a moment later and saw Dolores, a word formed on her lips. Eduardo shifted in his seat. Now they were all staring at each other, more or less the way she had imagined the encounter that was supposed to have occurred outside. She was surprised that shame was nowhere evident in their eyes. She considered how she looked to them. Could they see the trace of her emotions as she had theirs? If it were true the eyes were mirrors to the soul, why did they continue glaring so defiantly, hatefully, stupidly? If they saw what she felt and feared, the blue record of all those years, they could not look the way they did. So it must be a lie, a poetic device untethered to reality.

Sorano's touch brought her out of the reverie. Emilio de León was coming through the door from his chambers. Tall, bearded, grave in demeanor, he carried a thick folder under his left arm. She searched his face for a clue to his decision. It was blank. The smile he directed toward the boys held a meaning beyond her ken.

Hermione leaned close and whispered, "Be strong. It's almost over." Sorano patted her hand as Emilio de León settled into his chair.

After removing a pair of half-glasses, he deliberately opened the folder. Each page was either an indictment or a vindication of her, outrage or justice. Nothing in between was possible. The ritual was perverse, designed to inflict needless pain and suffering. There was no reason to be there because he had already reached his decision. She wondered if he had told the boys, if his enigmatic smile conveyed acknowledgment of what had happened in his chambers. They could have persuaded him to change his mind, offered up a single detail that tipped the scale in favor of Eduardo and Beatriz. What they had said about the sea after their blood was drawn had been persuasive, eloquent, and if she had sensed its pull on them, why would similar words not touch the judge's heart? She had no idea which side he had favored during the war but if priests could sympathize with the generals, why not a man of law? And even if he despised Galtieri and Guzmán and the rest, that did not guarantee he had decided for her. Today, in this courtroom, the odds of three out of three seemed as unlikely as winning the lottery. She was a fool ever to think otherwise, should have left the country with Roger and Joaquín. But even if it were somehow still possible it was too late. She could not move. Her arms and legs felt boned with lead. Flight was no option, nor was flying. That was the Ponces' mode. Would the judge's words send them into the air in a frenzy of delight?

With a sudden decisive gesture Emilio de León closed the folder and peered at the boys. When he looked up, his eyes were on her. She had a few moments left to believe. The wheel was still turning, the ball bouncing from notch to notch. Hermione twined their fingers together. She squeezed her hand and held the pressure.

"Señora Masson," said the judge, his voice so soft she had to strain to hear, "there are painful issues at stake in this hearing no court should have to address. That they must be, not for the first or the last time, is something history will consider. We as a people will not come off lightly, make no mistake about that. As an Argentine, a father, I am ashamed such things happened but they did. Now the court must deal with consequences even more complex than their causes.

"The DNA tests prove conclusively that you are the grandmother of these young men. You have certain rights. They have rights. By virtue of the years they cared for them, so do Señor and Señora Ponce. While the evidence in your favor is compelling, the court is also obligated to consider intangible matters of the heart. There is the letter of the law and its spirit. A just verdict must find a balance between them." He paused and gazed around the room. "I am not Solomon. I can only declare the truth as I have seen it."

The difficulty of what he had to do was etched on the judge's face. He was a decent man, she believed. On the other hand, his voice undercut her confidence. He should not be speaking so softly and dispassionately. The occasion de-manded stentorian tones, high rhetoric. Waiting for him to continue, she feared the lack of intensity might be calculated, part of a plan to ease the blow he would deliver to the Ponces or herself.

He looked at her and she tried to project an outward

calm, an appearance of assurance. The moment he shifted his attention to the boys Joaquín put his arm around Roger's shoulders. Emilio de León spoke kindly, his tone warmer, more intimate than before.

"As I told you this morning, there are no precedents for these cases. Each differs, presents a unique set of problems even though their prime cause rests with felonies committed under the regime. Your desires, your sense of who you are and of your future are critically important. So are those of Señora Masson and the Ponces. The only guide I could follow in my deliberations is natural law, with the end of discovering what I believe is most beneficial for you. Is that understood?"

They nodded. Had they told him their stories of the sea, or others even more compelling? The pleasure and longing she heard that day in memory seemed to approach the absolute. If they had spoken so passionately to Emilio de León, what could keep him from returning them to that life they so obviously revered?

Satisfied that he had made himself clear, the judge smiled again at the boys before turning his gaze to the Ponces, regarding them with an even more judicious expression than he had brought to bear on her.

"Your claim to be the natural parents of these boys is negated by the results of the blood tests. The use of false documents to establish your connection is a criminal offense. However, to some extent your actions are mitigated by the longevity of your relationship. These young men have testified that you provided a good home and raised them as you would have your own children. That is a strong point in your favor. Because of your commitment over so many years, a case could be made for you to continue your relationship, especially since they have known only you as their parents."

As Dolores followed the trail of words she saw the tension ease in Eduardo's face. He squared his shoulders. With

eager, rapt attention, Beatriz looked on with poignant hope-
fulness. The judge had spoken coldly of the evidence against
them. That was good. Yet in the next breath he seemed to be
complimenting them. If he were going to find for her, why
wasn't he concentrating on their crimes? That was what he
had meant about the letter and the spirit of the law, balanc-
ing claims. He was leaning toward them. No other construc-
tion could be put on what he said.

"I say this because the crux of this case rests on the idea
of the family, both the way it has traditionally been viewed
and the way it must be seen in the aftermath of our civil war.
Tradition, natural law, suggests that custody should be
awarded to their blood relative, Señora Masson, but tradition is a poor guide in this situation. More than a decade has
passed since the boys were given to you. During that time
they have known only you as their family. Because of that, it
is possible to argue that you constitute their primary family
despite the fact of how you came together. In a certain sense,
what is at issue here are the conflicting claims of blood and
time, their blood and their time. But none of this takes into
account the fact that we are here as a result of a crime spon-
sored by a military regime, a violation of law and human
decency so repugnant it is all but unspeakable."

Turning to the boys, he added, "You are products of
that crime, victims of it no less than your birth mother,
Marta Masson, and your father, Rubén. One can be a
Desaparecido without dying. You are. So is your grandmother."

When he looked down at his hands, as if concentrating
his attention, Dolores kept her eyes on him. The little white
ball was about to settle in its niche.

"Desaparecido," the judge repeated. "Argentina has become famous because of that word. It has made the rounds
of the world, given us, as a nation, a character the nation
does not deserve. It is the linguistic coin of the regime, bear-

ing the imprint of many hands. A simple word, you may think, despite its horror. But it is not simple. Its meaning is not exhausted when we think of those gone without a trace because there is another side of the coin whose meaning remains incomplete until we consider those left behind, like Señora Masson, as well as those taken into the gray space of lies, like yourselves. It means death. It means vanishing act. It means sorrow. That is the full meaning of *Desaparecido*, the final truth of it that I have followed to my decision."

Emilio de León engaged the spectators, his eyes roaming across the room as if he were intent on making sure everyone understood his definitions. When his gaze came to rest on the Ponces, Dolores closed her eyes and saw Eduardo dragging the boat through the sea by its painter.

"Your love for these young men reflects the spirit of the law. I have taken it into account, believe it is genuine, deeply felt. It would have been unconscionable to do otherwise."

The dripping rope glistened. In the distance a whale breached and its flukes went gold in the sun.

"But I cannot ignore the fact that your love was born of a crime knowingly committed, an unforgivable crime that has caused terrible pain. Therefore, you are charged with kidnapping, illegal imprisonment of minors, and falsification of documents. Custody is awarded to Señora Masson."

Out of the absolute silence that had fallen on the room she heard a rush of sounds take flight, breath expelled, a sharp cry, cheers, the scrape of chairs, clapping, a solitary whistle, all mingled so there seemed no source or focal point.

With her eyes still closed a vision came to her, the boys in their sailor suits, Marta and Rubén in their portraits. Then she was on her feet, though she had no recollection of standing up.

Sorano smiled broadly while Hermione gave her a bear hug. Surrounded by white scarves, *compañeras* were touching her arms, her shoulders, her cheeks. As she edged toward the aisle accepting congratulations, murmuring her thanks, Graciela said, "We have to celebrate."

"Yes, of course," Dolores replied, more aware each second of the power of what had happened, the meaning of the judge's words for everyone. But celebration was for later. All she wanted now was to take the boys home, close the door on the past.

In the aisle she had an unobstructed view of the whole room. The Ponces were on their feet facing each other, Beatriz with her hands clasped in front of her breasts, Eduardo standing straight. Dolores longed for one of them to return her gaze. It was not going to happen. The way their eyes were locked on each other so intently, so exclusively, reminded her of the moment couples exchange rings at a wedding.

The next instant Beatriz was imploring, begging. Dolores strained to hear her words and Eduardo's reply as he opened and closed his mouth, biting off a phrase. With an agonized look, Beatriz nodded. Eduardo spoke again and as she glanced away Dolores realized something terrible had passed between them.

Eduardo looked up at the ceiling with an expression that seemed half grimace, half smile, a mix of incomprehensible emotions. The cords of his neck stood out as he bent forward, turning slightly to the left so that she could see his face was tight with pain. Suddenly, he put his right hand to his chest. *A heart attack.* He was dying in front of her. Before she could react his arm uncoiled in one seamless movement, his fist swinging like a ball on a tether, blurring as it struck Beatriz square in the face. His momentum sent him reeling into the chairs and he reached out awkwardly, grasping one whose legs screeched just before Dolores heard the soft thud of Beatriz' fall.

Everyone turned in the direction of the sound. Someone gasped. "What happened?" cried Hermione. The boys stared wide-eyed as people rushed toward the far side of the courtroom and then they were up and running and she was running too.

Beatriz lay on her back, her eyes open, glassy. Blood trickled from her lips and nose. In the wake of the commotion, of chairs thrust aside, of people asking what had happened, an eerie silence enveloped the crowd circling Beatriz, as if now that they could see they could find no words. Heavy breathing, the shifting of feet, nothing more until Joaquín's voice came to her. "Please," he said, and then she saw the two of them pass between Sorano and the judge, their faces pale and slack. She could do nothing for them. It was their moment and she belonged in it no more than anyone else.

Beatriz blinked at the sound of Joaquín's voice. As he knelt beside her she tried to focus on him. He asked if it hurt and she waved her hand feebly, as though brushing away a fly. Roger bent down beside her and Joaquín raised his face, staring at Eduardo, who had collapsed in the chair that broke his fall. Dolores saw the boy's eyes fall on Eduardo's bloody hand.

"Why?" asked Joaquín.

Eduardo stared dully, abstractly at Beatriz, for all the world like a man lost in meditation. Joaquín looked on a moment longer, then took out a handkerchief and began to staunch the blood flowing from Beatriz' nose.

She flinched at his touch, then turned her head so that she faced Eduardo, forgiving him, Dolores realized, telling him with her eyes that he had done no wrong.

"Don't," Sorano cautioned the boy. "It's broken."

The officers forced Eduardo to his feet.

"No," Beatriz groaned. She rose on one elbow and looked pleadingly at Emilio de León.

"It's not his fault," she said thickly. She looked at the boys. "It's not his fault."

A policeman arrived with a medical kit. Joaquín

watched him remove tape, a bottle of antiseptic. Slowly he turned to confront Eduardo.

"Why?" he asked, inflecting the word in such a way that he seemed to be posing a question about some deep mystery.

Eduardo regarded the boy wearily, his lids heavy as someone in need of sleep.

"Aren't you going to say anything?"

Eduardo closed his eyes, opened them, blinked. He stared at Joaquín a long time.

"You wouldn't understand," he said finally. "Some day but not now."

"You bastard," said Joaquín, his voice choked with emotion.

"Please," Beatriz implored. "Forgive him. He had the right."

"To hit you?" Joaquín asked incredulously.

"Can you sit up?" asked the judge.

As she leaned forward and grasped her knees the officer said, "You'll need to see a doctor."

Eduardo watched him unroll a length of tape, snip it, and place the strip across the bridge of her nose. Then he shifted his attention to Joaquín and his eyes were eloquent with foreknowledge that whatever he said would be rejected.

"It's not what you think. Things happened a long time ago."

Dolores was as hungry for an answer as Roger and Joaquín but Eduardo's words explained nothing, had been offered not as a defense but a sheer rhetorical exercise.

"What is it, then?" Roger snapped back.

"Listen to him," Beatriz implored. "He's your father. It's the truth."

Emilio de León knelt down in front of her.

"If you want I'll have him arrested."

Beatriz leaned her head on updrawn knees like an exhausted child, defenseless, without resource.

"No," she said.

It should have been a supreme moment. In exchange for what this woman had taken, Dolores should return disdain, indifference, some phrase that would cut into her as the sword of the gladiator did his opponent while he held him to the ground with his foot on his neck. She had the power to do it. She had the right. Clear as a bell she heard Beatriz scream her wish that Marta had fallen from Scilingo's plane. But she could not bring herself to speak. Hatred intact, tempered as steel, she felt nothing but sadness. The truth was that she pitied Beatriz. Despite herself, her heart went out to her. No one should suffer as she was.

"Leave her alone," said Eduardo to the judge. "What happens between us is none of your business." Seething, emboldened, he challenged Emilio de León with a contemptuous look. "When is the so-called trial?"

"The court will set a date. As of today, you're prohibited from leaving Buenos Aires."

Eduardo nodded with mock gravity. He nodded again, smiling this time, his eyes all but glittering.

"It was an accident," he said to the boys. "Nothing more."

They regarded him as if he were speaking a language they did not know.

"Tell them," Eduardo said over his shoulder to Beatriz.

"It was," she said pleadingly. "It was an accident."

There was something so unsettling in her acquiescence, so disgraceful in her capitulation, that Dolores felt dirtied. She wanted to be free of this, wanted to be outside where the air was clean.

"You see," said Eduardo, smiling as he took a step forward, holding out his hands, palms turned upward. "It was nothing."

As Roger pivoted away from his reach the color seemed to drain from Eduardo's face. Clearly, he understood the meaning of Roger's retreat. It was burning in his eyes as he stared at the boy.

"That's enough," warned the judge.

"Forgive him," Beatriz said.

Eduardo searched their faces.

"Please," he said, his voice cracking, "you're my *sons*. I love you. This doesn't mean anything. We'll all be together again just like before."

"For Christ's sake," said Emilio de León, "don't you have any decency?"

Spinning around, Eduardo glared eagerly at the judge, happy to have a target.

"You talk about decency," he said incredulously, "after taking away my sons?"

"They are not your sons," Dolores said. "They never have been."

Until that outrageous claim escaped his lips she had been content to listen, as fascinated and appalled as she would be driving past a wreck on the highway. But Eduardo had overstepped his bounds and in doing so freed her voice.

To the boys she said, "It might be better if you waited outside with Sorano."

Neither moved. She regarded them, wondering whether she should insist. They had a right to hear, she realized, as much as she did to speak.

"All right."

With that, she turned to Eduardo.

"There are certain words you have no right to, that don't belong in your mouth. 'Sons' is one of them."

"Tomás and Manfredo are my sons," he said defiantly. "They love me like a father."

"They do," Beatriz moaned. "They always have."

"Invented names," Dolores said. "Names you made up and then ran from place to place to keep the lie intact."

"We love them," Beatriz cried. "We always have."

"And they love us," Eduardo added. "Don't you?"

Dolores looked at them. "It's all right," she said calmly. "What you felt and still feel is all right. Remember that."

Eduardo waited for her to continue. Now there was a trace of imperiousness in his expression.

"Your pleasure was all that mattered, wasn't it? Did you ever consider what it cost them? Me? Rubén? I thought about that once and decided you never did. Much as I hate you, I can't believe you did because you couldn't have kept them. Your conscience wouldn't have allowed it. You'd have understood that you had cut out my heart and given them back."

"Listen to this," he said to the boys. "Have you ever heard anything like it? She's crazy."

"You committed a crime, but stealing my grandsons wasn't the only one, simply the first. It began the night you took them and every moment afterward was another crime, every day I lived without them, every empty day that tormented Rubén until he couldn't stand living here. It was a crime I never knew where they were. A crime I missed seeing them grow up. You stole them but you can't steal a word that doesn't belong to you."

"They're our sons," Beatriz cried. "Always and forever."

Speaking caused her lips to bleed. She touched her fingers to her mouth and stared at the blood as if surprised to see it. Slowly she faced Eduardo. She raised her shoulders, opened her mouth, her eyebrows arched in supplication.

"How could I have known?" she said.

They exchanged a glance fraught with private knowledge. Then Eduardo looked at the boys. A gap had opened in his life, Dolores thought. The judge made it happen but she had widened it with her words, the boys with their silence. She saw it in his eyes, the gleam of the struggle to close what had been opened. He would do anything, absolutely anything.

"They talked about *evidence,*" Eduardo said disdainfully. "About *facts.* But only the ones that pleased them. Did they mention the *fact* that this Marta and Rubén were criminals, Communist subversives? No. They were in prison because they deserved to be. We never held it against you. You couldn't choose your natural parents. We saved you, do you understand? You could have gone to people who'd have mistreated you, ignored you, God knows what else. You could have been left at an orphanage with signs around your necks saying you were children of subversives. It happened, more than once. Or killed. What difference does it make that Beatriz didn't give birth to you? All that matters is that we loved you from the beginning, from the moment we set eyes on you. We sacrificed to keep our family together. You loved us. That hasn't changed. How could it change in a few months? Tell the judge it hasn't. Tell the old woman."

Dolores wanted to peel the skin off his lies. The boys' faces said everything, showed them trapped between what had been and what was coming.

"What are we supposed to do?" Roger asked. "We know what happened. We loved you. We still do. But she's our grandmother."

"She's old," Eduardo answered contemptuously. "She'll die soon. Where will you be then?"

"This is finished," said Emilio de León.

"*Nothing's* finished!" Eduardo yelled.

Emilio de León turned to an officer. "If he isn't gone in one minute I want him arrested for contempt."

Awkwardly, uncertain of her balance, Beatriz struggled to her feet.

"Please. Try to understand what this man is going through."

Dolores saw the consternation in the judge's face. He understood Beatriz no better than she did, pitied her as she did, but he was also disgusted.

The boys stared at her, unable to hide their distress at the sight of her bloodstained dress. Her nose flared to the left. Her swollen lips were already discolored.

Joaquín made a low sound in his throat, neither a groan nor a word, something newly invented to express his sorrow.

"We loved you," he murmured, drawing the words up with a great effort. "We still do. She understands." He inclined his head toward Dolores. "I don't know what to think about this but it was bound to happen, wasn't it? We couldn't have run forever."

A range of emotions passed across Beatriz' face. She brightened as Joaquín spoke of love but the glow faded with his question. Her lips parted in a crooked, pleasureless, rueful smile. A sound between a cough and a laugh escaped, as though in acknowledgment of a private thought. She nodded several times, and Dolores had the impression that was also in response to an inner voice.

"Yes, I suppose it was."

There was a moment when she seemed liberated, at rest, as though a door in her mind had closed. Then she teetered, reached out suddenly for Eduardo's arm.

"Time's up," the judge told Eduardo.

"It'll be all right," he told the boys. "Believe me. Don't ever doubt it."

His despair was plain to see but something else lay behind it, an idea or emotion no more decipherable than whatever had animated Beatriz. He put his tongue between his lips as if readying himself to speak, then thought better of it.

Emilio de León glanced at his watch.

Beatriz tugged on Eduardo's arm.

"Remember what I said," Eduardo told the boys, looking at them confidently.

With awkward dignity, he led Beatriz up the aisle, walking straight and stiff, his arm curved just enough for her to grasp.

This was one of the moments Dolores had rehearsed, imagined in half a dozen variations. They were walking out of her life and there was supposed to be a finality to it, like the last scene in a play, the last chord of a symphony, the sun slipping beyond the horizon, even death. But the curtain was not coming down, not all the way. They had left something behind, like a scent so vague it could only be noted, not identified. It remained after they passed through the doors, turned left, and disappeared.

Sorano stood between Roger and Joaquín with his arms draped around their shoulders. A fatherly gesture. She remembered the last time she had seen Rubén touch them. He had picked them up and carried them out to the car after a visit. If she knew where he was. She could not go down that road again with its curves and ruts and detours that ended in a vacancy.

"Let's go home," she said.

Hollow-eyed, utterly drained, aged since she had seen them off only hours ago, they assented with a nod.

"I'll take you," Sorano said.

The aisle led away from the past. She was walking in freedom, in happiness, though Eduardo was still nagging her. She thought of what he'd said to the boys, recalled the confidence in his voice. It had seemed only an isolated moment, a fragment of the ugly tapestry that had so unexpectedly unfurled, but it was more than that, more than a dismembered arm or leg, a horse's head, the lance of an unseen knight. His determination. That was what it was. His need, the desire in his eyes. Though she could not imagine its shape, it dominated the room, and the power of the room, what it represented, seemed to lessen as they passed into the foyer.

Sorano was going on about soccer. Names of teams and players floated in the air like wind-blown scraps of paper, whirling around but not obscuring the image of Eduardo. She needed to calm down. It was only natural to worry, she thought, after all that had come before. Like the last light of the sun, or the picture on a television screen when you turn it off, the way it shrinks from the margins to a glowing point before it disappears, that was what it was.

Through the glass of the revolving door ahead of them she saw the reporters.

"We can go out the side door at the far end," Sorano told her.

She was tempted to. The last thing in the world she felt like was answering more questions. There had been too many for too long. She had had enough questions, was surfeited, bloated with them.

But what she felt was not important. Her story was, especially the end. People should read about it. They needed to know that the idea of justice was still alive, breathing. They needed the end of her story to dilute the filth about Scilingo and his priest, to use it to wash the taste out of their mouths, clear the air they breathed. It didn't matter that she was tired.

"Take Roger and Joaquín. They don't need any of this. I'll talk to them a little. Where are you parked?"

"Near the back of the lot. Are you sure?"

"Yes."

The revolving door made a flat, fluttering sound as she entered one of the wedges. She took a few quick steps, keeping up with its speed, and was deposited outside.

The Ponces were still there, standing on the sidewalk beside their truck. Dolores was surprised they had not left.

She wanted the finality she had imagined, the blank screen, not their images. But it was naive to think it was over in the courtroom. She was still in her own ending and they were in theirs. Her assumption that they would flee the building and drive away as fast as possible, unable to look in the rearview mirror, had nothing to do with the story unfolding beneath the trees.

"Señora Masson!" called Julia Fuentes. A flashbulb went off in the corner of her eye.

Looking up at Eduardo, Beatriz tentatively raised her arms, embraced him. She rested the side of her face against his chest. Her bruised mouth was plain to see, the strip of white tape like a tiny flag. She was waiting. Eduardo remained rigid. Then, as if acting against his will, his right arm came up and he slid it around her waist.

Julia Fuentes stepped in front of Dolores, blocking her view.

"How do you feel?"

"Wonderful," she said, moving to one side.

Eduardo was getting behind the wheel, Beatriz making her way to the other side of the truck, steadying herself with one hand against the tailgate.

It was not the right ending.

"Please," said Julia. "Would you just answer a few more questions?"

"Ask," Dolores said.

They all started talking at once as she watched the truck disappear into traffic.

THIRTEEN

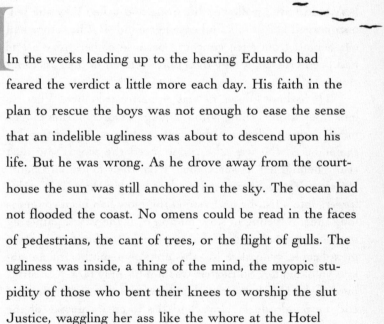

In the weeks leading up to the hearing Eduardo had feared the verdict a little more each day. His faith in the plan to rescue the boys was not enough to ease the sense that an indelible ugliness was about to descend upon his life. But he was wrong. As he drove away from the courthouse the sun was still anchored in the sky. The ocean had not flooded the coast. No omens could be read in the faces of pedestrians, the cant of trees, or the flight of gulls. The ugliness was inside, a thing of the mind, the myopic stupidity of those who bent their knees to worship the slut Justice, waggling her ass like the whore at the Hotel Bolívar for the small change of a sentimental view of history.

What relief this understanding brought was quickly

dispelled by his anxiety about Beatriz. Her words, the tone of her words spoken in the shadow of the plane trees echoed in his mind. *I want to die because of what I've done to you.*

He glanced at her. Bright-eyed, abstracted, deep in interior space, she stared straight ahead. Though she had staunched the bleeding with Manfredo's handkerchief, her lips were swollen, discolored. Her stoicism surprised him. She had never been good with pain, was felled by cuts and bruises anyone else would have barely noticed. The shock of the verdict, he thought—that even more than his blow had numbed her.

There was a time in another place, in another life, when he would have swallowed his pride and asked how she felt, encouraged her to talk and ease her mind. But her story had cut her off from such concern. Because of her story a line had been crossed, a new direction declared in their relationship.

He had not known he was going to strike her. When he looked up at the ceiling with the judge's words burning in his mind, seeking relief, a vision came to him of the earring. He remembered the way she pronounced the word, saw dust rising behind her as she walked from their house into Santa Rosalita. Yet as he pressed his hand to his chest, balling his fingers into a fist, he understood the blow had been coming a long time, traveling in slow motion over the years, gathering momentum like a wave, the rage behind it born of Beatriz' inexplicable sympathy for the unknown mother of an unknown daughter. So Beatriz was not his only target. In striking her, he also struck the daughter who died in the pampas and Fernando de la Hoya and the forensics people of the Ezekiel squad who exhumed the killing field. He struck Dolores and all the old witches who had haunted his dreams.

• • •

At a café he asked if anyone knew of a doctor. A waiter jotted down the address of a clinic.

In the parking lot he helped her out of the truck.

"We have enough trouble," he said. "If anyone asks, say you fell down the stairs, stumbled on a loose carpet. Understand?"

She glanced at him and quickly averted her eyes. "Yes, I fell," she answered, her voice flat as the calmest sea.

He filled out a form in the reception area and ignored the people gaping at them.

In the examination room the doctor took one look at Beatriz, then turned to Eduardo.

"Did you beat her?"

"I fell," she said quickly. "It was stupid. A loose carpet on the stairs."

"And his hand?"

"An accident," said Eduardo. "I was working on my truck."

"Bullshit," said the doctor, shaking his head in disgust.

He injected Beatriz with Novocain and Eduardo flinched at the sight of the needle entering her flesh. She stared placidly out the window. He watched her paleness against the white walls, her skin almost the color of the paint, while the doctor stitched the cut on the inside of her lip and replaced the tape on her nose.

After his knuckles were cleaned and bandaged the doctor gave Beatriz a prescription for a painkiller.

"The next time he does this," he told Beatriz, "have him arrested."

"I told you I fell."

The doctor looked at her sadly.

"Most women say the same thing. In fact, I don't remember hearing another story in years." He faced Eduardo. "It's pure luck you didn't break any of her facial bones."

"She told you what happened."

"I heard what she said."

"How much?" Eduardo said as he took out his wallet. The doctor told him. "Pay at the desk."

Tossing the bills on the examination table, Eduardo said, "Go to hell," and stalked out.

Their room was hot after being closed up most of the day. An unidentifiable odor hung in the air, probably from the stained carpet.

When he opened the windows Beatriz stood in front of the larger one, gazing down at the street. They had not exchanged a word since leaving the clinic and her stance suggested she was content with silence, that she had said all she intended to.

He, on the other hand, needed to speak. Even though it was clear she did not blame him, he wanted to make sure there were no lingering resentments that might flare up later.

He went over to her. "Look at me."

She turned from the window but could not meet his eyes.

"We should talk, get it out in the open."

"It's not necessary."

"What do you want me to say?"

"Nothing."

"You understand why?"

"The earring," she said, her voice hardly more than a whisper.

His impression was of distance rather than softness, as if she were so far away he should be shouting. He felt lonely, alone. He thought of the way the boys had looked at him. For the present, she was all he had.

He spoke conciliatorily, in a tone verging on the apologetic. "I wish it hadn't happened."

"I know."

"You forgive me? This isn't going to smolder?"

She looked at him, searching his face with deep earnestness.

"I made it happen. It was my fault. They're gone because of me. Sometimes I dream about it, the same dream, over and over. I think I see them in a boat but it's not a boat. It's the earring, big as a truck tire, and they're inside its circle, clinging to it. The current pulls them away. Because it's gold and the sun's always out I can see it until they reach the horizon. My eyes always hurt from looking, even after they disappear, after I wake up. Do you think I should have told the judge?"

He touched her arm. "It was only a dream."

She frowned and looked out the window, as if she were searching the sky. With her back to him she said, "You're right. Just a dream. I don't care about dreams."

She put her hands on the sill and leaned forward, gazing into the street, her grip so tight the tendons in her hands stood out. Slowly, almost languidly, she turned to face him.

"Sometimes I go in the water after them. I can't breathe and I can't drown. It's like I have to remember them disappearing forever."

There was neither condemnation nor self-pity in her voice, nothing he could interpret. The strangeness was to be expected, he supposed, in someone so high-strung.

"I'm going to call Guzmán. He'll want to know."

It was a relief to be away from her. The pain at the courthouse had been precise, specific. What he felt listening to her created an edgeless anxiety. It would soon be over, he thought. The wheels were already turning. He should look upon the day not as a defeat but as the beginning of a bright new life.

The city called to him as he waited for the light to turn green. Even the sights and sounds of this run-down district could charm an exile, turn his heart to longing. The question asked and answered more times than he could count returned, beguiling him with a freshness that gave rise to hope: Was there a way to disappear into the sprawl of Buenos Aires, some enclave where he could assume a new identity? Surely there must be dozens, hundreds of *porteños* living under adopted names, people who had shed old lives and their burdens and now could hardly remember who they once had been. But the time when it was possible ended the day he opened the door to Mendoza. Thinking otherwise was sentimental drivel. Buenos Aires was sealed to him.

Two boys about the ages of Tomás and Manfredo approached from the other side of the crosswalk. Bright-eyed, arrogant as only boys their age could be, they seemed to walk on air. By the time he looked away the pedestrians streaming by were blurred. He blinked, swallowed hard, surprised by the instantaneous rush of emotion.

The bar welcomed him with muted light and the smell of stale alcohol. He ordered a beer, drank it quickly, then walked back to the booth where he listened to four rings and the first part of a recorded message before Guzmán picked up.

"It's Ponce. The bastard found for their grandmother."

"I'm sorry, *amigo*. How'd the boys take it?"

Eduardo looked through the glass door at a neon beer sign, remembering. The telephone felt large and cumbersome in his hand.

"The old woman's filled them with lies."

"It doesn't matter. You'll be on your way soon."

"It's not that simple. He threw the book at us. And there's trouble with Beatriz. I hit her when it was over."

"Is she hurt?"

"She looks worse than she is. The real problem's inside. There's something the matter with her."

"Spend some time with her, *amigo*. Smooth it over. Did the judge set a date for the trial?"

"No."

"Good. It could take months. You'll be long gone."

"That's what I want to talk about. Can I see you this weekend?"

"I'm afraid not. There are some business matters I'm involved in, and Alicia's having trouble. Hugo's out of town, which means I'm on call if she has to see the doctor. She's due at the end of the month."

"You'll be tied up until then?"

"It's a girl, by the way. Ultrasound. I'm going to have two granddaughters. It'll be hell to pay for Juanito."

"I imagine," Eduardo said, unable to keep the disappointment out of his voice.

"Listen, *amigo*, it's not a good idea to rush this. The old woman's probably worried you'll try something."

"What makes you think so?"

"Put the shoe on the other foot. If it'd gone against her, would she have given up? She's been after your ass for thirteen years. And she's not the only one you'll be running from. You'll be skipping out on a trial, remember? Let her settle down, get comfortable. You need to make sure everything's right."

"I'm still worried about Beatriz."

"Explain it to her," Guzmán said irritably. "What's a few more weeks? I like what you've said so far about your idea but you haven't thought it through. The last thing you want is to go off half-cocked. Work it out. Once Alicia's delivered we'll take care of things."

The line buzzed like an angry fly as Guzmán hung up.

Eduardo looked at the bottles on the shelves. The taste

of beer still lingered on his tongue. He wanted to join the men tending their thoughts at the bar, slip into a pleasant haze of forgetfulness, but he remembered too clearly what Beatriz said outside the courthouse, the way she pressed her face against his chest and tightened her arms around him. Her words in their room had been even more disturbing.

Outside, he glanced left and right, squinted against the glare. Something from above attracted his attention. Looking up, he saw Beatriz standing by the window, extending her hand and dropping something too small to see.

No sooner had he begun telling her about the conversation than she said she doubted the general's commitment. Surely he did not have to spend all his time at Alicia's beck and call.

Eduardo asked if she had suddenly become clairvoyant. Guzmán had many interests. He was dedicated to his family, to them. Did he have to remind her how often he had helped them over the years? Guzmán's life had been devoted to strategy and tactics. Who were they to question such a man? Who else could they trust, rely on? There was no one else. They had to dance to his tune.

"He's not God," she said. "He's just a man. It's not good to trust someone so much."

Before the words were out of her mouth she understood her blunder. She looked the way she did whenever she dropped a plate. He knew she was waiting for him to twist the knife but she was too brittle for him to do it.

"I'll take care of this. Your job is to be patient."

Guzmán urged him to plan their route out of the country before taking up the question of how to free the boys. "I know you want to do it the other way around but if you work out how to get them first, you'll become impatient. You might miss something important."

Eduardo responded like a good soldier. Bright and early every morning for the next few weeks he took a bus to the public library where he spent hours pouring over an atlas and travel books. He had acquired new maps of Argentina, Central America, Mexico, pencils in half a dozen different colors, which he used to annotate the maps, drawing lines with the aide of a triangle, printing information about mileage between stops, road conditions, locations of police stations as carefully as if he were a medieval monk transcribing scripture onto vellum.

The work was calming, deeply satisfying. Time ticked away to the imagined rhythm of the heart beating in Alicia's womb.

Each segment of the journey laid down in red ink empowered him. He became so enthralled with maps that often when his work for the day was done he perused books of cartography, wondering why he had never become interested in this art. Maps were more than mere blueprints of the world. They were also stories, prefigurations of success. The old hand-drawn ones reproduced in the books were museums of fine detail, the cartographer's work as distinct from each other as that of the finest artists.

Sometimes, when he came upon a detail that charmed him—the rendering of a road, a stream, grasslands—he opened his map and revised his work, striving for the same effect. The day he finished a sadness came upon him akin to what he felt after making love.

After returning the atlas and travel guides to the shelves he set to work making lists, one for him, one for Beatriz, one each for Tomás and Manfredo. Everything that might possibly be required for self-sufficiency on the journey found its way into his notebook.

Once he bought and stored all the items in numbered boxes, he returned to the library and began the search for a place to live in Acapulco. The Mexican newspaper advertised houses and apartments whose rents were far beyond his means. The best they could do would be to stay in a cheap hotel until he found a job and got ahead enough to rent a decent place.

He called the manager of the Hotel Estrella and explained that he and his family would arrive in six or seven weeks. The man said he always had rooms. To reserve one, all Eduardo had to do was send a month's rent in advance.

That afternoon Eduardo bought a money order and mailed it at a post office near the library. For the first time since beginning to work on their escape, their transformation, the weight of his old life returned, settled squarely upon his shoulders. Thirteen years of penury, worry, flight, scars from rope burns on his hands, the legacy of fishnets. A vision came to him of the moonlit pampas, of the killing field divided into squares by ropes tied to wood stakes, a geography of death whose cause he was ignorant of but whose effect had brought him to this pass. Beatriz' mouth and the earring had led the Ezekiel squad to Santa Rosalita. The danger he had perceived that somehow their attention might spread beyond the site to his sons had sent him fleeing once again, leaving in his wake a decent wage, a home, hurling him down the face of the cordillera to that windy haunt where he had struggled to wrest a living from the sea.

Where was justice in all of this? Understanding of his fierce love for Tomás and Manfredo?

Questions without answers, questions that probed the quick of his heart.

He was poor but undefeated. Someday he would have enough money. The bounty of Mexico awaited him.

Guzmán was effusive in his congratulations when Eduardo described all he had accomplished. Unfortunately, because his affairs were more entangled than he had realized, it would not be possible for them to meet. Perhaps when the second stage of the plan was completed. "This is what you've been waiting for, *amigo*. Enjoy it."

They needed precise information about the old woman's house and neighborhood. The men Guzmán intended to hire to take the boys were old acquaintances, reliable, perfectly competent, but neither was a genius. Eduardo had to be sure he overlooked nothing.

He began with long afternoon walks to reconnoiter the district. Soon his notebook was filled with diagrams of roads leading to her street. He observed traffic at various times, jotting down when it was light and heavy. He spent a whole day walking along the connector roads, counting stoplights.

The library work had taught him patience. Whenever an image of Tomás and Manfredo interposed itself between his eyes and his maps, he had managed to suppress his longing, but now that he was close to them the discipline was lost. He wanted to embrace them, hear them laugh. He was starving for them and the hunger grew worse when he ventured into her neighborhood at night, arriving on different buses to avoid establishing a pattern that might draw attention.

Getting off half a mile away, he forced himself to attend to the times shops closed, whether their proprietors lingered after locking up or headed home. He had to check his progress, delay his arrival on her street. Guzmán had impressed upon him the importance of such care but even though he understood the general's reasoning—an observant bystander could provide the police with clues—his desire was always to hurry onward.

He learned the habits of her neighbors, observing when they went to bed. He passed her house once on the north side of the street, once on the south, never turning his head, learning what he could from the corner of his eye, the sideways glance of a casual passerby.

The curtains were drawn the first night, thick lacy curtains that glowed with soft yellow light.

He saw a shadow the second evening. Someone stood close enough to imprint the curtain with a hazy shape.

On the third they were open. Tomás was sitting on a couch, Manfredo standing beside him. The sight tore at his heart. It took all his willpower to propel his feet along the sidewalk, resist the desire to retrace his steps.

By the time he returned, the living room lights were out but two small windows along the left side were lit. Now he knew which rooms were theirs, the last piece of information Guzmán required. Yet having learned where their rooms were was not enough, not after seeing them. If he returned, there was a chance the curtains might be open and he could feed his love as he walked up and down the street.

For two nights running even shadows were denied him. He decided to try once more, give himself the gift of another possibility. If he did not see them, he would have to be content with memory.

He told Beatriz what he was doing and the use Guzmán planned to make of the information. He did not mention that he had seen the boys. It was something he wanted for himself, a private reward.

The next night, after dinner, he told her that he had to go out again.

"Take me."

"Don't be ridiculous."

"I could help. I might see something you haven't."

"No. Two people would look suspicious."

She did not argue. After a few minutes she went over to the window and stood next to the strip of flypaper he had attached to the curtain rod, absently giving it a spin. When it stopped, she sent it flying again.

"For Christ's sake. What's the matter with you? It's filthy. You could get an infection."

"What difference does it make? I live in this room by myself. And them."

She plucked a fly and held it to the light.

"Do you think they come back to life if they're tossed out the window? I do it sometimes. It makes me happy thinking that something in the air brings them back."

"It's late," he said as he pushed his chair back from the table.

This thing with the flies disgusted him. As he boarded the bus he decided to press Guzmán. He wanted an end to all this nonsense.

Her house was dark and so were most of the others. His carefully perfected routine, the measured stride, casual gait, the indirect observation of things were unnecessary tonight. The darkness was opening up, offering an unexpected opportunity.

He brazenly stopped in front of the house, excited to be standing there, a virtually invisible presence free to pause, assess. After glancing up and down the street, he resolutely went up the walk.

The stairs were concrete, the top one deep enough to stand on comfortably.

He was so close to them! They were breathing the same air.

Suddenly he felt a deep, shattering longing. He swallowed and tried to fight back his tears. The same air.

He pressed his ear to the door. With his eyes closed, with tears running down his cheeks, he listened. He wanted to be in their bedrooms. He wanted to bend down and kiss them.

He put his lips to the door. Perhaps an imprint would remain. Perhaps tomorrow they would see the outline of lips and know he had been there.

FOURTEEN

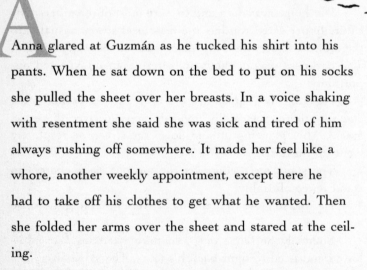

Anna glared at Guzmán as he tucked his shirt into his pants. When he sat down on the bed to put on his socks she pulled the sheet over her breasts. In a voice shaking with resentment she said she was sick and tired of him always rushing off somewhere. It made her feel like a whore, another weekly appointment, except here he had to take off his clothes to get what he wanted. Then she folded her arms over the sheet and stared at the ceiling.

Surprised—the accusation seemed to have come out of nowhere—he said that was nonsense, she knew he loved her. He wished things were different, too. It would be wonderful to have more time together. Since they couldn't, it might be nice if she tried to be reasonable. She knew what his life was like. He had done everything he could think of to make room for her in it.

She cast a skeptical look at him.

"Maybe we can get away for a weekend soon."

"That's not what I'm talking about. I'm talking about today. Right now. What is it this time?"

"I'm having a party for Father Von Claussen tonight," he said as he pulled on a sock. "He's been absolved. After the beating he took in the papers it seems miraculous. I thought he was finished."

"Like throwing away crutches?" she said in a taunting falsetto. "Like that? Parting the waters? *Walking* on them?"

He knew better than to take the bait. With as much patience as he could muster, he reminded her of the stink raised when Scilingo had implicated his own friend. As soon as he heard about it, he thought something had gone wrong with Von Claussen's head. An internal switch hadn't closed, his synapses had misfired. Nothing else could explain his failure of judgment in supporting Scilingo. If he had been thinking clearly, he would not have sanctioned the killings. They were beyond the pale. Shooting subversives was one thing, tossing them out of a plane alive was another. He himself had been sickened. Even now the thought of it made his skin crawl.

Anna plumped up a pillow and leaned against it. She looked bored and angry. He said the Church had seemed ready to throw Von Claussen to the lions in order to appease the public outcry. The damage of being cut adrift would have been incalculable. She ought to understand how relieved he was when the priest called and said his bishop had declared his words merely an error of judgment, overzealousness in defense of the faith. Except for Alicia's pregnancy, it was the best news of the year.

"Why?" Anna said flatly. "What's so special about him?"

"He has counseled and consoled me," Guzmán answered. "During the trial he was always by my side."

He pulled on his other sock before looking at her again. Raven black hair. Porcelain blue eyes that had locked onto him, what? a dozen years ago. Since then, he had learned to read them perfectly, and what he saw told him that he had definitely failed to appease her.

"I don't get it," she said. "Not that I haven't tried."

She said she had never understood this religious quirk of his. It really threw her for a loop, always had. Here it was the end of the twentieth century and men had walked on the moon and he still believed in things people did when they thought the earth was flat. That was bad enough but what really stymied her was how he could continue their relationship if he really believed. Unless he wanted something juicy to spice up the old pullet's life in the confessional. Had he told Von Claussen about her? How she looked naked? What they did?

Guzmán slipped his feet into Italian loafers and stood up.

"Are you finished?"

"Not finished. Fed up."

She put the back of her hand under her chin to show how much.

"Say I'm cute when I'm mad and I'll cut your balls off, Generalissimo."

"I've never mentioned you, with or without your clothes."

"What about your quirk?"

He looked at her steadily.

"Aren't you supposed to confess everything? If you don't, you'll go to hell, right?"

"I'll call tomorrow. Maybe I can stop by."

"I don't know. You might be roasting on a spit by then."

• • •

As the signal light turned red Guzmán smashed the accelerator to the floor. A florist's van loomed up on his left,
horn blaring, and slipped behind his Mercedes with no more
than a meter to spare. He glanced at the dashboard clock as
he pulled into the fast lane. An hour late already. If the
traffic did not thin out, it would take another twenty minutes
to get home. He bore down on the car ahead, flashing his
lights. When the driver pulled over and gave him the finger,
Guzmán returned the favor in his rearview mirror.

It had been stupid visiting Anna so late in the afternoon.
At the same time, he had to admit the pressure of time added
excitement to fucking her, something he seemed to have
needed lately. He wondered if it had to do with age. Whether
it did or not, if he knew what was good for him he had better
plan some long afternoons. And make her promise to lay off
his religion. When she ragged him about it he felt uneasy. He
had carefully, painfully worked out their relationship in his
mind.

She would never understand his beliefs. He would
never tell her how he had felt the draw of the priesthood as a
young man, how close he came to finding a vocation when he
succumbed to the pull of holiness from the stained-glass windows, the mysterious sound of Latin. The power to loose and
bind in the name of God, all of it seemingly inevitable until
he got a little older and realized he could not survive without
women, disappear into a life of renunciation. That was one of
the reasons he admired Von Claussen. The priest had been
able to do something he found impossible. She would laugh
if he tried to explain.

On his street flowering plants still glowed in the early
evening heat. The oranges on the trees in the walled garden
of the house across from his reminded him of Anna's breasts.

If Gloria asked where he'd been, he would say the shooting range.

Alicia and Hugo had picked up Father Von Claussen and were in the living room with Gloria. Guzmán apologized for being late. He kissed Alicia. With a smile he cupped his hand over her stomach.

"This is a big girl."

Alicia rolled her eyes and put her hand to the small of her back. "You're telling me. She weighs a ton."

"How do you feel?"

"Not well, Daddy."

"We were just talking about the christening," said Father Von Claussen.

"Which isn't far off," Hugo said with a glance at Alicia.

"The sooner the better. I'm so glad you'll be able to christen her," she said.

"That's how it should be," Father Von Claussen answered. "I feel part of this family."

"Well, you almost *are*," Gloria told him.

She looked at Guzmán, searching his eyes with an intensity he could not mistake, silently asking if today of all days he had been with Anna.

Fortunately, the doorbell rang and he quickly left the room, almost certain there had not been enough time for her to read him. When he returned with half a dozen guests she was smiling, which meant he was right. Still, to cover his tracks he made a point of staying close to her during cocktails. He had no intention of repeating the mistake he had made with Anna.

Throughout dinner, in the gaps between conversations, he replayed their argument. He hated fighting with Anna and usually capitulated rather than face a full-blown battle. He should have this afternoon but there hadn't been time to smooth things over. Now there would be hell to pay. Weeks of sullenness before she even started to think about making him crawl. He wished she were more like Gloria, who simply withdrew into silence for a while and then reemerged as if nothing had happened. Well, she wasn't, but he was damned if he was going to let their spat ruin the evening.

After they finished eating he led the men to his study. He offered a humidor of Cuban cigars, Napoleon brandy. "One more toast to our guest of honor," he said. "As far as I'm concerned, what happened was a little miracle."

"Hardly a miracle," said Father Von Claussen.

"Divine serendipity, then," suggested Cambio.

"It's more mundane," the priest said. "More earth-bound. The authorities recognized they made an error. Of course they were worried about the publicity but they're just men, and they saw to it that I received justice. The bishop understood, from the beginning, that I had not sinned in my heart, only in language. Semantic error, he called it. I admit to being imprudent but every one of you knows what lay behind my words."

"Here, here," Massina said approvingly.

Hugo said, "You knew we were all with you."

"I did. I thanked God for it."

They were quiet for a few moments, aware of the solidarity.

"You said you wanted to talk about Ponce," Violeta told Guzmán.

"I do. But wait a minute. There's something I want you to see first."

"Another bird trick," groaned Cambio. "They should be eaten."

Guzmán opened the cage and inserted his right hand.

"Maya," he called softly.

The canary leapt from its perch to his hand where it interrogated him with one eye, then the other.

Guzmán slowly withdrew her and with his left hand put a seed between his lips. The moment he raised her to his face she took the seed.

"Now," he murmured, "a kiss for Daddy."

Maya pecked his upper lip and Guzmán turned triumphantly to his guests.

"It took a month to teach her that. We worked on it every day, for an hour."

None of them understood the pleasure he took in birds. They were all dog people. Not that it mattered. He rather liked the idea of it being a private passion, something he shared with people at the bird market who appreciated the same things. Nothing was more soothing than a stroll down the rows of cages. He had perfect pitch when it came to bird songs, equal to any of the vendors'. He remembered once when he was talking to an old man about parakeets and there had been a great commotion. Someone had opened half a dozen cages and all the birds were scattering this way and that in the sky. It had been a terrible loss for the man, and he still sympathized with him whenever he recalled that afternoon. All that color and beauty disappearing, all those familiar voices never to be heard again.

Returning to his desk chair, he poured another brandy, then ran a hand through his thick gray hair.

"There is something I want to say about Ponce. I think everyone knows what happened in court."

"Outrageous," Massina said angrily. "A travesty."

"But predictable," the priest said, "after this Scilingo business. It had to have prejudiced the judge."

Guzmán said, "I'm sure that's right. In any case, it's water under the bridge. Here's the problem. If Eduardo and Beatriz stand trial, they're sure to go to prison. He was loyal to me, devoted, and I haven't forgotten. I've told him I'll help get him out of the country."

"I think I see what's coming," said Cambio.

"He's poor as a church mouse. Anything would make a difference."

"He must be devastated about leaving the boys," Father Von Claussen said.

"Of course," Guzmán answered, quickly adding, "But it's either that or go to jail."

"Poor bastard," said Cambio. "Sorry, Father."

"When do you need it?" Violeta asked.

"Fairly soon. A few weeks."

With their pledges and his own contribution Guzmán thought Ponce should be able to stay afloat until he found work in Mexico. He was pleased with the way he had managed things. The priest's question had slipped into and out of the discussion without making a ripple, which was good. What he and Eduardo had in mind was best left unmentioned.

"Well," he said slyly as he broke open a new deck of cards. "Are you chickens ready to be plucked?"

By the time Mariana appeared in the door and signaled to him, Guzmán had lost most of his stake to Cambio.

In the hall she said, "Señor Ponce's on the line. He's very upset. Something about his wife. I told him I'd see if you were in."

He checked his watch. He did not like it that Eduardo was calling at midnight. What's more, he was getting irritated with his constant litany about Beatriz. It was because he had expected such impositions would come more frequently as time passed that he had invented the story about Hugo's absence to give himself some breathing room. Even if it were serious, taking the call would set a bad precedent.

"Say I'm in bed."

Then he returned to the card table. An hour later, he recouped his losses.

FIFTEEN

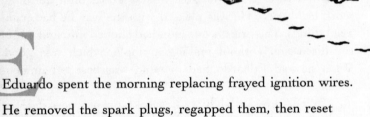

Eduardo spent the morning replacing frayed ignition wires. He removed the spark plugs, regapped them, then reset the timing.

Until the end of the war he had rarely looked under the hood of a vehicle. The life of near-poverty he'd lived since then had forced him to become adept at maintaining and repairing his truck and especially his boat, whose ancient engine was always failing, often when he and the boys were miles from shore. Because it was specific and logical, the work had a calming effect. This morning he was even more attentive than usual. The engine had to sing on the way north.

The road was all he had been able to think of after leaving Dolores' house last night, that and the imagined sound of the boys' breathing. The intensity of emotion that overwhelmed him on the stairs had almost frightened him. On the way back to the Hotel Bolívar he tried to be reasonable about what had happened, telling himself that they would be together soon, but as the bus lumbered through the night he began to fear something might go wrong, as if the darkened house had been an omen. And then, after he had failed to get through to the general, he had gone upstairs and found Beatriz weeping, saying over and over that it was too late, it would never happen. He had gone to sleep listening to her crying and awakened to it, her anguish so great it had driven him outside.

He started the engine. It sounded better than it had in years. He revved it and realized he did not want to turn it off. He wanted to leave it running while he packed the boxes and then drove away from the hotel, hustling the boys out of the old woman's house while she looked on dumbfounded and helpless. He thought of how wonderful it would feel, how the anxiety of what seemed like endless waiting would float off behind like exhaust.

Determined to force some kind of concession from Guzmán, he slammed the hood, quickly cleaned his hands with a kerosene-soaked rag, and strode across the street to the bar. The owner languidly polished a glass while he deposited his coins and dialed. The moment he heard Guzmán's voice he turned away from the prying eyes.

He made no effort to disguise his anger when he explained that he had called last night, that he had urgent things to discuss.

"Mariana told me this morning," Guzmán said. "It's too bad you tried so late."

"She was crying when I got back, hysterical. She started again as soon as she was awake."

He wanted to drop the ruse that this had anything to do with Beatriz. He wanted to tell Guzmán what had happened when he mounted the stairs, how longing for his sons had seized him.

"Tell her I've been looking into things. Tell her to be patient."

Was it possible she might be right? If she weren't, then why this delay?

"That's not enough," Eduardo said slowly, emphatically, "for either of us. I want to see you and go over the maps. She has to have some sense of progress."

There was silence on the line. Finally Guzmán said, "All right. I think I can make some time for you this afternoon."

Beatriz gave him an indifferent look when he came in. She had stopped crying but her eyes were fiery red, the lids still swollen. The moment he told her about the invitation she shook her head. "He's playing with you, with all of us."

He was aware of a tiny pang, the memory of his own suspicion. Her feelings ran so deep they were beginning to seduce him. He had to be very careful.

"I know some things," she added with a strange smile. "I listen. I hear."

The odd singsong of her voice swept away his suspicion.

"You don't know shit. Get dressed. We're leaving in twenty minutes."

While she was in the common bathroom down the hall, Eduardo removed from the strongbox the few pieces of jewelry they had not pawned.

He had assembled his maps by the time she returned. Her hair was done up in a bun but already wisps has slipped out of the barrette. She used to be fastidious. Now she always looked as if she had just gotten out of bed.

He held a black zippered bag with the jewelry.

"You know how important this is," he said as he slipped

on his jacket. "I want you to get hold of yourself. And put this in your purse," he added, handing her the bag.

"What's in it?"

"What do you think? The rest of your jewelry. We'll have to discuss money, and I want something to offer him."

At the door the housekeeper looked them up and down, her disapproving gaze clearly suggesting they were not the kind of people she was used to ushering into the general's house.

In response to her condescension Eduardo drew himself up and glared.

"Ponce," he said crisply. "Guzmán's expecting us."

She was offended that he used Guzmán's name rather than his title.

"Come," she said brusquely. "I'll see if the general is in."

"I told you he's expecting us."

She left without answering. A minute later she returned, chastened.

"His study is the last door on the left."

"I know," Eduardo told her icily. "I've been here before."

"He knows how to live," he mused, pointing to the hunting prints on the walls, the brass light fixtures. "He always has."

Guzmán stood in front of the cage, talking softly to the birds. He turned unhurriedly, keeping his eyes on Beatriz slightly longer than seemed necessary.

"It's good to see you," he told them warmly. "Would you like anything? A drink? Coffee? Tea?"

"We're fine," Eduardo said. He felt as if he were walking on eggshells and wanted to be as accommodating as possible.

"Well, if you change your mind," Guzmán said as he gestured toward the chairs.

Eduardo already felt better. It had been stupid thinking Guzmán would be irritated by the visit. The old affection was undiluted in his eyes. He almost looked avuncular.

"I knew you'd understand," Eduardo said. "The strain . . ."

"Of course," Guzmán said dismissively. "It's been hard on me, too."

Eduardo glanced at Beatriz, thinking she would be relieved. She gazed at the birds and gave no indication she had heard Guzmán. He watched her go over to the cage.

"They're beautiful," she said softly.

"They've always been a comfort to me."

"Do they have names?"

"Of course. That's Maya on the top perch. She's ruled the roost since I bought her."

"She came home to roost?"

Guzmán seemed not to understand her meaning.

"Like chickens are supposed to do," she explained, "when something's happened? I always wondered where that idea came from. I like things with names. It's so hard when they don't have them."

Guzmán's eyes narrowed. He seemed to be waiting for her to go on, to clarify what she had said.

Eduardo had no idea what she was talking about. Her speech verged on nonsense and to distract the general he spread the maps out on the desk. "Everything's here," he said. "I've been very careful."

Guzmán showed no interest in the maps.

"In a little while. Give me a sense of the house and neighborhood."

As Eduardo described the street, he had a vivid image of Tomás. Perhaps if he were to tell the general about the desire that had come upon him, the way he had kissed the door to leave a sign of his presence, the urgency would seem more real. But of course that was impossible. Guzmán would laugh.

"They're always alone. I've been there a dozen times, at least, and she has no visitors."

"That's true," said Beatriz. "He's been very busy. He went out every night and during the day, too. Did he ever tell you he dreamed about old women coming to take my sons? Every time he'd wake up shouting, sweating. It happened the first night you were in Mar Vista."

"Beatriz," Eduardo said as calmly as he could, "we need to focus on what's happening now."

"I am. Isn't it like your dream? The old woman came and took them away and there was nothing we could do, nothing anyone could do. The judge said it was right. He said, 'I award custody to Señora Masson.' "

"This isn't a dream. We're doing something now."

"That's right. It's not a dream. Tell him what you saw in the dark of night. Shine your light on it."

"Her house is the second from the corner on a side street connecting to a main road. The door's flimsy, tongue and groove lock. A man wouldn't have any trouble breaking it down. The boys' rooms are the first two on the left," he added as he handed Guzmán a sheet of paper. "I've marked them on the diagram. It will take less than a minute to get them outside and into a car. Twenty seconds, more or less, to the stoplight. We'll be waiting a few miles away, there, the place I've circled. These green lines are two alternate routes through the city. I've driven them at day and at night."

Guzmán listened attentively, nodding from time to time.

It was not a bad plan, he said when Eduardo finished. He especially liked the alternate routes.

"What do you think?" he asked Beatriz.

"It's fine. Anything you want to do is fine. I don't know about these kinds of things."

Her response was a little off-centered, but nothing like whatever she'd been talking about earlier. Now she seemed almost normal.

"Leave this here," said Guzmán. "There are some things I want to mull over." He rocked back in his chair and looked at Eduardo.

"I assume the truck's registered in your name."

"Yes."

"You can't keep it."

"But I just tuned it up."

"I'm not talking about how it runs. You can use it the first night, probably the second day. By then she'll have contacted the police. They'll have a description."

"You think she'll remember what it looks like?"

"She doesn't have to. The make and model are on file. The police will run a check. Rosario's a good place to buy a car but don't trade in the truck. If you do, they could trace your car. Leave it on the street. It's necessary, *amigo,* part of what has to be done."

Eduardo had never thought the truck would be a beacon. But buying a car! His savings would be devastated. If he had realized that, he would not have let the jewelry go for so little.

"You'll need to set up living when you get there. How much do you have?"

Guzmán shook his head when Eduardo mentioned the total.

"After a car you won't have much left. My friends and I can come up with enough for you to get by on for a while."

Eduardo felt his face turning red. The work he had done on the maps, his nightly forays, had given him a sense of agency. But he was still dependent on Guzmán.

"I'll make good on everything you lend us, *everything.*" Turning to Beatriz he said, "Give it to me."

He quickly unzipped the bag and spilled the pieces onto the desk.

"Take these as partial payment. It's not much but better than nothing."

"It's not necessary."

"It is. You don't know how this makes me feel."

"He feels bad," said Beatriz.

Guzmán searched her eyes, then swept the pieces toward himself with a cupped hand.

She watched him pick up the pearl necklace.

"It belonged to my mother. She only wore it on holidays."

She pointed to the gold broach.

"My aunt gave it to me when I was confirmed. And these," she said as she picked up the silver bracelets, "these were from my husband on our first wedding anniversary. Eduardo's not sentimental, but men aren't, are they? Nothing belongs to us anymore. We don't belong to anything either."

"Stop it," Eduardo said.

Guzmán regarded her awhile before he looked questioningly at Eduardo. "Listen, if they're so personal . . ."

"She's just upset," Eduardo replied as he glanced at her. "She wants you to have them, don't you?"

Beatriz did not seem to be listening. For the last few days her attention had drifted away like this. An intense outpouring would be followed by abstraction.

"We've talked it over several times," he told the general. He looked at Beatriz. "Haven't we?"

She frowned. "Yes. That's what I want. That's what I told Eduardo I wanted. But it's not all mine," she added as she pointed to the earring. "That isn't. It was never mine. It fell out of the earth but it's valuable. You can't believe what it's cost."

"Don't you think that's enough?" Eduardo said.

She looked at Guzmán. "Eduardo keeps his word. He keeps the faith. You have no idea how much he believes in you." She paused and contemplated the birds. "And so do I. You're a man of honor. You have my faith. I want my sons."

"Very soon. Arrangements have to be made."

Eduardo watched her lean forward. Her brow was furrowed, as if she were concentrating on a complex thought.

"But you've been paid. We paid you with all these things."

Eduardo and Guzmán exchanged a glance. He felt like cringing as he looked into the general's eyes but there was no need. Guzmán understood. He nodded slightly, and Eduardo was certain he meant for him to humor her.

"Remember, he's very busy. And his daughter's due any time."

She stared blankly at him.

"What does that have to do with Tomás and Manfredo?"

"Nothing," Guzmán said patiently. "It has nothing to do with them." He looked at Eduardo as if to say he would take care of this. "But I need to go over everything with the men I've hired to help us. I want them to make a dry run to get a sense of the place. This isn't the kind of thing you hurry. You want everything to go right, don't you?"

Eduardo felt boundless gratitude.

"Beatriz?"

She looked at him for what seemed a long time. When she shifted her gaze to Guzmán, Eduardo saw that the general was reaching the end of his patience.

Taking her arm, he forced her to stand.

"I'm sorry we took so long," he said. "I know you're busy."

"Call in a day or two. I should know something by then."

Eduardo's hand shook as he put the key in the ignition switch. He could not look at Beatriz as he backed down the long driveway. He thought the emotion burning in his gut was from anger but that was not it. Fear. Listening to her, he had learned something he had no desire to know. She was getting worse. She had been sliding away from him and the pace had increased at Guzmán's house. Giving vent to his feelings would be useless; she was beyond the effect of his words or Guzmán's or those of anyone else.

Their hotel was far across the city. She was happy about this. She never felt brave enough to leave it by herself, fearing her legs might give out, fearing that she might get lost and never see the boys again.

But this was different.

She felt safe in the truck. She loved the sense of movement. She looked greedily at the roads, the people streaming by on sidewalks, in cars. She loved the street signs, the traffic signals, the kiosks with their headlines going by too fast to read.

The truck smelled of oil but to her it was a chariot. Eduardo promised it would take them north. It would. She made herself believe it, forced the little hot fear thing away from her thoughts. Believed. Because when Guzmán put the jewelry in his desk and closed the drawer she had heard the sound. Anyone else would think it was only wood against wood. But it wasn't. It was really like dirt against wood, dirt being shoveled onto a coffin. The time the priest said ashes to ashes, dust to dust. The earring was going back to where it came from, out of her life, just as if it were covered with six feet of sweet-smelling earth. All those years buried in a moment, like the beginning of something.

SIXTEEN

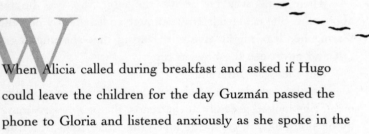

When Alicia called during breakfast and asked if Hugo could leave the children for the day Guzmán passed the phone to Gloria and listened anxiously as she spoke in the intimate tone she always used to discuss her daughter's pregnancies.

After hanging up, she reassured him that nothing out of the ordinary was happening. Alicia just needed to stay in bed.

"You're sure?"

"This is the way it is with her. Do you want the anatomical details?"

Her willingness to talk about her daughter's reproductive system always made him feel uncomfortable. He preferred the mysteries of the female body unexplained.

"No," he said. "I trust you."

As soon as Hugo dropped them off, Juanito and Catalina insisted on playing a new video game in the den. Guzmán was glad they found something to occupy them; he wanted to think about Eduardo's plan before discussing it with Sánchez-Macias and Berletti.

He had just settled down when the children came into the study and pleaded for swimming lessons.

"What about your video?"

It was over, Juanito told him. They didn't want to watch it again.

"There's work I should do."

"Please, Grandpa. I've been practicing what you taught me last time."

Guzmán looked at them and slowly shook his head.

"I've spoiled you. You'll never be good for anything."

"We'll put on our suits," beamed Juanito.

Catalina was still afraid to keep her face in the water when she swam freestyle. Guzmán worked with her for half an hour, swimming alongside and putting his hand gently on her head whenever she tried to hold it up.

He helped Juanito with his kick. The boy took instruction well and was getting the knack of it, learning how to ease the tension in his ankles. Unlike his sister, he had a natural grace in the water that could make him an athlete.

While Gloria gave them lunch Guzmán paused at the foot of the diving board, hands flat at his sides as he imagined the form his body should take. He strode forward and felt the board flex as it sent him into the air. He spread his arms at the top of the arc and for one brief moment it was as if he were flying, as if his arms were wings. Then he brought them together just before knifing into the water.

His entry was smooth, close to perfect. He swam underwater to the end of the pool, concentrating on the way his body moved, the feel of the water, but as soon as he executed a racing turn and the momentum from the push-off carried him forward, he lost the purity of sensation. He really needed to finish this business with Ponce. While he swam his laps he concentrated on the plan. Both routes were good, but the alternate seemed better, even though it would add half an hour to their drive out of the city.

As soon as he finished his workout and cleaned up, he called Sánchez-Macias and told him to bring Berletti over at four that afternoon. He would pay them half of the fee they had agreed on. Then he wanted them to drive both routes while it was still light. Sánchez-Macias could call him later and tell him what he thought.

The children appeared just as he hung up. Looking at them with mock seriousness, he said, "Don't you think it's time for a nap?"

"We're not sleepy yet," Catalina said. In a hopeful voice she added, "Do a trick with Maya first."

"Is that a bribe?"

"Yes," she answered defiantly.

"Which trick?"

"Something new," Juanito insisted.

He deadpanned, "I don't think she has any new ones."

"Please, Grandpa," said Catalina. "Don't tease."

He was always struck by her uncanny resemblance to Alicia. She would be a beautiful woman. On his way to the cage he wondered how the new baby would look. He decided to call Alicia later and see how she was doing.

He peered into the cage.

"Well, Maya? Do you have anything up your sleeve?"

The bird chirped and leapt to the highest perch.

"I don't think so," Guzmán said doubtfully.

"Yes, yes, yes," shouted Catalina. "She does!"

"What makes you think so?"

"You! I can always tell from the way you talk."

"And how is that?"

"I don't know, like you're keeping a secret."

"Is that right?"

"Yes," she said impatiently. "You know it."

"Well," he said, stroking his mustache. "I suppose there might be something in my desk."

"What?"

"I'm not sure. Let's take a look."

She watched him remove the earring from a small cardboard box. He winked at Catalina and then went over to the door where he reached up and placed it on the tip of the sword's scabbard.

"What are you doing?" asked Juanito.

"Wait and see."

The children cackled when he gave Maya a seed between his teeth.

"Doesn't count," Catalina said. "We've seen it."

"Maybe that's all she can do."

"Grandpa!"

He launched Maya with a flick of his wrist. She flew once around the room before landing on the sword.

"That's not a trick," Juanito complained. "No fair."

"Don't be so impatient," Guzmán said.

Maya looked at them for a moment, then edged her way to the earring and took it in her beak.

"Watch," said Guzmán. In response to his whistle, she flew down to the desk and dropped the earring in his upturned hand.

Catalina clapped. "Do it again!"

"Remember what you said?"

Crestfallen, she looked at him. "Yes."

"Would this make you feel better?" he asked, holding up the earring.

In a knowing voice, she said, "It's for pierced ears, Grandpa. Besides, there's only one."

"I know what," said Juanito. "Give it to Maya. Put it on her."

"What a good idea."

He unhooked the clasp and slipped the earring around the bird's left leg.

"Like a dancing girl," Catalina said.

"That's right. Just like a dancing girl."

Maya pecked at the earring.

"No," said Juanito. "She looks like a queen."

"The queen of dancers," Guzmán laughed. "Now. Nap time."

"Are you going to put Maya away?" asked Juanito.

"No. She likes to wander around while I work."

"I'm not very sleepy," Juanito said.

"I mean business this time."

"Come on," Catalina said. "You're making Grandpa mad."

As she took her brother's hand and led him to the door, Guzmán had to smile. Juanito was naturally inclined to push everything to the limit.

With the back of his hand he gently pushed Maya off the map. The notations were neat, almost calligraphic. Every line indicating the routes had been drawn with a straight-edge. Eduardo had even gone so far as to add contour lines where there were none on the printed page.

Given the fact that Beatriz seemed to be coming more unglued every day, Eduardo had done a remarkably thorough job. At the same time, whatever afflicted her had taken its toll on him. Eduardo was clearly reaching the end of his tether. He had tried to disguise his reaction to her odd comments but the effects were obvious in his eyes, in the tension of his voice. Guzmán's affection for Eduardo increased as he considered what he himself might have done in a similar situation. He could not approach Eduardo's patience.

The primary route out of Argentina was marked by a

thick red line snaking north. Beside each town where
Eduardo planned to stop for the night were the names of
hotels or inns along with phone numbers. There were notations with the exact distances between towns, others of the
number of miles he intended to travel each day.

Several of the calculations seemed overly optimistic and
he checked them against his atlas, erasing some of Eduardo's
notes and replacing them with more accurate ones. It was the
kind of work he liked—precise, logical, unambiguous. The
process of fine-tuning Eduardo's escape stimulated and excited him. In its own way it had the elements of a small
campaign.

He was still making notes when Mariana came in followed by Sánchez-Macias and Berletti.

SEVENTEEN

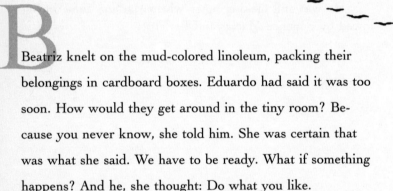

Beatriz knelt on the mud-colored linoleum, packing their belongings in cardboard boxes. Eduardo had said it was too soon. How would they get around in the tiny room? Because you never know, she told him. She was certain that was what she said. We have to be ready. What if something happens? And he, she thought: Do what you like.

She had hated the color of the floor a long time before it didn't matter anymore. The room, too. The yellow strip of dead flies. Now she hated only the old woman. Dolores. Dolor. The sound of funeral bells.

Everything had changed at once. The day of the hearing, was that it? The humiliation more than the pain, the justness of what Eduardo did to her. Like a high wind blowing away smoke. It must have been then. It was getting harder to remember what she wanted to remember, harder to forget what she wanted to forget.

She wanted to pack everything perfectly. She wanted to leave the room spotless, not like she found it.

An image drifted into her mind of her house in Mar Vista, always perfect, immaculate, not one watermark on a single glass, the surfaces of tables clean enough to eat off, the windows framing the sea transparent, as if there were only air and no glass.

She remembered what she had just seen in the dresser drawers, in the hollow spaces between the stacks of clothes she had removed and safely put away in the boxes. She looked toward the dresser. Beside it, the window blinds were lowered halfway against the sun, like the drooping eyelids of old women.

She was almost certain Eduardo was watching her, wondering if she would do this right. The radio was playing low in the background, a song that had once meant something to them. Did he remember? They had danced to it somewhere, sometime. Surely he must be thinking that, too.

Without looking over her shoulder, afraid of breaking the sweet spell that had descended, she said, "There are things in the drawers. You'll feel better after I've cleaned them."

But there was nothing in the top drawer, nor the second, nor the third. Only green oilcloth with yellow flowers.

He must have done it for her while she was busy with the clothes. She felt a rush of warmth in her heart at his thoughtfulness. "Thank you," she said as she turned around.

He was not in his chair. She was alone in the room full of boxes, the boxes full of clothes, knickknacks, keepsakes, and mementos she had brought from Mar Vista. Only her, the boxes, the radio now playing a song she had never heard. A roomful of emptiness and her and time that led nowhere, ticking in no direction except one more day and one more day and one more day.

When he came back she felt better, like herself again. He brought her food, a cardboard container.

He was drinking again and she was glad. He had endured more than any man should have to. He deserved happiness. Later, playing the aggressor, she gave him more with her body.

Afterward, waiting for sleep, she felt empty. Eduardo murmured something too slurred to understand. In her dream his fist floated toward her like a translucent bubble. There were scenes inside it, like the snowman in a glass ball.

She was standing in front of a glass door. Tomás and Manfredo were on the other side talking frantically, their faces contorted. They looked around as if they did not know where they were. Tomás saw her, touched his brother's arm. He said something she could not hear. A question, though. Clearly a question.

She told him it was her fault. She had brought it on them. Their father never knew what she had done.

They were listening. They seemed to hear.

She said she had put them there because of the young woman who stood beside them, a pretty girl, like her mother, who floated into the scene.

She had done it because of the mother, too, because she knew how the woman felt. They were mothers together, a special feeling, unlike any other in the world. She had not known what would happen. She had not thought about what would happen. All she had wanted was to ease this woman's pain.

The mother stared, offered no thanks with her eyes, only accusation.

She told her she had nothing to do with it. She didn't

know her daughter was in the ground until the boys found the earring.

Still without a word the mother stared. In a while, she nodded, and the gesture was eloquent. You were part of it, that was what it said. Your sons made you part of it.

She felt her pulse racing in the soft tissue on the inside of her arm. The moment she raised her voice in protest the glass became opaque, its surface hard and grainy, stonelike. She shouted the boys' names and the echoes were like fire searing her ears and the pain made her shout all the louder.

The dream stayed in her mind when she woke, every moment of it from start to finish, all its lusters and textures. Its words formed a circle from which she had to escape.

"What's the matter?" asked Eduardo.

It had to stay inside. She could not give him any of it. The smallest word, the least detail of anything she had seen would anger him, reopen the wound she had made in his life, her sons' lives, start the torture for him all over again.

Light would take the place of words. A roomful of sun.

She went from window to window, opening each after she had raised the blinds with the hope the dream would leave the room.

Eduardo struggled up on one elbow, squinting against the glare. He complained about the light, yawned, stretched, rubbed his eyes. Then he saw she was naked. She was standing there naked, dropping a fly out the window!

"Beatriz!"

She heard the surprise in his voice, the disbelief and censure. She was amazed by how clearly it came to her, how easy it was to distinguish the complexity of meanings in her name. The way animals heard, she thought. Cats and dogs. But better. Her understanding was boundless. That was something she could tell him. She would, soon, when she

knew whether the rush of air against the fly's falling body
had revived it, given it life, given her a reason to greet the
day more happily.

"For Christ's sake!"

She heard the springs creak, the sound of bare feet on
the linoleum as she leaned out to see what had happened.

The fly had vanished. She raised her eyes to the sky and
was scanning the horizon when she felt his hand on her
shoulder. She turned and looked into his sleep-reddened
eyes, following them as he glanced down at the street where
two men were looking at her.

"You look like a whore," he said as he pulled away from
the window.

"I had to try."

He would not ask what she meant. If he did, there
would only be gibberish. So he stared, trying to see something in her eyes that would tell him what he wanted to be
true, that once they had the boys she would get better. The
roads he had followed on his maps, the roads he had traced
with thick red lines suddenly seemed girded around by bars.

"It's only a matter of days. Can you understand that?"
He shook her by the shoulders. "Do you hear me?" There
was no resistance in bone or muscle. He could have been
shaking a rag doll.

When he understood that, he gave up. He was tired. He
felt older than his years. He had made mistakes in dealing
with her, done things he was sorry for. He had tried to fight
whatever was happening to her, done everything he could
think of that might bring her back and none of it was more
effectual than this shaking.

The problem was a matter of belief. He could not give it
back to her and neither could Guzmán. She needed proof.

Gently but firmly he led her to the closet. He removed a
robe and held it for her, handed her the ties. He led her to

the chair where she sat without a word while he prepared tea and bread.

When they finished eating, he said, "Would you like the radio on?"

"Yes. The radio would be nice."

He turned it on.

When he was dressed, he patted her on the shoulder and left, locking the door from the outside.

EIGHTEEN

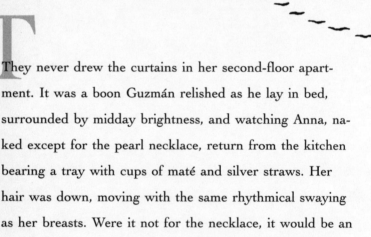

They never drew the curtains in her second-floor apartment. It was a boon Guzmán relished as he lay in bed, surrounded by midday brightness, and watching Anna, naked except for the pearl necklace, return from the kitchen bearing a tray with cups of maté and silver straws. Her hair was down, moving with the same rhythmical swaying as her breasts. Were it not for the necklace, it would be an ordinary scene, one even now being repeated in dozens of rooms in the city. But the pearls with their soft luster set her apart, added a certain theatricality. The image was familiar and a moment later he discovered the source; a blue film he had seen years ago.

He sat up and took the cup she handed to him.

"You remind me of someone."

"Who?"

"You won't have a fit?"

Half in earnest she said, "Are you sleeping with someone else?"

He smiled and shook his head. "Only you."

"And Gloria. We can't forget Gloria."

"A woman in an Italian movie I saw a long time ago.
She was carrying a tray of drinks and all she had on was a
hat."

"A whore?"

"It wasn't that kind of movie."

"But she was naked."

"As a jaybird."

"Who did you see it with, Gloria?"

"Some officers."

Anna laughed. "Horny soldiers playing with themselves.
Horny old goats."

"That's what you think I am?"

"When I'm mad."

She put the tray down and got into bed, carefully bal-
ancing her cup and saucer.

"But you aren't now."

"That was three weeks ago. I'm just preparing for the
next time you treat me like shit."

"I'm not leaving for an hour."

The necklace caught highlights from the windows. He
leaned over and carefully ran the backs of his fingers over
the pearls.

"They bring out the color in your eyes."

She cradled the strand in both hands, holding it away
from her breasts to see it better. "Where did you find them?"

"There's supposed to be an aura of mystery about
presents."

"They aren't new. I can tell from the old-fashioned
clasp."

"An heirloom," he said gravely. "They belonged to the queen of something or other."

Anna put down her cup and leaned against him.

"What do you give Gloria?"

He moved away a little so he could see her.

"Is this jealousy?"

"I'm just curious."

"Watches."

"Watches?" she asked incredulously.

"Some women are addicted to jewelry. Others to watches. She says the right one's essential."

Anna laughed mischievously.

"I'm not surprised. At her age she probably wants to keep track of the time she has left."

"I think you just insulted my wife."

"I'm entitled, don't you think?"

"I suppose."

"What's the last present you gave?"

"This," he said, fingering the pearls.

"Before today."

"An earring."

"You mean one?"

"Yes."

"She only has one ear? That must be attractive. What happened, did you bite off the other?"

"I didn't give it to her."

"Oh? You have a one-eared girlfriend?"

"I gave it to Maya."

"Birds don't have ears."

"She wears it on her leg. Ponce gave it to me as down payment on a loan and I taught her to fetch it from a sword on the wall in my study. I had her do it the other day for the kids and Juanito thought we should put it on her. I think she's proud of it. It sets her off from the other birds."

"I'd like the story better if Gloria had only one ear."

"Why are you after her today?"

"You've been talking a lot about her and Alicia, in case you didn't know. How do you think that makes me feel?"

"You should be grateful she's devoted to Alicia. It's given us extra time."

The afternoon that had begun so passionately was fraying at the edges. He heard it in her voice, the faint but unmistakable sound of resentment. After all these years she should accept things as they were but recently she had become more demanding.

"I spend every minute I can with you."

"You're always doing something."

"I'm not dead, Anna."

Apparently, she had expected another response. After a pause she went on.

"What about Ponce?" she said accusingly. "What about him?"

"You know the situation."

"Have you worked things out with Sánchez-Macias and Berletti?"

"Almost. There were some kinks in Eduardo's plan but I've fixed them. He's been pressing me, calling every day. Something's wrong with his wife. When they came over she was acting crazy."

"What?"

"I don't know. Eduardo says it's just because she misses the boys but I think there's more he isn't telling me."

"That's not why you're dragging your feet."

The comment surprised him as much for its conviction as its unexpectedness.

"You think that's what I'm doing?"

Anna made a dismissive gesture as if to say he knew better than to ask.

There were times when she seemed to understand him better than he realized, cutting straight to the heart of some matter in exactly this way. He was never sure whether he liked it or felt exposed.

He regarded her, intending to gauge the depth of her knowledge and whether it was possible to change the subject.

"Are you going to tell me why?" she asked.

"What difference does it make?"

"Because it distracts you. You've been distracted ever since this started."

She was serious, determined that he understand.

"And because it's gotten between us, in case you haven't noticed."

"If I say I want to get all the details right, make sure nothing goes wrong?"

"I'd say you were lying."

"That snatching the boys could mean trouble, that it's dangerous?"

"Another lie."

"What makes you so sure?"

"You're the most careful man I know. You move through life like a cat."

He laughed. The idea appealed to him.

"Like a cat?"

"You're trying to slip out of sight right now."

This was the Anna he loved, the ironic Anna who did not whine about things that were impossible to change.

"All right. I plan to enjoy every step, every moment. Does that sound like the truth?"

"Closer to it."

"This isn't perfect but it's all I have. There's a score to settle."

"Against who? The grandmother?"

"That's right."

"She never did anything to you."

"Against what she represents. Against disgrace, what

happened to me, to my friends. You know how I suffered during the trial, in prison."

"You have a long memory, Rodolfo."

"That's right, I do. Longer than my dick."

Now he was eager for the discussion he had wanted to avoid. As if a door had swung wide and the stories with all their attendant images and sounds and smells had tumbled out. The old woman's was only one, among the smallest, insignificant in itself but as a sign of what had destroyed his career powerful, epic. The mothers beating their breasts, carrying signs in the plaza below his office in a distorted version of a religious procession.

"The word 'fester.' What does it mean to you?"

She frowned. "Illness. Infection."

"Exactly. And it doesn't have to be from a physical wound. It can be inside," he said, tapping his forehead, his chest, "an open wound inside your mind, your heart. I was humiliated. I lost my honor, my reputation. If I'd been Japanese, I'd have fallen on my sword. Somehow I didn't exactly like the idea of my guts spilling on the floor. Every year things get worse. The army's insulted in the papers, the rights people bitch and moan. Scilingo gets this crazy idea he has to talk and the government tries to cover its ass. We were honorable men and the country pisses on us."

He paused, tried to calm himself. Every time he rehearsed the litany his heart thudded in his chest.

"You take revenge where you can. There aren't many chances, and when one comes along you better savor it. Beatriz might be a little nuts but Ponce's a good man. He sacrificed to have those boys, suffered. He's lived in poverty because of them. I help myself by helping him."

His outburst finished, he looked at her to make sure she understood. Suddenly, he felt very tired.

"I hope you get what you want."

"I will. I am."

"Be careful. Revenge is complicated. There always seems to be a loose end."

"If you don't pay attention. There's an old Italian proverb, 'Revenge is a dish best served cold.' Mine's been on the table a long long time."

Driving home, he was visited by a deeply appealing if implausible idea. He wondered why he had not thought of it before, when there would have been time to consider the problems that prevented him from getting rid of Sánchez-Macias and Berletti and doing the job himself. Half a dozen reasons marshaled themselves, all impossible to dismiss. But the charm of the notion held his attention and a solution occurred as he turned into his street. He could make some revisions in the plan so that he would be more involved. The effect would still be vicarious but closer to the bone.

He was considering where he might begin when he saw their other car barreling toward him.

Gloria slammed on the brakes and rolled down her window.

"Alicia went into labor. Hugo's taken her to the hospital."

"Park," he said.

She quickly got into the Mercedes.

"When?"

"Twenty minutes ago."

"Is she okay?"

"I think so."

"What is that supposed to mean?"

"There was some bleeding but she's done that before."

NINETEEN

Dolores was in the living room studying her atlas. It had an image of the globe crosshatched with lines of latitude and longitude on the cover, abstract grids that made it possible for seafarers, footsore travelers, wanderers of every sort to know their location anywhere on the face of the earth. She was not sure what she was looking for, only that she was certain she would know when she found it.

She had started an hour ago at the front of the heavy green book, diligently working her way through the alphabetized countries, skipping Argentina but no other, moving from Afghanistan to Austria, Belgium, Botswana, Colombia, Denmark, and now France, a preliminary survey, the first tentative action in response to an idea that had been nagging at her since the hearing. She was all but certain it was futile, childish, that she ought to leave well enough alone and be satisfied with what she had, yet whenever hopelessness threatened she would look at Rubén's portrait and his eyes seemed to lock on to hers and the idea flared again in the light of his eyes, the question changing from why? to why not? and she would tell herself *you have nothing to lose but time.*

So here she was, half an inch into the thickness of the world, staring at France, meditating on the shape of the country, noting its ports of entry, pronouncing, sometimes silently, sometimes aloud, the names of cities and towns and villages in the hope that sound might become a clue, that one syllable might open intuition.

She thought of old maps of the world with clouds like faces, heraldic devices floating over the sea proclaiming, Dragons Be Here.

She thought of sailors in wooden ships with little more to rely on than hope that land was somewhere and willing to take the risk of finding it.

She thought of herself as an old woman in the creaky boat of age, already out of sight of land in search of the light in the eyes of her long-gone son.

TWENTY

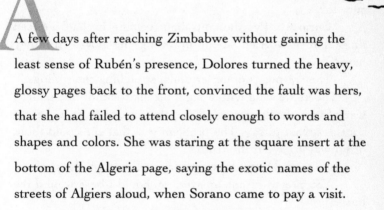

A few days after reaching Zimbabwe without gaining the least sense of Rubén's presence, Dolores turned the heavy, glossy pages back to the front, convinced the fault was hers, that she had failed to attend closely enough to words and shapes and colors. She was staring at the square insert at the bottom of the Algeria page, saying the exotic names of the streets of Algiers aloud, when Sorano came to pay a visit.

"I happened to be in the neighborhood," he said as she opened the door.

"Hunting criminals, no doubt."

He shrugged and smiled.

"Actually, I had to go out of my way."

"You can take time off just like that, in the middle of the week?"

"I'm a captain," he said, tapping the insignia on his jacket, "remember? So long as the work gets done nobody complains."

"They appreciate you, I hope."

He laughed. "Who's ever appreciated me as much as I deserve?"

"I have," she said seriously. "And you know it. Are you staying long enough for tea?"

"I was counting on it."

"Keep me company."

Sorano followed her into the kitchen. After putting a kettle on the stove she turned and looked at him.

"Well? Are you going to tell me what I owe this pleasure to?"

"Curiosity. I've thought about coming by half a dozen times but I worried about upsetting the boys. Are they here?"

"They're out running errands, stretching their wings."

The kettle sang with a high, birdlike sound. She poured water over the leaves, glad for the excuse it gave her to consider what to say. The problem was that she could think of no way to avoid the truth.

She waited until the water dripped through the strainer.

"You prefer a frank answer, or should I beat around the bush?"

"I think you've just given it to me."

"They don't talk about you, at least when I'm around."

"And when you aren't?"

"They know you were merely the agent, not the cause. As a matter of fact, it would be good for them to see you once in a while. They need to be around men."

She peered into the pot.

"I'm addicted to sugar."

"So am I."

Sorano carried the tray into the living room and put it on the table beside the open atlas.

"Algeria?"

"I'm studying geography, becoming reacquainted with the shape of the world."

"For a trip?"

"No." She pointed at his cup. "I make the best maté on the block. Everyone says so. Drink it while it's hot."

"How are you?" he asked. "Honestly."

"Better than you seem to think," she answered with a laugh. "As close to delirious happiness as I've ever been."

"Beyond the euphoria."

She looked at him sharply.

"I think we've had this conversation before."

"Yours is the third case I've been involved with."

"Did they spend as many years alone as I did?"

"No, but the strains are pretty much the same. People change over time. So do expectations and hopes. I worry about you."

"The people you're talking about, they wanted everything to be the same?"

"Exactly."

"That's where I have the advantage. I had enough time to learn it couldn't be. Whatever shape life takes is fine with me."

"I'm not sure that makes me feel better."

She smiled. There was a decency in Sorano, a pith of caring that always touched her.

"Of course there are strains. There probably always will be. But I'll tell you something. I'm grateful for everything, the good and the not so good and the downright ugly. The misunderstandings, the occasional anger and resentment remind me I'm alive. Remember what I told you about my archives? Roger and Joaquín are antidotes. Now I can walk into the blueness without being afraid it will destroy me, which was what was happening before we found them. If I get tired, and it happens, all I have to do is remember the alternative. Is that what you were worried about?"

"It crossed my mind."

"I'm being patronized. 'The old woman on her last legs.' "

"I didn't intend it as an insult."

She waved her hand as if to dismiss the idea.

"People don't know anything about being old until they get there. I suppose I would've thought the same when I was your age. Here she is seventy, arthritic, wearing out, two teenagers on her hands. There's nothing to worry about. I have a great deal of energy. The strength I needed to look for them has stayed with me. All my mechanisms are still intact. And living with young people peels away the years. It's like a face-lift for the soul."

Sorano finished his tea and put the cup on the table.

"Which tells me you've settled in together. I was wondering about that, too, how long it would take. I'm glad it happened so soon."

"It hasn't completely. There are still times I wake up not quite believing they're just down the hall. I remember the last thing we said to each other before going to bed but for a moment everything seems fluid and I remind myself that reality is malleable, capable of changing shape and direction in the blink of an eye. It doesn't last long. I feel on solid ground again and start thinking about luck. I have a dear old friend, Chloe, an astrologer, who keeps hounding me to let her do my horoscope. I tell her the only sign that means anything to me is the wheel of fortune."

She looked past Sorano to the street, aware that she had failed to convey the power of her conviction. There was no equivalent in language for the sense of jeopardy she was trying to describe. It seemed to exist as pure phenomenon, hidden beneath a thin veneer of normalcy. When she concentrated, tiny distortions became evident in the shapes of houses, cars, people, a certain tilt and blurring came upon them, the signatures of the sensation.

"I'm not intentionally being cryptic," she said apologetically. "It's just that I don't take my luck lightly."

"It didn't occur to me that you were," he answered as he refilled their cups. "I think I understand, though, why you call it dreamlike. It's interesting that's what we fall back on so often to describe the peculiar. I do it all the time. But as far as this is concerned, I'm more inclined to see it as a play than a dream. There's still the third act."

"The trial."

"There's a kind of balance thinking about it that way that's opposed to your open-endedness. And not to insult you, it seems more realistic. There's a finality to them going to prison."

"I suppose."

"Are you going?"

"It would be too complicated. I couldn't tell the boys. When I considered what I'd have to do to manage it, deceive them, I didn't like the way that felt. Besides, it wouldn't work. The atmosphere in this house is charged. We vibrate like tuning forks at the slightest provocation. They're intuitive, Roger a little more than Joaquín, and they're learning to read me. I don't have the slightest doubt that the second I came in the door they'd know where I'd been."

"They wouldn't understand?"

"My desires aren't the issue. It's how we are together. We've progressed as far as we have because I've been honest with them. Finding out I'd sneaked off to the courthouse would be devastating. They'd know the only reason I'd gone was for revenge."

"There are some things we deserve," he said flatly.

"I've already had it, the second De León announced his

decision. And the fact is that I don't want to see them again. There was a look in Eduardo's eyes. I don't know how to describe it but it worried me. Did you notice?"

"Nothing out of the ordinary. The losers never accept what's happened. They believe in themselves more than ever and the denial fills them with a kind of generalized rage. He probably would have hit you, if you'd been handy. You weren't, so he settled for Beatriz. In any case, he can't do anything to you now. They're as good as in prison."

Whenever she tried imagining them behind bars she conjured nothing more than a vague grayness. She knew why. Prison was superfluous compared with the punishment they had already suffered. She had never wanted to credit them with the capacity for true love, not the kind she felt, but she had seen it in the courtroom, and afterward, outside. The loss of the boys was a life sentence.

"You're going?" she asked.

"I'm made of lesser stuff than you are. Vengeance has a place in my world."

"Call me when it's over. I think I'd like to know the day and time."

"You'll tell the boys?"

"Of course. But I don't want to. It will set back the work we've been doing."

"Which is?"

"Reconstruction. I've been trying to reconstruct their memories, help them understand that what they remember is only part of their personal history. It's very, very difficult. In their heads, they know they lived in a lie. In their hearts, the false history still feels true. They have to rewind the clock of themselves, reexperience every moment with the knowledge that neither they nor the Ponces were who they thought they were. Remember how the Soviets airbrushed pictures of people who had fallen from grace? We're putting the pictures back."

"That's what Freud's all about, restoring memory, re-writing the story."

"There's a difference, I think. He worked with individu-als, family catastrophes. What happened to us can't be un-derstood on such an intimate level. It's part of the monster that was born in 1976. Roger and Joaquín are its natural heirs. What I suffered embodies part of it, but an old woman can't carry the weight of all that meaning. They need to hear it from me *and* my friends, in many different voices. I ask everyone I know to tell their versions. I take them to the sites where so much happened so they can see how deceptive history is, how normal these places look that were used as prisons, killing fields. It's painful but necessary. Some are overgrown with weeds. Others are busy, thriving. I tell them that the only way to keep history alive is through memory and speech, that there's an implicit pardon in silence, that silence can be as evil as what it refuses to name."

"I'm thinking of all that resistance I've seen in them."

"That's changing. For the last few weeks they've come with me to the plaza on Thursdays. I didn't invite them. One day they asked why I still marched. I said because other children had not been found. Because the government still refuses to tell the truth. Because years ago my *com-pañeras* and I agreed that all our children and husbands and wives were one person. The next week Roger came into my room while I was putting on my scarf and asked if they could go."

"Wonderful."

"It was. But that's not the end of it. For three weeks they stood on the margin of the plaza, watching. That's where I left them last week. When I march, I think of my *compañeras*, my blue archives. I feel reabsorbed in our his-tory, pulled back in time, out of myself and into a deeper self all at once. But something happened when I came out of the shadows of the Casa Rosada."

She regarded him over the rim of her cup, wondering if he knew.

"And?"

"They were at the end of the line. They'd joined the march. They were crying and so was I, for the same reasons. They were walking with us but they were also walking away from the past. It was radiant. That's the only word that does justice to the moment."

"What did they say?"

"I didn't ask for an explanation. It cost them, enormously. It was their first real acknowledgment of who they are. They looked so new. They'd had the freedom to come and go since we arrived from Mar Vista but they never went further than a few blocks from the house."

"And now they have."

"Yes. It began with the acknowledgment inherent in that act, that they belonged in history. Until then, they'd been afraid to accept their place in it. Once they did, the city was no longer an antagonist."

"They were afraid of it?"

"Of what it represented. Life beyond the Ponces."

"So you've gotten where you want to be."

"I'm approaching it. You know what an uncertain business this is. There's no such thing as unimpeded progress."

"When you get there, what then?"

A strange question, she thought, big enough to encompass the rest of her life. Given the nature of their conversation, it was inevitable he would ask. If anyone else had she would have let it slide, but she could not do that with Sorano.

"There's something I want you to see."

She led him over to the wall of photographs. Rubén's frame was slightly askew. After straightening it, she wiped a smudge of dust from the glass with the tip of her finger.

"He was thirty-five when they arrested him. He's forty-

eight now, almost forty-nine. We were very close. When he
left with Félicité it felt like part of my body had been torn
off. My friends thought it was shocking. They said something had to be the matter with him to abandon me but they
didn't understand his feelings or the workings of his heart.
He had no choice. Marta's death and the boys' disappearance sucked all the air out of Argentina. I didn't protest
when he went. I gave him my blessing. I knew how it was
with him. He would have died if he tried to stay."

She took a step back.

"Can you see the likeness between him and the boys?"

"Yes."

"So do they. They've started asking questions."

She paused, looked at him frankly.

"The answer to 'what then?' is that I'm going to try to
find him. I've gotten greedy, Sorano. I intend to live a long
time to make up for the years I lost. I have my grandsons. I
want Rubén and Félicité, too."

After walking Sorano to his car she went back inside
and stood in front of the photograph. She recalled the terrible guilt that came when she took it down, how the lighter-
colored square on the wall was a daily reproach, a sign of
absence so eloquent and insistent she heard it in every corner
of the house.

She let her eyes move from Rubén to the boys beside
him. More than ever before she felt the pull of blood uniting
them, the three mouths so alike in shape seeming to say *the
same the same the same blood* undiluted by distance or time. She
knew exactly how Rubén would feel when he learned his
sons were living in this house, how, as he traveled from
wherever he had been, he would imagine the door opening,
imagine them waiting, how Félicité, on the cusp of wom-
anhood, would be behind him, straining to see her brothers.

When was unanswerable. Beginning was all she could think of, visual interrogation of the world.

She returned to the couch and poured the last of the tea into her cup. Opening the atlas at the bookmark, she looked at Algeria again, then went on, casting her mind wide, knowing that was how she might sense the place, catch the trace of blood.

TWENTY-ONE

No sooner had Guzmán answered the phone than Eduardo began a breathless, nearly frantic litany of real and imagined slights.

He had called and called and never found him home.

Was this how he treated old friends?

If so, he was sure as hell glad he wasn't the general's enemy.

Irritated as he was by Eduardo's tone, Guzmán listened half-sympathetically. The poor bastard had a point. He had been left high and dry.

When there was a pause, Guzmán asked if he felt better now that he had gotten things off his chest.

He did not. In fact, there were more things eating at him than he had time to mention, things he did not think the general wanted to hear from the mouth of an old friend who had always given his best no matter the cost.

Then he said he felt terrible, ignored, pronouncing the word succinctly, drawing out its syllables in what Guzmán knew was a conscious effort to shame him.

Beatriz had thought all along that something was wrong. He had not believed her, refused to listen. He had chewed her out for saying such things. But if Guzmán wanted the truth he was beginning to wonder, yes, more than a little. They were ready, he said emphatically. For days they had been ready and waiting. If he had taken matters into his own hands he would be in Mexico right now.

"Are you planning to let me speak?"

"Go on," Eduardo said, the challenge clear in his voice.

"It's all arranged. Yesterday I went over everything with Sánchez-Macias and Berletti. As a matter of fact, I've been waiting for your call."

Silence. He imagined Eduardo processing the news. Any moment now he would apologize.

"When?"

"Did it ever occur to you there might have been a reason I wasn't here?"

"No," Eduardo said impatiently. "What difference does it make? When?"

Guzmán gazed at his desk calendar. He had written "Marpessa" in the square for Wednesday. He liked the look of her name, the exotic, feminine shape of it. He let the pause drag on, intent on letting Eduardo suffer a little. "Wednesday," he said finally. "They'll deliver the boys at nine o'clock."

"They know exactly where we'll be?"

"Of course."

"Thank God," Eduardo said.

"You sound surprised."

Just then the door opened and Juanito stuck his head in.

Guzmán waggled his finger. "Can't you see I'm on the phone?"

"What?" said Eduardo.

"I was talking to my grandson."

"I shouldn't have said what I did."

"Do you want to know what happened?"

"I panicked when I couldn't get hold of you."

"Alicia went into labor early, completely unexpected. The baby was in trouble, something about her breathing."

"I hope she's all right."

"She's fine. They both are. The christening's Wednesday morning. You're invited but I expect you'll be busy."

"You're sure everything's set?"

"There's nothing to worry about."

"Until it happens there is."

"Two days is nothing. Think about the satisfaction."

"I don't give a shit about that anymore. All I want is my sons."

Guzmán heard a quaver in his voice.

"Don't get sentimental."

"I can't help it. They're my life's blood."

"Well, you're getting a transfusion. It's the end of a long road," he said with a tone of finality, "for both of us. Write when you get to Acapulco."

"It's strange saying good-bye over the phone."

"Better that way."

"I'm sorry I yelled."

"It's all right. I understand. And stop worrying about your wife."

He put the receiver back on the cradle. Their conversation had worn some of the luster off the enterprise and he wanted to get it back, restore the sharpness.

Juanito came in and looked at him impatiently.

"You weren't eavesdropping, were you?"

"No, Grandpa."

"You seem antsy," he said, tickling the boy. "It wouldn't have anything to do with swimming, would it?"

Juanito giggled.

"I've been practicing my kick."

"Put on your suit. I'll be out in a little while."

Before changing he called the caterer. It had occurred to him while he was talking to Eduardo that he'd better order another case of champagne for the party.

Juanito was broad-shouldered for an eight-year-old, stronger than any of his playmates who sometimes came with him to the house. Guzmán admired the beauty of his arms, the reedy neck. A feeling of warmth suffused him as he thought of how this sweet young life was driven by his own blood. The boy was going to have a hard time over the next few months adjusting to Marpessa. They would have to spend more time together.

"I'm better, aren't I?"

"You've improved. Your ankles are still too stiff, but they'll loosen up with practice."

"Can I stay a little longer?"

Guzmán eased himself into the water.

"I want you to promise me something."

"What?"

"That you'll behave at Marpessa's christening."

"I promise. Watch me."

TWENTY-TWO

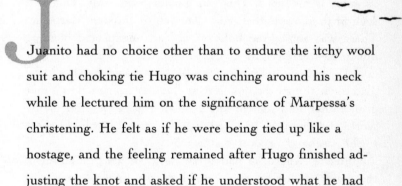

Juanito had no choice other than to endure the itchy wool suit and choking tie Hugo was cinching around his neck while he lectured him on the significance of Marpessa's christening. He felt as if he were being tied up like a hostage, and the feeling remained after Hugo finished adjusting the knot and asked if he understood what he had told him.

He said he did, though the idea of the Church being a body that would absorb Marpessa's soul when she was anointed with holy water was out of his range, like a radio playing so far away he could hear only intermittently and had no sense of the melody. His family was very religious. His grandfather had almost become a priest. He had already learned that to be ignorant of things associated with religion meant longer talks than the one his father had just delivered. Someday he would know everything. In the meantime, he said he did, affecting a deeper belief than he felt in his heart.

At the church Guzmán took him aside. They had something to discuss, he said, man to man.

Juanito liked it when his grandfather said that, even though it was always a prelude to something about his behavior.

Did he remember his promise a few days ago?

He did. He would behave and sit up straight.

Guzmán said he would hold him to it. A man was only as good as his word. This was a solemn occasion. God had seen fit to allow Father Von Claussen to christen Marpessa. There was something holy in this, an unexpected blessing not to be treated lightly.

He patted Juanito on the back and said he should be glad such things did not last as long as a mass. His other grandfather told him to cheer up, it wasn't the end of the world and that if he behaved well they might just find tickets to the weekend's soccer match.

Inside, where he had to sit between his grandfathers, the smell of flowers could not hide the lingering scent of incense that sometimes made him sick. There were many family friends and three generals who often visited Guzmán, men who carried themselves with the same dignity and assurance he admired in his grandfather.

Once all the guests had arrived there was nothing for him to do but stare at the stained-glass windows, the ceiling with its beautiful curved arches. When he grew bored counting them he turned around to see where the priest was and Guzmán put his hand on his knee, squeezing it hard enough to let him know he meant business.

Out of the corner of his eye he stole a glance at Catalina, who had a prissy expression he always hated. He waited until she looked back and made a face at her.

After what seemed like hours Father Von Claussen, resplendent in his vestments, took his place at the altar. Juanito respected him because Guzmán had once said that the priest was his special guide and counselor, that he had opened to him mysteries about the nature of God he would never have discovered by himself.

Juanito had not thought about the priest again until a few months ago when he overheard Guzmán talking to another general in his study about Father Von Claussen blessing a man for killing people in the ocean. Juanito did not understand how he could be holy and do that. When he asked his mother she had gotten very angry and demanded to know how he knew about it. He admitted to listening outside his grandfather's study one day. She told him he must never do that again. He said he would not but why had the priest done it? That was when she made him go to his room.

Now there was music and Alicia looked very beautiful in her blue dress. Juanito knew she was crying because she was happy. She told him she would and not to be upset. So were his grandmothers. They sniffed and blotted tears with white handkerchiefs.

He was glad when the ceremony began. It made him feel important that his parents were up there in front of everybody, that they were so happy even though the object of all the attention was almost invisible. The crown of Marpessa's head sticking out of the blanket reminded him of the end of a melon. A cantaloupe. She cried all the time and smelled and threw up on his mother's shoulder. He wondered if she would when the priest touched her but she only cried and he felt disappointed.

When it was over and they were outside women in

bright dresses and floppy hats spoke in baby talk to Marpessa. They told Alicia and Hugo how beautiful she was, how lucky they were to have such a perfect child. As soon as he could Juanito asked Hugo when they could go home and his father said when it was time and that he had better not make a scene.

There weren't any boys his age. Catalina was whispering with some girls and told him to leave them alone. Because he was feeling lonely and ignored, he sought out Guzmán only to be told that his grandfather had important things to discuss with the priest. They would have time together later on at the party.

By the time they finally got home Juanito felt hot and tired. His mother told him to hang up his suit if he was going to lie down so it would look nice for the party. He felt sad in his room but it was better than having to listen to his grandmothers going on about Marpessa.

He read a comic book. He was playing with some plastic racing cars Guzmán had given him when he heard the caterer's truck arrive and went back out to the living room.

They brought in aluminum containers, folding tables, coffee urns, silver platters, a crystal punch bowl, dozens of long-stemmed champagne glasses. Once the tables were set up, they put out all kinds of meats and pastas and sweets. When Alicia said he could not touch anything his grandma Miara told her not to be silly, this was a special occasion and it wouldn't hurt him to have a small piece of cake. The housekeeper cut it and gave him a glass of milk. Marpessa was in a crib in the living room so everybody could see her and he offered her a tiny bite. Alicia shouted when she saw what he was doing and told him to stop it, he knew better.

Some neighbors stopped by and they all talked about Marpessa this and Marpessa that. He asked his father to go outside and play soccer but Hugo looked irritated and said there wasn't time. Catalina refused because she had on her party dress.

He went out by himself and tried kicking the ball like Madragora but it was boring playing alone. He wished Guzmán would come. He wished they all lived together. His grandfather wouldn't talk nonsense to Marpessa, who couldn't understand anything and went to the bathroom in her pants.

Juanito kicked the ball and disconsolately watched it roll into the bushes near the sycamore tree. He liked to sit high up on the thick branches where no one could see him and let his legs dangle in space while he looked down at the neighbors' houses. His father had forbidden him to climb it anymore because it was too dangerous.

After retrieving the ball, he looked toward the house. Through the glass doors that opened onto the patio he saw the first guests had arrived. There were people he had seen at the christening, distant relatives, strangers, all with thin glasses in their hands. He saw the housekeeper open the front door for half a dozen people bearing bright packages, which they put on a nearby table. The sound of laughter carried out to the backyard, the sound of music from the stereo. Hugo was holding Marpessa, smiling broadly at an old woman with a big hat and pearls around her neck. It was a happy time, a celebration that seemed to have nothing to do with Juanito, as if he were supposed to be out there looking in, ignored as he had been at the church.

He put down the ball and took off his jacket. Mounting the low crotch of the tree as he did a pony, he climbed straight up to his hiding place, determined to stay there until his grandfather arrived.

Birds with red patches on their throats were perched on the far end of the branch. Sitting very still so as not to disturb them, he started talking to them the way Guzmán did to

Maya, in the same low voice. As one cocked its head and stared, Juanito thought how surprised his grandfather would be if he caught one and put it in a box with holes so it could breathe and gave it to him when he arrived.

He scooted closer, telling the bird not to be afraid. As he grabbed for it he began to slide off the branch. He threw his outstretched hand out behind him for balance and saw the bird hop into the air just before the ground rushed up to meet him.

TWENTY-THREE

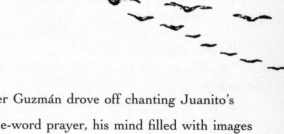

Two hours after Guzmán drove off chanting Juanito's name like a one-word prayer, his mind filled with images of Marpessa's christening, a tree swaying in the wind, a jagged white bone, his grandson's piercing scream, Pablo Sánchez-Macias and Guido Berletti parked in the street in front of his house.

Sánchez-Macias led the way up the drive, rang the bell, and knocked for good measure. Since he had already put so much time into this venture, he was more than a little irritated that Guzmán had made him wait until to-night for the rest of his money. He muttered to himself when there was no answer and told Guido to go around to the back door. The general was probably in the kitchen.

Berletti returned a minute later. Lights were on all

over the house but he hadn't been able to rouse anyone.

"He can't have forgotten," he said, "not after all the trouble he's gone to."

"It's a big house," Sánchez-Macias said as he tried the bell again. "Maybe he can't hear it."

He tapped his hand on his leg. A minute later he said, "Christ," and went out to the lawn where he surveyed the house. Guzmán's regimental flags were visible through an open window. He pushed his way between some bushes until he reached the study and called Guzmán's name only to be greeted with silence.

"No luck," he said when he returned to the porch.

Berletti glanced at his watch.

"We'd better get going. We can come by afterward for the money."

"No," Sánchez-Macias said angrily. "I don't do anything more till I'm paid."

"What about Ponce?"

"As far as I'm concerned, he can fuck himself."

Berletti regarded him apprehensively.

"Guzmán'll be pissed out of his mind if we don't go through with it."

"That's his problem. He screwed up, he can deal with it."

"I don't like it," Berletti said. "Something must have happened."

Snorting incredulously, Sánchez-Macias said, "That's brilliant. I didn't know you were a genius."

"Well? Have you got a better explanation?"

For a moment, Sánchez-Macias stared at the door. Then he shook his head and went down the stairs. When he reached the walk he turned around and regarded Berletti.

"Are you coming, or would you rather walk?"

TWENTY-FOUR

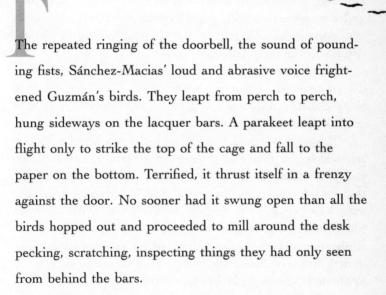

The repeated ringing of the doorbell, the sound of pounding fists, Sánchez-Macias' loud and abrasive voice frightened Guzmán's birds. They leapt from perch to perch, hung sideways on the lacquer bars. A parakeet leapt into flight only to strike the top of the cage and fall to the paper on the bottom. Terrified, it thrust itself in a frenzy against the door. No sooner had it swung open than all the birds hopped out and proceeded to mill around the desk pecking, scratching, inspecting things they had only seen from behind the bars.

Maya took to the air and soared around the room faster than she had ever done to the general's commands. With a whir of beating wings, the others followed, dodging the chandelier and grazing the walls until, on her third pass, Maya led them through the open window.

They circled the trees that in the daytime shaded Guzmán's pool.

They flew low over nearby houses, darting in one direction and then another as they released their pent-up urge to fly in dizzying ascents and wild plunges that gave them the look of feathered comets.

Only after they had explored every inch of space in Guzmán's neighborhood did they set out in search of new discoveries, following the gold beacon on Maya's leg into the heart of the city and descending upon the trees in the Plaza Durango where lovers walked hand in hand, groups of men and women passed each other exchanging flirtatious words and glances, all oblivious of the derelict talking to himself while he rummaged through a trash bin.

He alone noticed the arrival of Maya's flock. With eyes drawn upward by songs and the beat of wings, his face showed unveiled pleasure in what he saw while his soliloquy continued in the same unbroken pace.

Eduardo watched him through the truck's windshield, repelled by his rags and chatter but grateful nonetheless for the distraction. He forced his mind away from the thought that had made his gut ache and tried to imagine what the man was saying so reverently to the trees. With his head tilted back, he looked as if he were having a vision. Suddenly, the powers that had directed his eyes upward abandoned him. His lips were still moving when he turned his attention to things he had rescued from the bin, placed them carelessly in a sack which he heaved over his shoulder as he departed toward the center of the park.

Eduardo raised his left arm from the steering wheel. The green glow of hands and numbers on the luminous dial of his watch seemed brighter than ever, invested with unmistakable authority: ten o'clock.

The feeling that Beatriz' eyes were fixed on him was an actual physical sensation, like vague heat. In the semidarkness of the cab he saw her face glowing with the reflected lights of neon signs from bars and cafés across the street, pulsing reds and greens and yellows. The dominant color was a soft and lustrous blue.

He turned his wrist so she could see the time. She stared, slack-faced as someone who had suffered a stroke, her brain no longer capable of sending signals to animate the muscles of lips and cheeks. When he said, "They're just late, that's all," his voice sounded pinched, scarcely like his own.

She regarded Eduardo long enough for him to see the shadow of an expression creep into the blankness, a weird sign of private knowledge. He tried to understand what it meant as she slowly buttoned her sweater from top to bottom. When she finished, she put her hands flat on her thighs. Except for the rise and fall of her chest, she could have been a statue, a stone woman meticulously sculpted into the shape of a living one.

"I'll be back in two minutes."

His legs felt weak and shaky as he waited to cross the street at the intersection. By the time the light changed he was surrounded by people, all of them laughing and chattering without a care in the world. He wanted them to shut up, wanted to yell at the top of his lungs that he was suffering and frightened and had no idea what to do. He wanted attention to his plight, sympathy, and knew it would not come, not even if he stood in the middle of the street blocking their progress. They would look at him in exactly the way he had the derelict.

In the bodega he bought a bottle of brandy and ordered a shot, which he drank standing up while he gazed out the window at the truck. His heart thumped wildly when he thought a car was stopping beside it, but it had only halted for the traffic light.

Settled again behind the steering wheel, he dug his thumbnail into the lead seal and tore it off. He raised the bottle, swallowing greedily, grateful for the brandy's warmth and sting, the wetness it brought to his eyes.

He wiped the back of his hand across his mouth and held the bottle out for Beatriz. "It'll do you good."

She gave no indication of having heard. She crossed her arms beneath her breasts. Usually the gesture signaled anger but that was not the case now. She did it because she was cold. He noticed that she was shivering; a vaguely perceptible vibration was evident all the way from her shoulders down her body to her legs.

He envied her reaction. His was locked inside, along with the unspoken shouts. Maybe he should hug her. Maybe putting his arms around her would encourage his own body to respond, like paper takes flame from a match. But it would change nothing. The car had not come. All he could do was wait and hope.

Out of pity, he started the engine and slid the heater lever all the way to the right. He had another drink while it ran and this one tasted smoother than the first, more satisfying. Still, he felt no easing of the knot beneath his heart.

Bells chimed. He counted each ring, felt the numbers accumulating, the weight of so many hours.

When the twelfth struck, Beatriz responded with a strange sound, high-pitched and piteous.

He said, "We'll wait another hour," and then he began to talk. He was afraid it would be like swallowing when he had a sore throat, that the words would abrade the soft tissues, but he had no choice. He had to talk for her and also for himself, construct an explanation for why they were not out of the city, speeding north.

He told her there could have been car trouble.

There could have been a misunderstanding about time and place.

There could have been an accident that snarled traffic.

Dolores might have taken the boys out for an evening on the town. He laughed and said of all the nights to choose, of course, it would be this one.

Sánchez-Macias and Berletti must be waiting in their car, cursing and fretting.

"They're probably afraid we've given up."

Each of his imaginings seemed more far-fetched than the last. He wondered what Beatriz was thinking, if she were thinking. From the look of her he doubted it. He stared out the window until the bells chimed one o'clock.

The brandy burned in his stomach. He thought of throwing the bottle away, just rolling down the window and tossing it into the street. The sound of breaking glass would be a perfect expression of his emotions. At the same time, it seemed unlucky. Everything had consequences. Acts of destruction were repaid in the same coin. So, too, were acts of kindness.

As he put the bottle on the bench next to the trash bin he saw the boys in his mind's eye, felt again the touch of his lips on the door. What if they had waited too long? What if the old woman sensed something was about to happen and had gone into hiding?

Beatriz made the sound again when he returned. Inside himself he did it, too, except his was manifested in a distinct phrase. *They aren't coming. They are not coming.*

The derelict appeared on the path, lips moving, eyes growing wide when he saw the bottle. Without speeding up, he changed direction and made his way haltingly to the bench where he picked it up, sniffed, tipped it, drank. Without screwing on the cap, he put the bottle in his bag and was on his way again, leaving a trail of brandy on the walk.

The bells chimed the half-hour. Eduardo thought he heard birds singing. The steering wheel felt huge and unwieldy in his hands. The traffic was thinner now. There were longer pauses between the rush of cars along the avenue.

When they chimed again he reached for the ignition with fingers thick as sausages. The engine burst into a sweet smooth purr.

TWENTY-FIVE

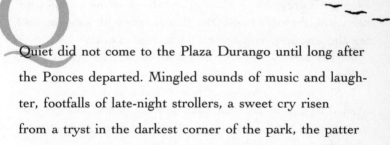

Quiet did not come to the Plaza Durango until long after
the Ponces departed. Mingled sounds of music and laughter, footfalls of late-night strollers, a sweet cry risen
from a tryst in the darkest corner of the park, the patter
of the derelict's speech kept the night alive for many
hours.

At first light, the birds woke, preened, descended sin-
gly and in pairs to feast on crusts of sandwiches, the remains of treats in plastic bags. When they left they flew
serenely, rising high above the city on their way to the
port where they touched down in the shadow of a German
freighter. There they strutted, perched on cranes and
trucks, watching the stevedores until the clatter of a fork-
lift frightened them away.

They toured the city, circling domes and steeples and causing a great commotion at the bird market.

They passed over the avenues of Recoleta's crypts, then rode a current to the telephone pole across the street from the Hotel Bolívar, squawking loudly as they fought for space along the lines.

Eduardo watched them descend. The first thing he thought of when he opened his eyes was calling Guzmán, yet no sooner had he rolled out of bed than he saw Beatriz sitting in a chair and staring out the window, shoulders slumped, head tilted slightly to one side. There she had remained all morning without so much as stirring or acknowledging his presence. A plate of uneaten food he brought for her lay on the table beside the chair, along with a cup of cold tea and a saucer with crystal-white sugar cubes.

"Do you see them?" he asked, hoping to distract her. "They look like musical notes on the wires."

She neither glanced at him nor the birds. Much as he needed to talk to Guzmán and disabuse himself of the fear that they had waited too long, this latest stage of grief tethered him to her. He was afraid to leave.

In the conciliatory voice he would use with a troubled child, that he had used, time out of mind, with Tomás and Manfredo, he told her nothing was wrong. It had only been a mistake, a misunderstanding. Everything would be fine once they were reunited with the boys. He told her to think of what it was going to feel like as they headed north, crossing borders.

"It will never happen," she said.

Spoken without inflection, her words managed to convey an authority all the more strange because it seemed so wildly at odds with her appearance. The uneasiness he had battled since nine o'clock last night crept further into the light of thought. Did what she say have the ring of truth? Was that what he heard? He told himself it was impossible.

"A mix-up," he said. "A mistake."

"You know why," she answered in a voice filled with self-recrimination.

"I don't know any more than you do."

She was looking at him and there was no way to mistake the meaning of her expression. She pitied him for his stupidity.

"I brought it on us."

His mind took him back to the first time she uttered the phrase. Then, it had the sound of terrible discovery. Now he heard immutable conviction, the statement of a scholar.

"You had nothing to do with this," he said quickly.

"Liar," she answered, whispering the word in such a way that he knew she was not challenging his veracity but merely explaining a belief.

She moistened her lips with the tip of her tongue, closed her eyes. At first, he thought she was only blinking, but they remained closed for upward of a minute. Opened, they were gelid, their focus turned inward on something beyond his powers to conceive. *Guzmán's fault. No one else's.* Eduardo wanted to tell him what he had done but he could no more leave her alone than fly.

He sank down on the bed and flipped through the pages of a newspaper retrieved from the lobby days ago. The sentences had nothing to do with him, swam incomprehensibly past his eyes. Nothing was important except the place on the road where they should be. He remembered the name of the inn and exactly where it was on the map. He remembered circling it with a red pencil, then neatly jotting down beside the circle the distance in kilometers to the nearest gas station.

Beatriz was sitting very straight, her hands resting stiffly, awkwardly, on the chair arms. Her hair looked like a bird's nest. This, too, was new. She had been fanatical about it. Even after the boys were taken she had gone through the ritual of combing it out before making breakfast.

When his old life began playing across his mind he longed for the ease of it, the predictability of the days. He saw his house with the startling clarity of a good photograph, his boat rocking on the tide, remembered sanding and varnishing its deck, his pride in the boys' seamanship and how their legs had mastered the movement of the deck.

He refused to believe it was gone. In Mexico he would have it again. There, he would re-create their old life and everything would be fine. The old woman had sucked her spirit dry. That would have devastated anyone but it was worse for Beatriz, who was overly sensitive and followed her heart too much. She had been strong before Dolores came, strong in ways he had not realized. And she had suffered because of the secret she kept from him, the stupid blunder that had gotten mixed up in her mind with the boys.

A twinge of guilt emerged when he recalled striking her. He would be more patient. Once they were together, he would talk to the boys privately and explain what she had been through. He would never forgive Guzmán for his self-ishness, his fucking daughter, all his lame excuses.

The tendons in the backs of Beatriz' hands stood out against the flesh. Her shoulders tensed and the muscles rippled beneath the thin material of her dress. She rose. While he tried to interpret these signs she ran her hands deliberately through her hair, breaking the tangles with her fingers, smoothing them with her palms. She tugged at the front of her dress and tried to brush out the wrinkles at her thighs. There was something erotic in these acts. He longed for her, wanted to ease her down on the bed and make love to her until she forgot her sorrow.

"You seem better," he said, hoping she would turn and acknowledge his desire as she used to with her eyes.

Instead, she went over to the window and delicately touched the strip of flypaper. He watched it turning, then shouted, "Leave those goddamn things alone!" The words were barely out of his mouth when he understood she had no intention of indulging in her filthy habit.

Minutes later, as he rushed downstairs, he would remember how she had walked from her chair to the window with an unmistakable intensity of purpose.

He would remember thinking that what he saw was only a husk in the shape of a woman moving across the room.

Now his attention was focused on the way she delicately slipped the index finger of her right hand into the pull. Released, the curtain made a dull sound as it rolled around the rod and the pull swung lazily back and forth while she pushed the window up.

For a moment she stood there with her arms raised. Then she bent and dove.

Her flight was wondrous to the birds, the plummeting of an exotic sister whose folded wings would soon spread, catch the air, and send her soaring. They watched, cock-eyed, chattering, expectant, until she struck the pavement with mingled sounds of breath suddenly expelled, snapping bones, the soft collapse of organs. Frightened as they were by the failure of instinct that kept their kind aloft, it was the sight of Eduardo framed in the window, screaming Beatriz' name, that sent them into the air, frantically beating their wings to escape a sound unlike any they had ever heard.

Eduardo ran for the stairs with her name still echoing in his ears, his lips still fresh with the feel of screaming it. A voice welled up from deep inside, guttural, devastating, accusing. He should have guessed from the way she walked. There had been more than enough signs. He remembered begging Guzmán to get on with it, how his fear that something was wrong had prophesied last night, everything forming a pattern detailed as a blueprint but meaningless now, too late, history. It all clattered behind him like a string of bones as he passed the startled clerk and threw the lobby door open on the run.

People emerging from the bar across the street brought music with them, a tango he often heard when he used the phone. With a small white towel the bartender gestured to a point off to his left. The eyes of pedestrians who had stopped in their tracks were filled with shock and wonder.

Eduardo pivoted slowly on his left foot, aware that he was stretching out the last moments before he had to confront the consequence of her flight, that until he saw her he was somehow keeping her aloft, her hair smoothed back by the wind, hugging her head as if she had put it up in a bun. A vision of her combing it with her fingers brought a cry from his throat.

Already a circle of people had gathered on the sidewalk. He heard a woman crying, saw a man leaning with both hands against the side of the building, supporting himself while he vomited. Beatriz' shoeless right foot, bent at an angle, was visible through the spectators' legs.

He walked toward her, absently pushing people out of his way.

Somebody yelled, "Call a doctor."

Another answered, "It's too late."

Beatriz lay face down with her arms thrust slightly upward, knees bent. *The posture of sleep.* A trickle of blood seeped from her clothes.

He did not remember kneeling. He was aware of it only because he now felt the heat of the pavement on his knees and hands. His fingers were splayed out like a runner's at a starting block, the skin conforming to the tiny imperfections in the concrete, burning slightly. There was a smell of exhaust and the sound of car motors left running by drivers who had stopped in the middle of the street. Horns blared in the distance. The warmth and smells and sounds formed an atmosphere that surrounded but did not penetrate the space he occupied.

A man asked if anyone knew who she was.

A glass of brandy appeared in front of him, accompanied by the bartender's voice urging him to drink, it would make him feel better. He had said the same thing to her last night. He struck the glass with the back of his hand and smelled the brandy when it spilled.

He could not bear to touch her. It was a terrible place to die. Better if she had been on Scilingo's plane. He imagined the surface of the sea disturbed by concentric circles, then the smooth sweep of the swells, all of it over in seconds. *Whereas this*.

She had fallen into a spectacle. From all sides people leered as they would at a dog struck by a car. It was an end and also a beginning. Kneeling over her was only the first of the obligations that would follow. He should remain on his knees, weeping and beating his breast until they brought a stretcher. He should insist on riding in the back of the ambulance with her, yelling at the medics and hoping for a resurrection. He should listen to a doctor at the hospital informing him she was dead and then somehow arrive at a funeral home to see to her laying out, a place where strangers would politely inquire about his wishes. It was all part of a predetermined ritual for someone lucky enough to have the leisure to mourn, for whom time had stopped in its tracks.

His own was ticking forward, *careening*. He had squandered it, spent it stupidly, irresponsibly. Now what was left was on the run. Soon the police would arrive. There would be questions. No matter how carefully he phrased his answers, assuming he could do anything but howl and babble, they could never understand what he was saying about time and how everything in his life had changed and if he did not rescue the boys now it would be too late. Besides, for all he knew, a warrant might already have been issued for his arrest. The police would begin with saying how sorry they were and end by putting him in handcuffs and then his last chance would disappear.

He knew how long it took to reach her house. If he left soon, they could be on the road within the hour.

With one last glance at Beatriz he rose and headed for his truck. The spectators backed away, making a corridor, a gauntlet for him to pass through. He felt their eyes boring into him.

The desk clerk was standing by the truck's door. In a shaken but resolute voice, he said, "You're packed."

When Eduardo tried to step around him the clerk blocked his way. "I'm sorry," he said apologetically. "You owe a week's rent."

Eduardo grabbed him by the front of his shirt and heaved him out of the way.

He thought there was just enough room to slip between two cars parked in the middle of the street. After backing up to get a better angle, he drove forward and heard the sound of metal scraping against metal quickly followed by an angry shout. In the mirror he saw a man running after him. Behind him, an ambulance was approaching with a crown of flashing blue lights on its roof, presentiments of disaster, thwarted love, the end of the boys' desire to be his sons.

He wanted to believe that nothing would have made Beatriz happier than his manic drive through the city, that she would understand his obligation was to Tomás and Manfredo, that once he had gotten them he would mourn her properly. But he could not believe it because it was absurd, a way of speaking the living used to console themselves. Beatriz had neither wishes nor desires nor benefactions to offer.

Dolores clouded his mind, her face smug in its certainties, victory shining like a banner in her eyes. He groaned as he thought of the time he had lost. But Dolores could do nothing. A push would send her sprawling. If she tried to resist he would blow her brains out. Because of her, because of Guzmán. He ached to confront the general with the consequences of his fine talk, ask what he had felt last night, demand an explanation for why he had let them sit in the truck for hours.

He would tell the boys about Beatriz in a day or two. This afternoon, once they were on the road, he would say she was ill and planned to join them soon. After they were safely out of the country he would explain that he had only been trying to spare their feelings and then they would grieve together and it would be terrible but also the prologue to a new life. He would tell them about the solace of peace awaiting them in Acapulco. He would name their new boat Beatriz.

An old couple standing by the bus stop at the intersection gazed at him with mild interest when he turned onto her street. As soon as he parked in front of her house he removed the pistol from the glove compartment and slipped it into his pocket. He felt the sun on his face as he strode up the walk, confident that the moment they saw him coming their faces would break into ecstatic smiles. He glanced at his watch so that he would always know when he had set them free. Five to one.

The spot he'd kissed was just to the right of the house number on the door and that was where he knocked, a loud rapping whose authority was guaranteed to summon Dolores, announce the freedom of his sons. He would embrace them, bury his face in their hair, inhale their scent, tell them everything was going to be fine.

Of course they would be overcome. They would weep, and so would he. Already, he felt the sting of tears. They would look at each other and then he would say they had five minutes to get whatever they wanted because they had to hurry. Anything they forgot could be replaced in Mexico. To her he would say nothing. No hasty words that might come to his lips, however sharp and devastating, could compare with the pleasure of silently watching her realize what was happening.

It was very quiet. He listened to birds in the trees and the hum of traffic on the connector road that would take them out of the city, glad she was slow to come to the door because the delay let him build in his mind a series of images of her face. First surprise, then confusion, then fear born of terrible knowledge, exactly the sequence he had suffered that morning in Mar Vista.

He stepped closer to the door because he wanted to hear the muffled sound of her footsteps, the brush of metal against metal as the tongue of the lock slid free.

He knocked again, harder this time, and heard the sound reverberate inside where it seemed to compete with nothing but silence. He listened, still caught up in the imagined scenario, fighting with all his strength against the meaning of what he did not hear. His heart began thumping. He felt blood tingling in his arms and fingers and then a terrible, wrenching wave of disappointment. He stood as if paralyzed, silently cursing himself for being so stupidly shortsighted. It was the middle of the afternoon. People go out.

There was nothing to do but move the truck a block away. He had a clear view of the house and the sidewalk all the way to the intersection. Soon they would come along. He would not even have to enter the house. He would snatch them off the street and leave her howling.

The sun beat straight down. Heat haze shimmered on the hood. Eduardo lowered the windows and the sluggish but welcome breeze brought a vision of the crowd surrounding Beatriz. In quick succession, he saw Mar Vista, the sea, the great rise of the cordillera. He saw the dock, his boat, Beatriz piling the table with food while he and the boys came in the door. They would work in warmer waters under a softer sun.

The heat was drying him out and soon he could no longer ignore his thirst. He looked down the block and saw a hose coiled neatly on the lawn of a nearby house, went to it, turned the faucet on, and let the water run until it was cold, drinking first, then splashing some on his face. When he turned off the faucet, he noticed a woman staring at him through the window. He smiled and carefully recoiled the hose. Then he left, walking slowly down the block in the opposite direction of his truck. He had only taken a little water. There was nothing to fear. Still, it seemed like a good idea to stay away awhile.

The neighborhood was served by a dozen small shops across the intersection. He walked there and saw that he still had a clear view of Dolores' house. He would be able to see her and the boys coming from either direction. There was something wrong with the way she walked. Not a pronounced limp. She simply favored one leg. Which meant that wherever they were she could not traipse around very long. It was more than reasonable to suppose they would return before dark. Like all old people, she would be a creature of habit. She would want dinner. He would serve it to her. There was a satisfying irony in the notion. *Give her her own heart on a platter. Take and eat.* He would be the priest of her misery.

He stopped at a newsstand and scanned the front pages of the papers displayed face out in metal racks. Memory seemed to reach out from the black type of the headlines and pull him back to the bed where he had tried to read while Beatriz was preparing herself. He quickly looked away, telling himself he could not think about it, that he had to keep his grief at bay. He would let her return once they were on the road, let her pour into his being. Until then he had to focus solely on the boys, blot everything else from his mind. They would need food and drink. There was no telling when he would feel safe enough to stop for a meal.

At the grocer's just up the block, produce and fruit were stacked in neat pyramids on wooden boxes. Inside, a few customers shopped while a clerk in a long blue apron chatted with an old man. He went inside and requested some bags from the clerk who regarded him quizzically as he handed them over.

After filling them with apples, bananas, and some blood oranges for the boys, he returned to the counter and asked for three large bottles of mineral water.

"What kind?"

"It doesn't matter."

While the clerk made change, Eduardo noticed that the old man was looking at him. *Sorrow showed*, he thought, *but did intention, desire? The smallest things can trip you up*. There was always something in the papers to that effect. He wondered how he looked and decided his face was giving him away. He quickly smiled at both of them and said, "It's hot for this time of year."

"Worse than usual," the old man agreed. "It's because there aren't enough trees."

"That must be it."

He was careful to walk slowly out of the store.

He felt better once he was in the truck. The old man was simply bored. He had overreacted to him and the clerk.

They would be here soon. Whether they approached from the direction of the intersection or the other end of the street, he would drive to where they were as soon as he saw them. That way, he would gain an extra minute or two before she could use a phone.

• • •

Shadows from the trees advanced from the middle of the street until they reached the cab. The heat was less intense, the light softer, easier on his eyes.

He turned on the radio in time for the seven o'clock news and found himself wondering what to do with Beatriz' clothes.

He turned the volume up and tried to concentrate on the shapes of the houses. The sky was the color of a bruise. *Keep or sell. Remember or forget.* He knew he could have stayed and dealt with everything. Was that why he thought about her clothes? That he would have had time to rummage through the boxes and find something proper for her laying out?

He longed for the solace the strangers had offered with their eyes, the words that would have helped dull the ache of loss. He saw Beatriz lying on the sidewalk, surrounded by people who did not even know her name. Then, as suddenly as the vision appeared, she and the spectators vanished from his mind. Out of the aching emptiness she left, a void that seemed deep as space, came a question he stopped midway because he could not bear to complete it: *What if?*

He had to keep the jagged words from joining the unspoken ones. The pressure of the day was loosening all sorts of stupidities. He needed rest for what was coming. He would have to protect them from so much, be father and mother.

Lights were on all along the block. He had a terrifying image of her empty house. He refused to look at his watch. Seeking relief in the darkened sky, the two words and the imagined sentence of the empty house merged, became a statement— *They were gone!*

She had gotten wind of his plan, or intuited it. In a frenzy she had taken his sons into hiding, perhaps out of the country. But why would the boys have given in? They would have refused, fought. *Unless.*

The word distilled the fear he had wakened to, that had tracked him over the last few weeks: What he feared might happen to their hearts during all those wasted days. In the house he could no longer see she had wheedled, cajoled, lied, taken advantage of their innocence to poison them against him, used the time Guzmán gave her to kill their love. He remembered the talk about friendship, the money given with just the slightest hint of condescension, how he had groveled. He heard the steady, songlike refrain of Beatriz saying it would never happen. There was a certainty in her words he had not noticed, a timbre at once calm and oracular. And what she knew had been shared by Dolores, the two of them possessed of some instinct beyond him.

Eduardo was aware of a weird disjunction between the calmness of switching on the ignition and the rage exploding inside. As if he were two different people. Was that why Beatriz had leapt out the window, taking the only way she knew to regain her wholeness? Was it what the boys felt when their lives cleaved in two before Dolores tricked them with her honeyed words?

He averted his eyes from the glare of headlights coming toward him. After the car passed, he watched their glow in the rearview mirror brighten the undersides of branches until they, too, returned to darkness.

He drove slowly, carefully, a perfect citizen of the road. After the turmoil of the day, a calm sense of purpose had settled in his heart. Everything was immutable, carved in stone. The cab was a little oasis cooled by the night air coming through the windows, the blue glow of the instruments reassuring sources of the only truths that mattered now. He was a devotee of speed, oil pressure, voltage.

The scent of flowers and freshly cut grass welcomed him to Guzmán's street. He recognized night-blooming jasmine, wisteria, and their scents took him back to his last visit and the excitement he had felt, the certainty that everything was coming together, that great forces were guiding him toward the end of his ordeal.

A party was in progress across the street from Guzmán's house. He heard music when he turned the engine off, peals of laughter, and more closely the cries of birds. Looking up, a few pale shapes were visible in the branches. *Song birds.* He remembered the ones on the telephone lines who watched her jump, and their calls and cries turned harsh, as if they were the broken parts of a single scream.

Without knocking, he went inside. In the living room he paused by a table crowded with family photographs. There was one of Alicia sitting between Juanito and Catalina, a formal portrait of Gloria, Guzmán in uniform. He looked around, breathing in the intimate feeling of the room. It had a lived-in quality, grander by far than his house in Mar Vista, but close enough to rekindle memory.

At the far end of the hall a sliver of light glowed at the bottom of a door. The knob felt cool to the touch and a little slippery, as if it had recently been polished. He pushed on it and through the opening saw the kitchen. Copper pots and pans hung from cast-iron hooks half the length of one wall. The stove and refrigerator were burnished aluminum. A work space beside the sink was crowded with rows of bottled spices.

He had to open the door all the way before he saw Guzmán sitting at a table in pajamas and a dark blue robe. In front of him was a bottle of wine, several glasses, a plate of antipasto, a caged bird. Guzmán was talking to it, but his voice was too low for Eduardo to make out his words.

Now that he was here, he was content to watch, no longer in a hurry because time had ceased to signify. He could stand there as long as he wanted, savoring his freedom.

He had thought he would enter whatever room the general was in and deliver himself of his rage in a tirade that would put the fear of God in him. Now, to his surprise, he realized that the desire was dead, that he had no more use for words than he did for time. He wondered if that had been on Beatriz' mind.

As he closed the door, Guzmán turned with a startled expression that quickly gave way to a smile. His face was haggard, darkened by the stubble of a day-old beard.

"Eduardo!" he said affectionately. "I'm glad you came in. I can't hear the doorbell back here."

"I was in the neighborhood."

"Good, good." He pulled out a chair. "I thought you'd call, but this is better. Sit down and let me explain. You won't believe what happened."

"Something bad?"

"Juanito broke his leg last night. To top it off, my birds escaped. My own fault. I never thought I'd see them again but they returned a little while ago. Maya was the only one who'd come inside."

"I saw a few of them," Eduardo said as he glanced at Maya. It was hard to believe his eyes but there was no denying the earring on her leg. For an instant he felt as if he had been pulled into some insane world, lost all connection with reality. Then he laughed at his shortsightedness. It had followed them all the way from Santa Rosalita. Why did he think it would vanish? It was part of his past and his past was part of his present, and Guzmán was the curator of this sign that his life had come full circle.

"What's so funny?" Guzmán asked.

"The earring," he said, his voice breaking as he pronounced the word.

"Do you feel all right?"

"I feel fine."

"It was Juanito's idea. Let me pour you some wine and I'll tell you what happened. I've been worried sick."

Eduardo watched the wine rise in the glass. It was the color of wheat.

As he put the pistol to Guzmán's head, he had a vision of the pampas stretching as far as the eye could see.

TWENTY-SIX

Dolores, on her way to the newsstand this Saturday morning, can't help smiling at the irony of her little excursion. After all those years of straitjacketing her days, militarizing her life, censoring thoughts like a priest on the lookout for blasphemy, the last thing she ever thought she would do again was live with rituals. Finding the boys was supposed to free her from proscribed routine. As soon as she saw them in Ponce's house she thought she could toss away the jacket and finally take her days as they came. Well, that was just one more example of how her thinking had been distorted, as if the belts had been pulled so tight they'd reduced the blood flow to her brain.

The chaotic early days of living with the boys when all their desires were at odds had gradually smoothed out as they got used to each other. First, the weeks took on a definite shape, then the days. Before she knew it, they had adopted routines, none weighty, but surprisingly satisfying, and the reason was not hard to come by. There were guarantees in repetition, a sense of security. Rituals like today's were roads into the future. Every Saturday morning Roger and Joaquín played soccer with a pickup team. Every Saturday morning, after seeing them off, she walked to the newsstand for a paper before stopping at the grocer's, an unremarkable half-hour made pleasurable because it was part of a continuum. After they outgrew soccer, there would be something to replace it and her morning walk.

At the newsstand the taciturn owner, a refugee from Lebanon who, after ten years of acquaintance finally told her his name was Rashid, removes a paper from the rack, folds it in the usual way, and leaves his hand out, palm up, for her coins.

He thanks her with a nod.

She asks how things are in the world today.

"Always the same," he answers with a shrug.

This exchange, with the slightest variations, is all they ever say.

On her way down the block Dolores hopes he saves his breath for his wife, a pretty woman she has seen a few times. It amuses her to think that closed-mouth Rashid, peddler of the world's unchanging news, becomes gregarious at home, entertaining his wife and friends with jokes until tears run down their faces. Rashid, secret comedian of the city's Levantines.

With his usual skill, the grocer, Jorge Valenzuela, has arranged his fruit in pyramids atop wooden crates on the sidewalk in front of his store. Unlike Rashid, at least the public Rashid, Jorge is a lover of words, indefatigable source of neighborhood gossip and advice. Utterly open about his own life, he demands the same from his customers and friends. As a consequence, he long ago pried from Dolores everything there was to know about her story and all its names, uncovering in the process a special bond between them: his brother, a sculptor most renowned for carving the doors of the Children's Theater, was among the Disappeared.

Today he greets her with uncharacteristic reticence. Avoiding her eyes, he describes what is good this week in a flat, humorless voice. "The apples and cantaloupes are average, but the blood oranges are perfect."

He quarters one with a pocketknife and hands her a slice.

The flesh is a deep ruby red, glistening with juice. When she bites into it, the taste is amazingly sweet.

"Even better than the last shipment," she says enthusiastically. "Give me half a dozen. No, a dozen. The boys love them."

He regards her with a pained expression. For a moment he seems on the verge of saying something, then apparently changes his mind as he quickly bags the fruit and heads for the counter.

After ringing up her purchase, he hands over the change, looking even more miserable than before.

"All right," she says in a motherly tone. "Out with it. What's the matter with you this morning?"

Jorge nods at the newspaper in her mesh bag.

"Have you looked at it?"

"I never do till I get home."

"You'd better."

"Why?" she says with half a laugh. "Did I win the lottery?"

"You didn't win a thing."

Her curiosity piqued, she puts the bag on the counter and removes the paper. The headline announces another massacre in Sarajevo, this time in a crowded marketplace. A photograph in the middle of the page shows bodies littering the street like burned flowers.

Obscene as it is, she cannot take her eyes off it, for as she scrutinizes the carnage, she thinks of Rubén. In response to the question that suddenly arises she tells herself that she is being silly, he would not have gone there. But why not? It was safe in those days, a beautiful cosmopolitan city where a man and his young daughter might build a new life.

The meaning of the burned flowers changes with her apprehension. Now there is an almost unbearable intimacy in the shapes. She knows that all the years of absence would not keep her from recognizing the least thing about them. Anxiously, she looks at the shapes again and a weight lifts from her heart. They are not among the dead and dying.

"It won't stop until everyone's gone," she says while thinking, They're alive, somewhere. A place of oranges. Let it be a place of oranges and lemons.

Jorge regards her with a rigid expression.

"It doesn't have anything to do with that."

She glances at the paper again, and this time a headline halfway down the page catches her attention.

"MURDER-SUICIDE NEAR SAN TELMO. FORMER ARMY GENERAL RODOLFO GUZMÁN SHOT TO DEATH."

Though the words are clear as day, though her eyes remain fixed on them, they refuse to signify, seem to have no connection to the name. Since first hearing it, Guzmán has existed for her as in a castle keep through whose slitted windows he watched and laughed, waving a copy of the presidential pardon. Impossible as it seems, someone scaled the walls. She feels a shock of pleasure too complex to fathom, too fraught with history, wonders if he heard footsteps, a door creaking open, how he felt when he realized what was coming, whether he knew the person.

In a tone that expresses her surprise and the lingering vestiges of disbelief, she says, "So someone got to him." She pauses, then more forcefully adds, "I wish I'd been there."

The matching pleasure she expects from Jorge is nowhere evident, only exasperation.

"I don't understand," she says. "You ought to be kicking up your heels."

"That's only the beginning," he tells her in a strained voice. "Read all of it."

Without his injunction—for that is how his words sounded—she's not sure she would, at least for the present. How Guzmán died is only of passing interest compared with the fact of his death.

The first paragraph, in stolid journalese, describes how neighbors heard a shot and first discovered the body of the unidentified assailant on the lawn before going inside where they found the general on the kitchen floor. Although the officer in charge of the investigation had no clues to suggest a motive, he reminded reporters at the district police station that General Guzmán had played a major role in the *Proceso*. Absent evidence to the contrary, he personally believed it had been an act of revenge undertaken by a grieving relative.

The idea appeals to her and she hopes it's true. The scene she had just conjured becomes more vivid. She imagines a confrontation this time, an exchange of words, imagines Guzmán reduced to tears as he begs for his life. Why would whoever shot him kill himself afterward?

She reads on slowly, savoring every detail.

A truck parked in front of the general's house contained household goods and clothes, some of which investigators thought would fit the assailant. There were also women's clothes, and clothes that appeared to belong to young men. Annotated maps detailing a route to Mexico were discovered in the cab, along with a bag of fruit and a receipt from a suburban market.

The police were investigating connections to another in-
cident that occurred on Thursday morning at a downtown
hotel. A woman had fallen to her death from an upper floor
of the Hotel Bolívar. The day clerk, Santiago Flores, identified her as Beatriz Ponce. He said that her husband,
Eduardo, had rushed downstairs. "When I went out to the
sidewalk I noticed his truck was packed. He was in a bad
way but he owed a week's rent and I had to ask him for it.
The boss makes me pay for anyone who skips out. When I
did, he knocked me down. They didn't get along. He beat
her. I wouldn't be surprised if he pushed her out the window."

The conclusion, that the truck's registration was being
checked to see if it belonged to Señor Ponce, floats by,
hardly noticed. From the moment she saw Beatriz' name she
has not been aware of breathing. Her chest feels tight, painful. She gulps in air but there is no pleasure in it, only necessity. Her body and mind seem split off from each other. Now
she understands why Jorge was so hesitant. He knows what
I have to do. The prospect flares into a sense of panic, and
the panic spawns a vision of Beatriz plunging to the sidewalk, screaming into the rush of air. How can I?

"I should have just told you," Jorge says apologetically.
"But I thought it'd be better if you read it."

She shakes her head.

"I'm grateful to you."

Had he said nothing it was more than likely she would
not have looked at the paper for hours, maybe not until after
they'd come home. What if she had opened it while they
were all in the living room, felt what she was feeling now in
their presence? Her face would have given her away. They
would have asked what was wrong. She cannot bear thinking about what might have happened.

"There's more," Jorge says tentatively, as if trying to
gauge her resilience.

He pauses. In the silence another scene comes to her, this time of the boys staring at her in the wake of her revelation.

"He bought the fruit here. The police came yesterday and asked if I remembered selling a man blood oranges. They described him but I said they didn't need to. I knew who it was. I told them yes, that I'd never seen him before and that he seemed nervous. It shocked the hell out of me when I saw the paper this morning and realized it was Ponce."

Her head is spinning from the news. The dread of having to repeat the story to Roger and Joaquín spreads wider, encompassing a half-formed idea or a question, she's not sure which, only that she needs to thrust it away.

Jorge says, "What do you think he was doing here?"

"How should I know?" she answers brusquely, aware that it's a rude effort to avoid the thought she sidestepped a moment ago, which has loomed up again. She had dreamed over the last month of a shadowy presence hovering nearby, of someone on the porch late at night. Surely they're what she thought at the time, remnants of the old nights when her mind fed her anxiety stories from dark to dawn. They had to be.

"Well, it wasn't an accident."

With an effort, she tries to put herself in Eduardo's place. What if the shoe were on the other foot, if she were the one facing prison?

"Maybe he wanted to see them before the trial," she says, feeling a chill because she is almost certain this is more than speculation. "Maybe he wanted to talk." I would, she thinks. I'd have walked across hot coals.

"What about her?"

Still thinking about what she would have done, *anything*, she isn't sure what he's getting at.

"Do you think he killed her?"

Slowly but emphatically she shakes her head back and forth, once in each direction. About that she has no doubt.

"Why not?"

"Because he loved her."

Jorge makes an impatient gesture, raises his eyebrows skeptically.

"After the hearing I saw them together outside the courthouse. Her face was bloody, swollen. She said something, and I knew from the way he put his arms around her that he did."

"You told me he'd slugged her no more than ten or fifteen minutes before."

"You'd have to have seen it to understand."

Unconvinced, Jorge presses on.

"People don't just fall out of hotels. When someone takes a dive, it's either to get rid of the taste of the world or because they're pushed. The clerk said he beat her."

"That doesn't matter," she says emphatically. "He couldn't have done it."

Frustrated, she glances out the window. He's only trying to help her grasp what happened, solve the mystery. Then why this sudden irascible mood? Because she doesn't have time for speculations, needs to concentrate on what to tell the boys. No, not what. What is obvious. What is three bodies. How. She invents explanations, each more platitudinous and evasive than the last. Eventually, she'll have to come to the facts, stop trying to protect them. When she does they will be like pieces of steel, bright and gleaming. Knives. The words will cut them like knives.

With a catch in her voice that does not begin to express her anguish, she says, "I can't stand what this is going to do to them."

"You have a choice. Maybe you shouldn't say anything."

"No, I don't. We have no secrets and they have a right

to know. Besides, it's the kind of thing that will be in the papers a long time. Even if I didn't tell them, they'd find out. How do you think they'd feel when they came across it? That would be even worse than hearing it from me."

He hesitates, then goes on in a brighter tone. "They'll be all right. They're good boys. This will beat them up, but they'll survive."

"I don't care about survival," she tells him heatedly. "I care about their suffering."

"They're part of the same thing. Survival first. Then healing."

Silence falls between them. She can't believe she's arguing with Jorge, feels like an ingrate, but much as she wants to accept what he said it's superfluous as far as today is concerned. The clock behind him says eleven. There's no more time to talk and not enough to think about what she has to do.

"I'm sorry. I'd better go. They'll be home in two hours."

"I could tag along."

"That's kind of you, but this is between the three of us."

"You're sure?"

"As I am of anything."

The moment she steps outside she is amazed by how everything has changed in half an hour. On the way from Rashid's, the array of storefronts, trees receding in the distance, passing traffic, all objects and sounds and smells were part of an undifferentiated presence, the backdrop of one more Saturday morning. There's something alien about it now, the familiar intimacy replaced by objectivity, pure phenomenon. She feels no connection to any of it.

Two strangers are buying papers from Rashid, an act that is being repeated all over the city at other newsstands. How many hundreds of people are reading, curious about why Guzmán was killed but regarding it as just one more act of violence and as unconcerned about what it means as they

will be by the soccer scores? The world seems lopsided, distorted, colors run together the way they do when she's had
too much to drink. In a little ecstasy of impatience she rushes
across the street, intent on getting home as fast as possible
and shutting out this strangeness.

   In the sanctuary of her favorite chair she rereads the
column, greedily devouring the words. After the questions
Jorge raised, after considering them on the way back and
feeling the way she imagines she would if she had stumbled
into quicksand, the sentences seem so freighted they might as
well be independent of each other, starting the story over
after every period.
   One thing is clear; none of the facts even begins to hint
at an explanation. Why did all three die in a single day? Why
one? She is certain Eduardo did not kill Beatriz, nagged by
suspicion that it began with Beatriz' leap. Did that mean her
death precipitated the others? Was there an equation, Beatriz' death equals theirs, hidden in all those unaccounted-for
hours?
   Like so many colored balloons the questions hang in the
air, bobbing away each time she addresses them. She rubs
her temples, lets her eyes roam over the furniture, the pictures of Rubén and Marta, the snapshot of the boys. Staring
at the blank face of the television, she's reminded of the
confusion when she's interrupted watching a *telenovela* and
doesn't get back until it's almost over. You have the beginning and the end but no idea what went on in between. If
this story begins with Beatriz, what's the middle? Eduardo
shooting Guzmán. What could have happened for him to
murder the man he owed so much to? Confusion like this is
the stock-in-trade of her soap operas, which always rely on
something going wrong, ending in a way it isn't supposed to.
Betrayal? Of what? By whom?

The seemingly infinite regress of questions makes her feel guilty. It would not be so bad if there were a reasonable chance of finding answers yet she is all but certain that is impossible. Instead of worrying them to death, she ought to be using the time to think about how to break the news. On the other hand, anything she discovers, even if it's only a fresh supposition, might ease her anxiety.

She wonders if she has taken the wrong tack in looking for reasons. Maybe she should concentrate on the facts. There is the truck packed with their belongings, a map outlining a route to Mexico. They were ready to leave with everything they could carry and no wonder. Staying meant prison. But that does not account for Eduardo's presence in the neighborhood, nor does it shed light on why they had the boys' clothes. As mementos, their equivalent of her photographs?

She wonders what they might have done with those cloth shrines. The clothes take on a pathetic status in her mind. Though it is against all her instincts, thinking about the Ponces has put her in an elegiac mood. She knows more about their feelings than she would like to admit. She recalls the range of their expressions and from their numbers one emerges to grip her attention: Eduardo in the courtroom.

Though she has thought about his eyes time and again, she has never succeeded in pinpointing what it was about them that bothered her. Today they are clearer than ever, precisely defined, brown, with tiny green flecks in the irises. Moreover, she can make out a register of emotion she had not noticed before. That he did not look like a man who had lost everything has occurred to her before but there's something else, the smugness of certainty, *as if he were telling me something.*

She remembers Eduardo saying that nothing was over and how she thought he was speaking out of desperation and defiance, the bravado of defeat. Now she is not so sure. She had missed a confidence in his voice that undermines her assumption. Signifying what? That the way he looked at her and what he said were not separate things, but connected in some way?

The green flecks are really multicolored, complex as peacock feathers. His eyes are positively glistening, their mirrorlike surface seeming to reflect buildings and streets rushing by, vast open spaces. When she closes hers, the darkness intensifies the vision. *They had no intention of erecting a shrine. They had planned to take the boys, start the story all over again.*

Leaning back, overwhelmed with fear, she imagines sitting there with no hope of seeing them again, no idea of where they were.

She ought to be happy. More than happy. Ecstatic. She ought to laugh, dance, but what almost happened, the rewinding of history back to the night Guzmán gave them away, has her by the throat. It would have been her death. About that she has not one scintilla of doubt. The concreteness of her fear suddenly gives way to breath-robbing sobs. She raises her shaking hands to her face as spasms wrack her body. She weeps with the inexplicable despair born of her delivery.

After what seems like hours she draws a shuddering breath, coughs. Somehow, she has managed to reach a calm backwater, as if she is in a cove, safe from the roiling waters of the storm, the trees swaying back and forth. She ought to be relieved it is over but a numbness at the center of her being tells her that it isn't.

Something has happened. Something inside her has broken. She ought to be down on her knees with gratitude that she was spared. The feeling is there, bobbing on the calm surface of the cove, a little boat without oars or sail or port, but there is no satisfaction, no warmth, no relief in sourceless gratitude. It is merely there, pointless, drifting, unless she

can understand why she has been allowed to remain alive
and sit here waiting for the boys. She knows that is how it
will remain because the key to that part of the story is gone
with Beatriz and Eduardo and Guzmán.

Dolores has no idea how long she has sat there grap-
pling with this intolerable feeling when she hears their voices
followed by footsteps on the stairs. How could she have
squandered the time she should have used thinking about
ways to blunt their pain?

Sweaty, happy, their faces flushed, they drop their gym
bags on the floor, describe their prowess.

She listens until this first rush of pride ends with laughter and a joke. Then, in as calm a voice as she can manage,
she says, "There's something I have to tell you."

They regard her good-naturedly, still full of their exploits on the field. To ease the blow she begins with a prologue about chance, explaining that one can never prepare
for it since it sits where it likes on the wheel of fortune. She
says that she is going to bring more pain, that they have to
suffer again, that it makes no sense.

Never has she spoken so carefully, in such a modulated
voice, uttering every syllable in a way that softens the sound,
muffles accents. She hopes they will intuit the direction of
her words, sense where she is about to take them. But they
don't. They look at her attentively, confused, ignorant.

"Eduardo and Beatriz are dead."

This much she has rehearsed in her mind, the only
words she could assemble in advance. When she tried to
imagine their response, she had glimpses of every expression
she had seen from the moment she entered the Ponces'
house. All are strangers to what she sees. From uneasiness
their faces bloom into surprise. Another petal unfolds. Pain.
Another. Loss. Disbelief.

"What?" Joaquín asks as if out of breath.

"They died Thursday."

As Roger gapes at her with reddening eyes, she remembers telling Sorano how the blue glow would outlast her lifetime. It will outlast theirs, too. Perhaps only in the minds of their children will it sputter and fade.

Roger shakes his head in an odd way. In a trembling voice he says, "Please. What happened?"

She parrots what she knows from the paper, trying to summarize, get through it as quickly as possible, afraid the facts will stick to her, that the boys will imagine her implicated more deeply than she is.

When she finishes, a silence falls between them, the phenomenon of grief that makes one mute. They take each other by the hand and for a long time they avoid her eyes.

Finally, Joaquín says, "Why?"

She shakes her head slowly. The gesture does not seem merely a sign of sorrow but the thing itself.

"Aren't there clues?" he pleads. "Anything?"

"Here," she says, handing him the paper. "Maybe the two of you can see something I missed."

When they finish reading they look worse than before, the power of the words on the page even more lethal than those she spoke.

A van passes on the street. She absently watches an old couple who live at the end of the block stroll by, unremarkable events, she wants to think, part of the normal flux.

But behind this thought another is already forming. *This is how it would have been with him, this simple.* She feels the chill of the idea entering her bones as she imagines Eduardo coming up the walk. *He came so close you could have heard him breathing.*

Her mind takes her back to Thursday and her last-minute decision to take the boys to Graciela's birthday party after the march in the Plaza de Mayo. One day forward or backward on the calendar, Graciela's arrival in the world hastened or delayed by twenty-four hours, and it would have happened; he would have come striding up the walk, a terrible determination blazing in his eyes, the full bloom of what she had seen but failed to interpret. She imagines him mounting the stairs and kicking the door in and how she would have heard him breathing as he took them away.

One day, either way.

Her mind suddenly throws up visions of bottomless wells, chasms, the ocean floor. They seem so real she can almost smell the damp of the well, the wild grasses in the chasm, the seaweed forest, her fear of the imagined no different from what would have been her fear of the real. There is a fascination in what she sees, a giddy desire to close the distance between herself and the precipices so she can confront what is down there in the hope that the reason she was saved lies at the bottom, like a rusted car, a sunken, worm-eaten boat. *Because if it was pure chance, where is meaning in such a world?* Not even her love for the boys can signify in a place where Eduardo almost came striding up the walk.

A car blaring music goes by. The heavy insistent bass penetrates the walls, surrounding her with its thudding monotony of ugly duration. Even when the beat has dissipated she still hears it in memory.

What does it mean if the world really is bound together by nothing but winds and tides and seasons?

The view out the window reminds her of the way things looked when she left Jorge's store. Her knowledge of Eduardo's plan has increased that sense of emptiness. *Winds and tides and seasons, the earth hurtling through space, the clouds of superheated gases surrounding Mars,* all of it undermining the foundations of everything she believes, eroding her balance.

She is about to turn away from the window when she sees Hermione's car pull up in front. Four women get out, all in black, save for their white scarves. Hermione locks the door and joins the *compañeras* on the sidewalk.

A minute later another car arrives, and then one more, the women in them also dressed in black. They are too far away for her to make out the names of the Disappeared inscribed on their scarves. At this distance, they are merely abstract designs, meaningless swirls and circles. As they come together and face the house she has the impression that they are girding themselves, that something is being coordinated.

Roger and Joaquín question her with eyes full of resentment that their grief is being intruded on. She feels the same. She has no desire to see anyone, wants to let this afternoon play itself out undisturbed.

Racking her brains for an explanation, all she can think of is that a calamity must have befallen one of her *compañeras*. That would account for the invasion, the black clothes, the scarves. It is the kind of thing Hermione would orchestrate.

No matter the cause, they should not have come unannounced. She is of half a mind to go out and tell them their visit could not have been more ill-timed as Hermione adjusts her scarf and runs a hand down the front of her dress. Then she turns her back on the house and faces the others who share a grim but determined expression while she speaks. Whatever the reason for their being here, this is no casual undertaking. Her mind runs through the list of *compañeras* who are not there. She is all but certain that something has happened to one of them and feels a knot of anxiety in her stomach. She wishes she knew who it was.

Hermione starts up the walk and the others fall in line behind her. Tall, short, lean, fat, wearing oversized sunglasses or squinting against the glare, they unspool like a black thread from a bobbin. When they are closer, her eyes are drawn to their legs, some thick, some tattooed with varicose veins, some so thin she can't believe they could have endured so many years of walking. Though they keep the same distance between each other as they do in the Plaza de Mayo, there is something different about the way they walk today, more formal, ceremonial. Their dresses seem like vestments. They would not be moving with such formality if they had come to deliver bad news. There is an unmistakable air of a procession in every step they take, the way they hold themselves as if they were bearing some object necessary for a rite.

Her mind steals back to her thoughts before they arrived, to meaningless salvation, the winds of chance. Once again, despair looms up, worse than before, and with it a terrible thought: Will this be the cast of my mind from now on? And then, when it seems that she has not only lost her balance but is actually falling, an idea flickers, strengthens. As she recognizes her stupidity the truth takes hold, rising up from her consciousness wreathed with humility, gratitude. The change this forces on the direction of her thoughts, her emotions, is too sudden, too complete. Though she has regained her equilibrium, she is still caught between despair and what she can only think of as salvation.

In a husky voice she says, "For you. Because of what happened."

The boys regard her with stunned surprise, then shift their attention to Hermione, who has just come into the room.

Wisps of carrot-colored hair escaping from under her scarf frame her eyes. Dolores wants to thank her but she is too overwhelmed. The best she can do is nod at Hermione, who smiles as she walks over to the couch where the boys are sitting, stops in front of Roger, puts a hand on his shoulder. His face is a mosaic of pain and confusion, the look of someone who wants to believe what he has not yet understood. Hermione bends to kiss his cheek. As she straightens up, Dolores sees a faint imprint left by her lipstick. She whispers something to Roger and then moves on to Joaquín, the *compañeras* following, bestowing the same touch, the same kiss. When they come to her, repeating the ritual, she smells perfume, rouge, garlic. She inhales the scents of her friends, the breath of condolences.

Those who have passed move through the house. From the kitchen they bring in chairs with chrome legs and yellow vinyl seats, wooden chairs from the dining room. Once they have placed them in a rough circle connecting them to her and to the boys they sit down, carefully gathering their skirts around them, folding their hands with the deliberateness of priestesses.

The formality of their arrival, their entrance, the creation of this circle suggest there must be more. Dolores looks at Hermione, expecting that any moment there will be a signal.

A minute passes, then another.

She hears the sound of a car passing on the street, the more muted hum of traffic farther away at the intersection. There is no movement, no further development. She thinks that perhaps it is all *ad hoc,* that they had nothing in mind until they gathered on the sidewalk and spontaneously decided on their procession and then what they would do when they got inside. But there is an unmistakable intensity in their silence. It is, she realizes, part of whatever is happening.

Because no one needs to speak.

Because the room is already filled with words.

She hears the hum of traffic, the faint sound of breathing, an occasional cough, the squeak of a chair when someone shifts her weight and above it all what seems like a mournful yet defiant voice calling, *Argentina, Argentina.*

It is the voice of each of her *compañeras,* and all of them together, of people everywhere in the city, the pampas, on

the coast, the voice of exiles in other lands, Rubén's, Félicité's, mourning what has happened, what is still to come,
what has been seen, what remains hidden. In it she hears a
prayer, a damnation, a dream, the clatter of metal on the
hardest rock of the real. Hate and love. Torture and defiance.
Clandestine prisons and the free light of morning. A cate-
chism for her grandsons in the ways of the world and the
consolations of solidarity.

   In the lengthening shadows of the afternoon her *compañeras'* dresses have become indistinct, fading into the background. As if in compensation, their scarves reflect light
from some unseen source, the way it is in old paintings. The
light is fragile, vulnerable, but it is there. It is enough.

ABOUT THE AUTHOR

Lawrence Thornton received the 1987 Ernest Hemingway Foundation Award for his first novel, *Imagining Argentina*. His other published works of fiction include *Under the Gypsy Moon*, *Naming the Spirits*, and *Ghost Woman*. He lives with his wife in Claremont, California.